Kelly Elliott is a *New York Times* and *USA Today* bestselling contemporary romance author. Since finishing her bestselling Wanted series, Kelly continues to spread her wings while remaining true to her roots and giving readers stories rich with hot protective men, strong women and beautiful surroundings.

Kelly has been passionate about writing since she was fifteen. After years of filling journals with stories, she finally followed her dream and published her first novel, *Wanted*, in November of 2012.

Kelly lives in central Texas with her husband, daughter, and two pups. When she's not writing, Kelly enjoys reading and spending time with her family. She is down to earth and very in touch with her readers, both on social media and at signings.

Visit Kelly Elliott online:

www.kellyelliottauthor.com
@author_kelly
www.facebook.com/KellyElliottAuthor/

Also by Kelly Elliott (published by Piatkus)

The Love Wanted in Texas series

Without You

Saving You

Holding You

Finding You

Chasing You

Loving You

The Cowboys and Angels series

Lost Love

Love Profound

Tempting Love

Love Again

Blind Love

This Love

The Austin Singles series

Seduce Me

PIATKUS

First published in Great Britain in 2018 by Piatkus

1 3 5 7 9 10 8 6 4 2

All characters and events in this publication, other than those clearly in the public domain, are fictitious and any resemblance to real persons, living or dead, is purely coincidental.

A CIP catalogue record for this book is available from the British Library.

ISBN 978-0-349-42240-4

Printed and bound in Great Britain by
Clays Ltd, Elcograf S.p.A.

Cover photo: Shannon Cain, Shannon Cain Photography
Cover design: RBA Designs, www.rbadesigns.com
Interior Design & Formatting: Christine Borgford, www.typeaformatting.com
Editing & Proofing: Hollie Westring, www.hollietheeditor.com
Proofing: Callie Hamilton

Papers used by Piatkus are from well-managed forests and other responsible sources.

Piatkus
An imprint of
Little, Brown Book Group
Carmelite House
50 Victoria Embankment
London EC4Y 0DZ

An Hachette UK Company
www.hachette.co.uk

www.littlebrown.co.uk

Seduce Me

NEW YORK TIMES & USA TODAY BESTSELLING AUTHOR

KELLY ELLIOTT

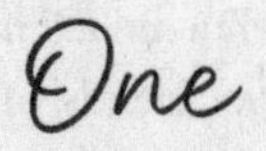

CHARLESTON

HE STOOD ACROSS the room and talked to Angie Reynolds like he had no idea he had shaken my entire world this past weekend. Maybe he did know. The truth was, he'd never know the real reason behind my leaving without saying a word to him. I gave him nothing. Not even, "Hey, thanks for the most incredible weekend of my life."

The only thing I did leave him was a letter because I didn't have the guts to be honest with him.

When his eyes drifted over the room, I looked away before he could see me watching him. I swore my lips still tingled from his kisses. Closing my eyes, I tried like hell to push the feelings away.

I cannot fall for Tucker Middleton.

Who was I kidding? I'd already fallen for him a long time ago.

Peeking toward him again, my breath caught while watching his hand run through his brown hair. My stomach tugged with that familiar desire that Tucker always pulled out of me.

I was struck by Tucker the first moment I ever laid my eyes on him. I turned into a complete mess. He made me feel things I'd never felt before, and that rattled me even more.

My father's voice played in the back of my head over and over. A constant reminder of why I couldn't give in to my feelings for Tucker.

"Charleston, do not be bothered with these boys in college. Focus on your future. Your future is with CMI. You can fall in love later."

When Tucker invited two friends of ours and me to his parents' lake house in Marble Falls, I was foolish enough to think I could resist him.

Yeah, I couldn't have been more wrong. I spent more time in his bed than on the lake.

My eyes closed. I could feel his scourging touch even now. Those magical fingers lightly running over my body. Deliciously soft lips against mine. His hands exploring every inch of my body.

Stop. This. Now. Charlie.

Drawing in a deep breath, I exhaled and glanced around the room. I pressed the beer bottle to my lips and finished it off. It didn't matter how much I drank; I'd never be able to forget the way his body felt. The way he pulled out my first ever orgasm and forever rocked my world.

Ugh, think of something else!

Taking another look around, I found him again. This time he was talking to Lily, my best friend and his sister. My gaze dropped to his soft plump lips. The things he whispered into my ear would replay in my mind for the rest of my life . . . making me feel a high like I'd never felt before.

And therein lies the problem.

I need to stay focused. With Tucker, I cannot focus for shit.

Someday I would be taking over my father's billion-dollar global consulting firm. The last thing I could afford was a distraction. And boy howdy, was Tucker Middleton a distraction.

Feeling someone bump my shoulder, I glanced to my right to see Lily standing there.

Geesh. I was so lost in thought I hadn't even seen her walk over here.

Note to self: Don't daydream about Tucker.

"So, what happened between you and Tucker last weekend?"

My heart stopped. With Lily being Tucker's sister, I had no clue what all he told her.

"Why?"

Looking between me and Tucker, who stood across the room, she focused back in on me. "Because he's been pissed ever since he got back. He said something to Nash about you being the biggest bitch he'd ever met. Then he told him if he never talked to you again, he wouldn't lose any sleep over it."

Ouch. I deserved that.

Snapping my head back over to Tucker, I saw he was now talking to a group of guys. I would never admit I was happy to see Angie had moved on and left Tucker alone.

"So . . . are you going to tell me what happened?"

My cheeks heated as I looked at her.

"Oh. My. God. Did y'all sleep together?"

When I didn't answer, she yanked at my arm. "Charlie, wait. I've never seen that look in your eyes before." She gasped then slapped her hand up to her mouth before dropping it again and saying, "You like him!"

With a curt laugh, I rolled my eyes and said, "Please. I do not like Tucker."

Lie. I think I'm in love with him.

She lifted her brow. "But y'all slept together?"

I shrugged. "Maybe."

Grabbing me, she pulled me down the hall and into the bathroom. "Okay, I'm so confused. I know Tucker has the hots for you, but I didn't think you liked him. I mean, you get all weird around him and all but . . ." She gasped again. "Oh no."

My eyes filled with tears, and I quickly looked away. "Charlie, what happened? He acts like he can't stand you now."

I instantly felt sick. "What did he say?"

"Pretty much the same thing he told Nash. That you were cold hearted and didn't care about anyone but yourself. He just told me he didn't care if you ever hung out with us again."

Squaring off my shoulders, I took in a deep breath as I tried to bury the sting of his words. I deserved them, though. "Well then, that's for the best. Takes the awkwardness away from the situation."

Narrowing her deadpan stare, she asked, "What . . . situation?"

How did I tell my best friend I was in love with her brother, had the most amazing weekend of my life with sex that was mind blowing, and then snuck out Sunday morning without so much as a word? Well. There was the note I left, which is probably why he hates me.

"Um . . . well . . . we, ah . . . things got a little . . . you know . . ."

Shaking her head, she responded. "No. I don't know, and you're babbling." Her brows pulled in. "You never babble."

I jumped and pointed at her, causing her to shriek. "See! That's the problem. Your brother brings out this whole other side of me, and I can't think straight when I'm around him. I trip on shit and say the stupidest things. You'd never know I was going to run a huge corporation someday by the way I act when he's near me."

The smile that spread over her face made my stomach drop.

"Oh. My. God. You *really* like him."

I frantically nodded my head. "Yes. No. Oh God, I don't know. No! I don't like him. I cannot like him. We had an amazing weekend with the best sex of my life, but it's over. I told him in my note I wanted to forget it ever happened and that it was best if we were just friends."

Swallowing hard, I looked away as I chewed on my lip. Oh, how I tried to talk myself out of kissing him that first night. We were both a little drunk, and damn it if he didn't look hot as hell in his stupid Dallas Cowboys baseball hat turned backward. *Do guys have any idea how hot that makes them look?*

For the last three years I fought my feelings for Tucker. I had a moment of weakness. Okay, it was more than a moment. It was three days' worth of moments of weakness.

"Friends? So you're saying you're not attracted to my brother?"

Attracted? Pfftt. Boy, was she off. I had fallen for Tucker the first time he grabbed my hand and walked me into a movie theater with our little group of friends. To him it was a friendly gesture . . . to me it made my entire body come to life. I knew then he was going to be my kryptonite.

Innocent touches here and there I could handle, but this past weekend took everything to a DEFCON level 5. All I heard the entire weekend were sirens going off in my head. Not to mention my father's voice warning me to stay focused and not get involved with what could only amount to a fling. After all, college relationships never lasted, he said. It didn't matter he had met my mother in college and married her. Or that they had been happily married for thirty years. He made me promise I wouldn't date and that I would solely focus on school.

I had kept my promise too. Kept it as long as my heart would allow.

Well, until last Thursday night when I let my betraying bitch of a body control me.

But Tucker was different. So very different. He made me want things I never desired before. He was a weakness I couldn't afford to have in my life. Not if I wanted to pursue my dreams. Well, my father's dreams.

"Hello? Earth to Charlie? Are you even listening to me?"

I shook my head to clear my thoughts. "Sorry. Listen, I messed up this past weekend. Things got a little hot and heavy with Tucker. It was a mistake that I . . . that I . . . regret."

I wonder if that sounded convincing to her? It sure as shit didn't to me.

Her mouth damn near dropped to the ground. "Wait, did you say you told him you wished it never happened in the note? The note you left him, Charlie?" Her eyes nearly popped out of her head.

Damn. This is where the shit is going to hit the fan.

"I, um . . . well. I left super early."

The look of disappointment on her face about killed me. I knew if I had waited for Tucker to wake up, I wouldn't have been able to leave. I would have found myself wrapped up in him another day. And that would have turned into another night, which would ultimately turn into more days and nights. There was no way I would have been able to look him in the eyes and say it was a mistake we were together because deep down in my heart, it was exactly what I had been wanting. There wasn't one ounce of regret in my body over the time we spent together, but my mind was flooded with all the whys and hows of why we could never be more than friends.

My blank stare was answer enough.

She closed her eyes for a brief moment before glaring at me with pure anger in her irises. "So, let me get this straight. Y'all made love, you led him on, then got up and left without so much as saying goodbye?"

The way she said it made me feel like such a slut, and truly the world's biggest bitch. Tucker was right when he told Nash I was a bitch. In fact, he was being a tad bit generous in his assessment of me.

Note to self. Sleeping with a guy and then getting up and leaving without so much as a thank you for the multiple orgasms is a bitch move. A total bitch move.

I didn't like the way she looked at me. Anger quickly raced through me. It was the only choice I had. "We didn't make love, Lily. Don't try to romanticize it. We *fucked*. He wanted me; I wanted to see what it would be like with him. Itches scratched. End of story."

Lily slowly shook her head. "You know it was more than that, Charlie. I see it in your eyes. You're just too damn scared to admit it. Maybe next time you want to get laid, go find some asshole who won't care when you get up and leave. Someone who will actually slap your ass on the way out the door. Tucker had feelings for you. How could you do this to him? How could you lead him on all weekend and then leave him high and dry and say it was a mistake?"

My chest squeezed thinking Tucker might no longer have feelings for me. That if he had feelings for me, I'd crushed any chance of ever being more than what we are right now. The thought that I had ruined a friendship I valued so much for a few hours of pleasure was fracturing my already broken heart. I had to keep telling myself it was for the best; it was the only way I'd be able to put one foot in front of the other around him.

Forcing myself to keep a steady voice, I replied, "Tucker wanted in my pants as much as I wanted in his, Lily. I can't help it if he thought there was going to be something more out of it. There were no promises made between us; it was just two adults doing adult things with no strings attached. Plain and simple."

Her head jerked back and she wore a shocked expression before letting out a scoff. "Wow, Charlie. You really *are* a bitch. A heartless bitch with no feelings at all. You've mastered that at the ripe old age of twenty-one. You're going to make a great addition to your father's company with that attitude."

With that, my best friend spun around on her heels and stormed out the door. I couldn't even be mad at her because every single word she said was true.

All of it.

Two

Seven years later

CHARLESTON

THE DING OF the elevator door pulled me from my thoughts. Mindlessly stepping in, I heard a female voice speak.

"I'm so sorry for your loss, Charleston."

My blank stare met her warm eyes. "Charlie, please call me Charlie."

She nodded and gave me the same smile I'd been getting for the last week. That's what happens when both of your parents unexpectedly die at the same time in a car accident. People give you that sad look that says they really don't know what to say, and "I'm so sorry for your loss" is the only thing they can muster. Do they think it helps? It doesn't. It's only a reminder of what's missing. A reminder of what I was left with.

No one. I was all alone.

They thought their whispered questions went unheard by me, but I heard them all.

What will she do now? How will she be able to handle it all? Is this place going to stay open? One of the world's largest consulting firms . . . is she capable of running it?

Alone.

I was totally alone. I had no one.

"Your father was an amazing man. Not to mention your mother; she was so caring and everyone loved her."

With a weak smile, I nodded in agreement. The ache in my chest knowing my mother would never see me walk down the aisle or hold a grandchild in her arms nearly had me bursting out in tears. But crying was something I didn't do. Then you had my father. Oh yes. My father was amazing. He was a lawyer, a businessman, a husband, and a wonderful father. But he demanded everything out of me and expected nothing but perfection from his only child. Needless to say, it was a no-brainer that he talked me out of taking the swimming scholarship to Notre Dame and instead head to his alma mater, The University of Texas. I went to school and achieved my business law degree with a minor in math. I'd do anything to make my father happy, even give up my dreams of owning my own small business and becoming a wife and mother. I didn't want a corporate life; I wanted a simpler one.

Instead, I dutifully did what I was told and got a degree from The University of Texas. Then I went on to law school . . . again . . . at The University of Texas.

The woman cleared her throat, I guess to pull me out of my thoughts. It wasn't until then that I really took her in. She was older; her blonde hair was pulled up neatly in a tight bun, and her makeup was perfect, as well as her nails. Glancing down at my nails, I hid them behind my back. The evidence of my grief chipped away on each fingernail.

Note to self: Make a spa day appointment. You fucking deserve it.

When the elevator opened onto the top floor, I stared at the numbers. I didn't even remember hitting a floor number when I walked in.

"I hit the floor number for you, Charles- . . . I mean, Charlie. The board members are all waiting for you. You'll meet with the lawyer first in the main conference room next to your father's office."

Then it hit me. "You're Marge, my father's executive assistant."

With a warm smile, she nodded politely and used her hand to urge me out before the elevators shut again.

"Yes, now your executive assistant."

"Oh, right. Sorry," I said as I quickly walked out and into the main reception area. It wasn't like I didn't know where in the hell I was going. My office was down from my father's. Hell, I even knew that was Marge, my father's right-hand woman.

For the last few years he had groomed me to take over our family business. I soaked up everything he said and then some. I thought I knew everything I needed to know to run CMI Consulting, at least what I needed to know for now. I'd still have plenty of years of learning under my father's wing . . . at least, I thought I would. However, being the CEO of a billion-dollar business was not something I was ready to do at twenty-eight years old. Now I was being thrown into it—frying pan meet fire—and I was scared shitless.

Or was I? This was what my father pushed me so hard for. Day after day he pounded it in my head about running the business his father had started. It was to stay in the family . . . and the family was to stay in control. Always. Ever since I was a little girl, he would tell me that over and over again. I swear if he could've woven it into a bedtime story, I was pretty sure he would have.

"Don't ever let go of this company. It's your future. Your children's future. Your children's children's future."

There was one promise I had made to myself a long time ago. If I was ever blessed with a child, I would never pressure them to do what I wanted them to do. They would have the choice to decide. Not that I wasn't grateful my father trusted me with his company, because I was. There wasn't anything I could ever want for; he made sure of that. And this company was the reason.

Swallowing hard, I smoothed out my pencil skirt, tucked my white satin shirt in a little more, lifted my shoulders, and headed to the conference room.

Glancing down at the *New York Times* on someone's desk, I stopped in my tracks. *Will twenty-eight-year-old Charleston Monroe soon be one of the top five richest women in America? Did we mention she's single?*

Marge gently took my elbow and led me on.

"Just ignore the press. They're going to want to chew you up and spit you out. Don't let them. They are just trying to sell a few thousand papers is all."

Turning to look at her, I was positive I wore a horrified expression. I was on the cover of the fucking *New York Times*!

I am so screwed.

Daddy, why did you leave me?

No.

No. I wasn't screwed because I was a strong woman just like my mother and father raised me to be. I didn't take shit from anyone. I was going to kick ass at this.

At least, that's what I kept telling myself.

"Your father always believed you were ready to take over. There wasn't a day that didn't go by where he didn't say to me, 'Marge, my Charleston is going to take this company even further than it is now. She not only has the brains, but the guts to do it.'"

My mouth lifted at the corners. "He said that to me all the time. Of course, I thought I was going to have a bit more time to take on the role." I didn't like how shaky my voice sounded. This wasn't me.

Weak. Lonely. Scared.

Over the last few days, thoughts of Tucker entered my mind every now and then as I fell into a lonely pit. I'd pushed them—along with him—to the back of my mind, but the pain was certainly still there. Even after so many years, I thought about the "what-ifs" and "what could've beens" that were possible between us. Instead, here I was, about to walk into a boardroom full of old-timers, and they all expected me to wear the crown of ownership with pride and aplomb. On the inside I was crumbling from all the emotions that were overwhelming me. I could do this. I didn't have a choice as I looked to Marge for silent encouragement.

Marge gave me a smile that made my chest feel warm.

This was not the woman my parents raised me to be. I needed to snap out of it and walk into that boardroom like I owned it. Well, hell . . . I did own it.

After a few seconds of deep breaths, I finally said, "Come on, Marge, let's go show these assholes who's boss."

Her smile faltered a bit as her mouth dropped open slightly before she said, "Okay, well, first thing worth mentioning, let's keep the swearing to a minimum."

Oh. Shit.

"Right. No swearing. But we're going to kick ass in there."

Her eyes widened. "Oh my. I'm going to have to get used to your . . . expanded vocabulary."

Note to self: Don't swear in front of Marge.

FIRST, I MET with the lawyer. Alone. After twenty minutes of Mr. Knots telling me everything my father wanted done with certain possessions, he handed me two letters.

My heart dropped when I saw it was my mother and father's handwriting. "What are these?"

"Letters your parents wrote to you. They asked for them to be given to you if anything was to ever happen to them. I was to hand them over to you after the funeral, and they requested you read them when you were alone."

I barely acknowledged his request. With a racing heart, I ran my fingers over my name on each letter.

Why did you leave me?

My father's personal lawyer got up and left the room, leaving the lawyer from CMI in his stead.

"Your father was the CEO and chairman of the board; that responsibility now falls on you." He cleared his throat and moved about in his seat like he was nervous.

Placing the letters on the table, I dropped my hands to my lap and began wringing them. *Did he think I was going to tank the company?* He sure was looking at me like the sky was about to fall.

Shit.

I was going to do my father proud. My mind was filled with ideas on where to expand the company. We were already in aerospace and defense, energy power, telecom, media, and technology, as well as financial institutions. My idea was to expand to environmental, health care and life science, and agriculture. Daddy laughed when I mentioned the last one, but I knew it was an industry we needed to get into. I was going to get this company caught up with the times. Not that my father lacked in that department, but it was time to shake things up. Expansion was something my father was leery of. It was a good thing I wasn't. It meant more profit for the company as a whole, and that would make for happy employees.

Marge got up and opened the side door that led to the smaller conference room. The board members all filed in. *Jesus, they're all so damn old. How am I just now realizing this?*

Paul Ricker, executive vice president and chief financial officer, sat and cleared his throat. "Ms. Monroe, how are you doing?"

Squaring off my shoulders, I gave a slight grin. "I'm doing as well as to be expected, I guess you could say."

He moved about in his seat and nodded. "Of course. Would you like to handle all of this another day? Maybe you need more time? Sometimes it's hard to jump into such a leadership role if your mindset is not all there."

What. An. Asshole.

I wasn't some weak woman who couldn't handle a damn meeting. Especially one that had to do with my future. What would the board think if I said I needed more time? I needed to show them I was up for the task.

With a slight grin, I replied, "No, Mr. Ricker, my mindset is perfectly fine to handle all of this today."

With a tip of his head, he motioned for Mr. Knots to speak after the other board members all came and sat down.

"Ms. Monroe, according to a bylaw that was put into place by your grandfather, there is a stipulation on when you can acquire full control of CMI."

My brow lifted. "And that is?"

I couldn't help but notice how he glanced around the room. I followed his gaze. More than half of the board members looked down. Cowards didn't have the balls to look me directly in the eye. Well, that was except for Mr. Ricker and Mr. Potts, the chief of ethics and compliance officer. They both wore smug expressions.

"Your grandfather felt very strongly about this. When he found out that your father would no longer be having children, specifically a boy . . ."

Motherfucker.

This was not going to go where I wanted it. Dear old granddaddy always made it known he was pissed I came out with a vagina instead of a dick. He felt like the role of a woman was at home, ready to provide her man with a cigar and drink when he returned home after a long day of work at the office.

"He wrote it in that if you were to inherit the business from your father due to unforeseen circumstances before you were of the age of forty, that in order for you to become chairman of the board and CEO, you would need to be married."

My jaw dropped.

The fuck did I just hear?

Mr. Knots cleared his throat and kept reading. "And that your husband would possess at least a Bachelor of Business degree and serve on the board of CMI, t-to, um, well, to assist you if need be."

My eyes darted to Mr. Ricker, who wore a look on his face that almost seemed like he wanted to laugh. I looked back at Mr. Knots.

"Are you fu—"

Marge, who was standing next to me, placed her hand on my shoulder. "Oh, Charleston, remember our conversation."

Shutting my mouth, I shook my head, took in a deep breath and laughed. "Are you kidding me? Did my father know about this little . . . stipulation?"

Now it was Mr. Ricker's turn. "He did."

Narrowing my eyes at him, I asked, "And he agreed with it? Because I'm going to tell you right now, I know for a damn fact he would *not* have agreed for this to remain a standing contingency in the corporation's bylaws."

Marge let out a soft grumble.

"He did not agree with it, Charleston."

Jerking my head to the right, I looked at Mitchel Landing, a chair member my father had appointed not long after he took over as CEO from my granddaddy. Mitchel continued to talk. "He had asked that the bylaw be taken out, since it was never voted in, and that Mr. Ricker was to see to it. From what I understood from your father, he felt it was just a bitter statement his father was trying to make."

Oh, this keeps getting better.

I had mentioned to my father I didn't like Ricker. He was old-school and didn't like change. More than once I said if I had control of this place, his ass would be gone.

"Is that so?" I asked. "And why was this never done, Mr. Ricker?" My voice was strong, and he heard it. What these old bastards needed to remember was I now held more stock than any of them. CEO or not, I could make their lives a living nightmare.

"Your father kept putting it off, Ms. Monroe."

Liar. He probably told my father it was taken care of, and my father trusted him and never questioned his actions.

"Let me guess, with my father gone and me unwed, you fall into the leadership role. Am I correct?"

He let out a nervous chuckle as Mr. Knots answered. "Not exactly. If at the time of your father's death you are unwed, you will be the acting chairman and CEO, but only for four months. At the end of that time period you will need to be legally married in the state of Texas in order to remain in that position. If you are not married, then the position falls to Mr. Ricker."

I scoffed. "Wedded to a man who holds a business degree, let's not forget. This is the stupidest thing I've ever heard, gentlemen. This isn't the 1950s. I'm very capable of running this company without being married."

A few other board members nodded their heads in agreement.

Laughing, I shook my head. "I can't believe we're even having this conversation in the twenty-first century."

"As it stands, it was the founder of this company who wished for it to be this way," Mr. Ricker snapped back.

I pulled in a deep breath. "Well, it is no surprise to me that my grandfather thought so little of me. After all, I didn't have the right equipment to play in his sandbox, or so he thought."

Marge groaned and a few chuckles echoed in the room. "I'll fight. Take it to court and have it thrown out."

"That could take years to work out in the court system, Ms. Monroe," Knots reminded me.

"Mr. Knots, are you certain this is legally binding? I'm not a lawyer, but this doesn't even sound right. It was never voted in. It seems to me we can all place a vote and dismiss this issue right now." A voice from across the table interjected.

I smiled at Melanie Prescott. I had always liked her. I also liked the fact that she was the only one with balls to speak up, besides Mitchel Landing, and that was because he was my father's best friend.

Clearing his throat, Knots replied, "I wish it was that easy, but unfortunately the legal process with the untimely death of Mr. Monroe," everyone looked at me and gave me a sad smile, "will slow things down."

Shaking my head, I glanced around the table. My grandfather actually required me to be married in order to take over the business I had worked my ass off for and earned the right to be sitting in this position. The business I had given up my entire life for. Hell, my own damn dreams. The business that was rightfully mine!

Swallowing the giant lump in my throat, I let out a chortle as I closed my eyes and shook my head.

Married.

The word itself made my skin crawl. The idea of giving up my freedom to let some asshole of a guy try and run my life was not one that ever appealed to me. I had my beloved cat, Mr. Pootie. He was all I needed. Not some damn guy who would throw his wet towel on the bed and scratch his balls and yell out, "When's dinner ready, baby?"

I shivered at the thought.

No. Thank you.

"So, when does this four-month time period begin?"

Mr. Ricker leaned forward and flashed me a smile that made my skin crawl. "The day your father passed. You're now down to three months and three weeks."

Every ounce of good sense immediately left my body . . . with anger quickly replacing it.

For the rest of my life, I will never forget the look on poor Marge's face when I stood and uttered my next sentence.

"You've got to be fucking kidding me."

Three

CHARLESTON

MY KEYS MADE a loud crash when I dropped them onto the table. Mr. Pootie, my orange cat and the *only* man in my life, came running up to me. He didn't rub around my legs like a normal loving cat would. Oh no. He had his priorities. First came food, then came loving on me. He jumped up at me, begging for food as he let out a meow that sounded more like a dying calf.

"Well, look at you, my sweet baby boy! You got your hair cut today."

Mr. Pootie responded with a drawn-out meow. "Don't act like you don't like it. We both know you sat in the mirror and looked at yourself all day."

It was true. I'd caught my cat on more than one occasion staring at himself in the mirror. He was worse than me. The first time I ever got him shaved, Lily threatened to commit me. I thought it was adorable and have had it done ever since. If anything, he was a topic of conversation when I threw dinner parties.

Mindlessly, I walked to the pantry and grabbed a can of cat food. Mr. Pootie ran in and out of my legs, attempting to trip me, because apparently I wasn't moving at the speed he preferred.

Bastard.

Once I opened the can, I dumped the food onto the plate and sighed. "Happy?"

He didn't even say thank you. He simply dug into his food like he hadn't eaten in weeks, when in reality, it was eight hours ago.

Rolling my eyes, I mumbled, "Men."

Making my way to the sofa, I fell face-first across it. That may have not been as thought out as it should have been because my face landed on a decorative pillow with little diamonds that stuck out and embedded into my cheeks. I let out a groan.

With a quick flip of my body, I stared up at the ceiling. The words from my father's lawyer swirled around in my head.

"In order for you to become chairman and CEO, you would need to be married."

Married! What in the hell?

The look on Ricker's face was enough to make me hurl. He thought he was going to win, but I had other news for him.

Of course, the worst of the news came after my initial shock. I had to prove it wasn't an arranged marriage. How in the hell was I going to do that? They expected me to find a man, fall in love, and plan a wedding in three months and three weeks' time? The only good thing that came out of this was I found a flaw in good ol' granddaddy's evil plan. I only had to be married one year. If after one year I divorced, I was still able to maintain control. What he didn't know was divorce was nothing these days. Hell, I've had friends marry and divorce a week later without so much as batting an eye.

My phone rang, causing me to sit up quickly. I recognized that ringtone. Jumping up, I ran over to my purse and pulled out my phone.

I smiled when I saw her name.

Terri.

"Hey," I said as I made my way to my bedroom. I lived in a historic loft apartment in downtown Austin. It had killer views and cost more money than should be legal, but it was my place. I rented it from a friend of my father's who owned the whole historical building. I had spent countless hours on Pinterest looking for ideas on decorating it. My parents thought I was nuts investing so much money restoring a penthouse loft I was renting, but I was working on the old man into letting me buy the place. My pappy, my mother's father, owned half of Texas, I swear. His love of buying and selling real estate was passed down to me. I just never had the time to really learn more about it. I'd love to someday buy old houses and restore them. Then flip them and make a shit ton of money.

Another dream I had given up for this clusterfuck of a situation I was in now.

"I got your text. What's up?"

Heading to my closet, I pulled open the doors and walked in. I needed a dress, a sexy dress.

"I need two things." Really I needed three. The last one I would keep to myself. I'd spent the last week hiding in my apartment, crying endlessly for my parents. I needed a night out in the real world. Something to take my mind off the hole in my heart.

I could hear Terri's boyfriend, Jim, in the background. "Wh-what two things do you need?"

My hand came up to my hip as I stopped what I was doing. "Are you having sex right now?"

"What? No! Oh my God. I'm at Jim's parents' house. I just walked outside."

"Oh. Well, it sounds like moaning in the background."

Terri giggled. "I wish. Now what are these two things you need?"

Smiling, I went back to scanning my closet. I knew I could count on Terri. She had been part of my large group of friends from college, and we'd been close ever since freshman year. We had all stayed friends and got together once a week still, even if it was for drinks only. It was hard because most of the time that meant seeing Tucker. My heart ached every time I saw him. Especially when he had his latest girlfriend on his arm.

Ugh.

"I need to get laid, and then I need to get married."

I had to admit, I wasn't too surprised by the silence on the other end of the line.

"You still there, Terri?"

"Ah. Yeah. I got the get laid part; it's the get married part that's thrown me for a loop."

I let out a frustrated moan. "Can you meet me for drinks? I really need to talk to someone."

"Sure, babe. Where did you want to meet?"

"I don't care. I need a hard drink and an even harder dick, which I'm not even sure I know what that is anymore. It's been so long since I actually had sex. After that, then I need to get married."

"Jesus," Terri said, scrambling with something. I was pretty sure I heard something crash on the floor. "My God, Charlie! I had it on speakerphone."

Rolling my eyes, I took a red cocktail dress off the hanger and headed over to my bed. "Why would you have me on speakerphone? You know the shit that comes out of my mouth."

"Well, I didn't at first, but then I needed to come back in and help Jim and Tucker move something, and I needed both hands."

I froze in place as my hand covered my mouth. It felt as if an elephant sat on my chest. "*Please* tell me they didn't hear me say that."

Please tell me Tucker *didn't hear me say that!*

"Everyone heard you say it, which is why I dropped the phone," she mumbled.

Shit.

Note to self: Always make sure I'm not on speakerphone before talking about sex.

"Am I *still* on speakerphone?" I asked.

"No. I quickly walked off. I'm pretty sure it was only Tucker and Jim who heard you."

My hands started sweating. *Great.* The last person I wanted to hear me say that was Tucker. Not that he would care. He hardly ever even looked at me, let alone talked to me.

"Well, that's nice. Now they both think I'm a slut."

Terri chuckled. "I'm pretty sure they don't think that. I will say though, Tucker sure perked up when he heard you needed a 'hard drink and a harder dick' and then the whole married thing. I'm thinking he wouldn't mind helping you out with one of those needs. Hell, it's been long enough for you two, maybe both!"

My lower stomach pulled. I'd been with two guys since I slept with Tucker in college. While all my friends had revolving doors of boyfriends, I was stuck in law school studying my ass off. The first guy, Sam, was more of a fuck buddy, and that didn't work out so great after I found out he had a girlfriend. The second guy was Josh. We met in law school and dated off and on for four months. It would have never have worked out for us. He wanted a commitment, and I had no desire to be tied down. Plus, he wasn't . . . Tucker.

With a frustrated sigh, I sank down on my bed. Jesus. My grandmother's vagina saw more action than mine.

Swallowing hard, I cleared my throat. "I doubt that. In case you haven't been around for the last seven years, you'd know that Tucker Middleton can't stand me."

"Uh-huh. If you think so. At any rate, be ready in an hour. I'm heading home to change then coming to get you. I have the perfect place to go tonight."

I stood and pushed my skirt then slip off and kicked them away. "Good. The sooner I forget this day the better."

~

WHEN THE TAXI pulled up, I glanced up at the blue neon sign that read *Sedotto*. "What's this place?"

"New bar. Just opened."

Stepping out of the car, I read what it said under the name. "Sports bar and craft beer. I like it already," I said with a big smile. The fact that it was in a historical building also piqued my interest.

"Ready?" Terri asked me as she wrapped her arm around mine.

"Most definitely. By the way, Sedotto? What does that mean?"

"Seduced in Italian."

I let out an awkward-sounding laugh. How fitting was that, seeing as I had a little more than three months to do just that? And I couldn't forget it had to be to a man who held a fucking business degree. "That's perfect. But why not just call it Seduced? What's with the Italian?"

With a wink, she replied, "You'll have to ask the owner."

What the hell did she mean by that?

The moment we walked into the bar, I took it all in. It was sophisticated and sexy as hell, yet most of the bar maintained that old historical feel to it. I could totally see why they picked the name they did. The ambient lighting set the perfect mood. I loved the Warehouse District in Austin and was glad to see we would have a new place to come and hang out.

My eyes scanned the place. The place was packed. From what I could see, there were two bars. Large-screen TVs were all over with every kind of sports game on you could imagine. "This place is pretty cool. Better not let Tucker see it. He'd be jealous."

After college, Tucker had decided to piss away his degree. He became a bartender in one of the places we hung out in our last year of college. Needless to say, his father, a prominent businessman in Austin, was not too pleased with his son's decision to continue that occupation rather than pursue an actual career by going to work for him at his marketing firm. Lily did, though, and she was making a name for herself in Austin. We'd even used her for a few of our clients, and I hoped to utilize her even more now that I was in charge.

My stomach twisted.

In charge for now. I have to keep reminding myself that.

Terri pointed to a half-round booth toward the back corner. "There's our table. Come on."

"Our table?" I shouted at her. Trying to keep up with her in my new Jimmy Choo shoes was proving more difficult than I anticipated. Even though money wasn't an object, I was still tight with it. My mother always told me the sky could fall at any moment and if it did, you had better be prepared. I didn't own a lot of expensive shoes or purses. I gave myself gifts, like the shoes I had on, when good things happened. I didn't go crazy, and my closet wasn't filled with overly exaggerated expensive items. I was by no means frugal, but more logical.

But I'd took my mother's sense of urgency to heart. I'd bought two hundred acres out in the hill country last year without telling my parents. The small cabin that sat on the property was stocked with freeze-dried food that would last me for years. I wasn't one of those prepper fanatics, but damn if I wouldn't be ready if shit hit the fan.

Terri pulled my arm. "Yeah. The owner held it for us."

"Do we know the owner?" I asked as I let her lead me like a dog.

It was right then that something in the air changed. My body came to life as I quickly looked back over my shoulder. That never happened unless *he* was nearby. No matter how much I tried to fight it, I couldn't. He had to be here somewhere. I was going to strangle Terri, I swear.

As if this day couldn't get any worse, right before we got to the booth, I slipped and started going down.

Great. I was going to bust my ass right there in front of everyone to see.

But at the last minute, I was saved. My body caught on fire when his arms grabbed me, preventing me from falling with utter embarrassment.

I looked up and his gray eyes met my blue.

Tucker.

I smiled, and he quickly looked away.

Ugh.

How long was he going to be pissed about what happened between us in college? It was ages ago, for Pete's sake.

Note to self: Buy Tucker a book about forgiveness and never wear these fucking shoes again.

Tucker looked back at me quickly and said, "You always were a klutz, Charlie."

That warm fuzzy feeling I had from his touch was extinguished by his shitty words of reprimand. Snarling my lip at him, I shot back, "You probably tripped me, Tucker."

He winked and my insides melted. Yep. They melted.

Damn him!

"You would have deserved it after what you did to me," he whispered against my ear, causing my lower stomach to heat up.

With a sigh, I shook my head. "Get over it, Middleton. It was ages ago."

His unshaven face brushed against my cheek and caused my breath to hitch. The way his eyes flamed, he obviously noticed what his touch still did to me.

"That's funny, seems like only yesterday to me."

My body shuddered. His voice had a bit of sadness in it that rocked me to the core.

"By the way, Pumpkin, I'm sorry about your parents."

Pulling back, the only thing I could do was stare at him as I swallowed hard and reminded myself I needed air. Tucker had given me the nickname the very first day I met him. I never told him that my father called me Pumpkin too. Of course, Tucker hadn't called me that since our last weekend together all those years ago. Until tonight. Tears threatened to fall as this shitty day came flooding back to me along with all the guilt I had for walking away from the only man I'd ever cared about. Add in the bitterness that was slowly replacing the sadness of my parents being taken from me too early, and you had one emotionally fucked-up woman.

I tried like hell to get my mouth to move. When it finally did, I whispered, "I'm sorry."

His brows lifted, then pulled tight in confusion.

"I mean, thank you for the sorry. I'm not sorry. Well, I mean, I *am* sorry about my parents and all, but . . . thank you for *your* sorry. That means a lot to me that you said sorry, and I've really said the word sorry a lot in the past twenty-three seconds, so I'll stop now."

For some strange reason, I couldn't pull my gaze away from him. *What in the hell?* I was a very educated young woman, and I just sounded like a goddamn teenager trying to figure out how to talk to her crush.

Terri pulled me into the booth as Tucker shot me a funny look and turned, walking over to the bar. I hadn't fumbled over my words like that in at least seven years. Of course, that was the most Tucker had talked to me, or touched me, in the last seven years.

"Jesus, sit down before you fall again," Terri said.

Feeling humiliated, I let out a frustrated groan. "Are Jim and Tucker joining us?" I asked, looking back at her with a dirty look. I had wanted this to be a girls' night only.

Terri grinned an evil grin. "Yep."

A waitress walked up and flashed us both a huge smile. "What can I get ya?"

"I'll have a Blue Moon," I said with a grin of my own.

"Same for me! Thanks!" Terri blurted out all chipper sounding.

My body sagged. I wasn't in the mood to be around Tucker. I didn't have the energy to pretend like I was okay. Not tonight. Tonight I needed to talk to Terri and get her advice on this fucked-up situation. I didn't need members of the XY gender joining us and offering their sage words of wisdom that always involved their penises.

"Why, Terri? I needed a girls' night out, and I needed to talk to you about something very important, like life-or-death important."

Before she had a chance to respond, Jim slid into the booth. "So, what do you think about Sedotto, Charlie?"

I couldn't help my reaction to Jim, though; he was infectious to be around. With a wide grin, I glanced around the bar again. "I love it! I foresee this being our new weekend hangout."

"Hope so, since it's my bar."

His voice alone sent shivers down my spine. Turning around as I peered up, I got a better look at Tucker and swallowed hard. A few moments ago my eyes had been pinned to his, not allowing me to take him in fully. Now I got to study him closer. Something I enjoyed doing very much.

He was dressed in jeans and a white button-down shirt with the sleeves rolled up to his elbows. He looked completely fuckable. Then again, he could have a bag over his head and I'd think he was fuckable. And gorgeous.

No, I don't mean that. Yes, I do. No. No, I don't.

Then his words replayed in my head.

It's my bar . . . My mind did a double take.

"What do you mean, it's *your* bar?" I blurted with a noticeable amount of time between when he said it and when I spoke. I hadn't meant for it to come out so bitchy and condescending, yet I knew he would take it that way.

"I mean, it's my bar, Pumpkin. I am capable of owning and running a business, not just serving drinks."

Thud.

There went my heart . . . straight to the ground. My cheeks heated at the memory of Tucker whispering into my ear as he sank balls deep into me.

"Does that feel good, Pumpkin?"

Tucker stared at me with a small smirk tugging at the corners of his mouth. That bastard. It was almost as if he knew the endearment would bring back that memory.

Oh, Jesus, Charlie. Stop this! Focus.

"You . . . own . . . this place?" It felt like I had to force the words out.

His smile grew bigger and those damn dimples appeared. "I sure do."

That voice made my insides heat up. It didn't help he hadn't shaved in a few days either and from our previous interaction and him rubbing that scruff on my cheeks, all I could think about was that scruff roughing up the inside of my thighs. Damn, he looked hot as hell. I was suddenly fixated on wondering what his face would feel like between my legs. Would he take his time or quickly bring out an orgasm? I could still remember what it felt like to have him buried deep inside me, and I longed for that again.

My mouth went dry as I let the mental image of Tucker buried between my legs play out.

Terri leaned over and whispered in my ear, "What in the hell are you thinking? Because your face is turning ten shades of red, and I can practically feel the lust pouring off your body, you whore! Are you about to orgasm in front of Tucker? If so, I need to excuse myself."

Shaking my head, I got a grip on myself.

Note to self: Pick up batteries for BOB on the way home. Rechargeable ones.

Glancing over to Tucker, I smiled. He stared at me. Almost as if challenging me to question his ownership of a bar. I didn't want to act like a bitch around Tucker, but it was almost as if it was expected of me by him. Plus, it pissed me off that he treated me like an outcast.

I shrugged and casually said, "Huh."

His head pulled back. "What does that mean—*huh?*"

With a smirk, I answered, "I'm surprised with all the girlfriends you filter through that you have time to commit to something so . . . long term and serious."

His eyes turned dark, and heat pooled in my lower stomach. Leaning in closer to me, he spit out, "Committing was never my problem. That's all on you. Remember?"

My lust quickly turned to anger. Heat swept over my body as I tightened my fists.

"Besides, I'm not the one out tonight hunting for another quick fuck. Or were the exact words a 'hard drink and a harder dick'? But that's what you do best, right, Charlie? Fuck 'em and then leave without so much as uttering a word. Take what you want and screw what's left behind." Tucker challenged me to a stare-off when he finished his almost silent tirade in the bar that he owned.

My heart raced. This was not where I was going to finally have this out with him. For years I had wanted to talk to him about that night and explain why I left like I did. Tucker refused to take my calls, and my texts went unanswered. After seven months of trying, I called it. I wasn't going to beg the bastard to listen to me.

"Jesus H. Christ, Tucker. It was years ago. If you remember, I did try talking to you, and you ignored me. So, you and your dick need to get over it."

Standing, he placed his hands on the table and leaned in closer to me. Hell, you could put me in front of a bunch of old men who could take me down with their experience and knowledge and I'm not the least bit afraid of them. But have Tucker lean over and look into my eyes and I was a complete mess.

"Oh, I am over it. And over you."

"Good!" I spat at him.

"Good!"

I shot him the finger. "Good plus a million."

He pinched his eyebrows together. "What are we in, grade school? And this, coming from a woman who holds multiple degrees and is now being touted by major newspapers around the country as being one of the richest women in America. Kind of sad. Probably why you're still single. Maybe I'll give the *Times* a call and let them know why that is."

Standing, I went to hit him when Terri grabbed my arm.

"Oh, for shit's sake. Would the two you just stop?" Terri said as she looked between us.

Tilting my head, I gave him a look that dared him to keep going. He took the challenge and won.

"I'll let you go, Pumpkin, but since I'm providing that hard drink, I'll leave you to your mission so you can find that harder dick you need to forget all about your shitty day."

"You're the biggest asshole I've ever met!" I hated that my voice cracked, and he noticed it. I thought he would let me have the last word, but when I narrowed my eyes at him, he proved me wrong again.

"And you're the biggest bitch."

Terri stood. "Tucker, maybe you should keep greeting your guests."

Giving her a tight smile, he nodded in agreement then walked away.

I let out a gruff laugh and sat. "He really thinks he has the business sense to run a bar?" I blurted it out, but I knew Tucker did. With a sigh, I took a drink of my beer and scanned the place. I knew a good thing when I saw it . . . and this was a good thing. My heart rate was through the roof. *Damn, why did I let him do that to me*?

Terri chuckled. "Well, he does have a master's in business, so I'm sure he knows what he's doing."

My heart stopped.

Snapping my head back to Terri, I asked, "What did you just say?"

"Uh . . . about Tucker having a business degree?"

I grabbed her and pulled her up. "We need to talk. Now!"

"Ah, okay. Ladies' room?"

Shaking my head, I searched for Tucker. When I found him talking to some blonde, I dragged Terri behind me and made my way over to him.

"Be right back, Jim!" Terri called out over her shoulder.

Tucker ignored me when I stopped in front of him.

"Excuse me, Tucker?" I asked politely.

The girl looked my way, but he didn't. "Tucker. I need to ask you something."

He turned his body slightly away from me and kept talking to the girl.

"Oh, look at you acting like a ten-year-old. Who's in grade school now?" I spit out.

He whipped back around and pointed to me. "You drive me nuts! I swear if I could sew your fucking mouth shut, I would."

I gasped and turned to the girl. "Did you hear what he just said to me?"

She shook her head. "I certainly did. Asshole."

I couldn't help but smile from ear to ear as we watched the pretty young thing stomp away.

"What in the hell is your problem, Charlie? Jealous that someone other than you was getting my attention?"

With a roll of my eyes, I responded. "Hardly. I need to use your office. It's an emergency."

He stared at me like I was nuts.

I sucked my lower lip in for a brief moment, then said, "It's about my parents."

Ugh. I didn't want to use the *my parents just died* card, but I knew he was pissed at me and wouldn't let me in his office if I didn't. Plus, it was kind of true.

His eyes softened immediately and for a moment I saw something pass over his face. It was too quick for me to catch it before he went back to giving me a blank stare. The same one he had mastered so many years ago.

"Sure, no problem. It's down the hall to the back, the passcode is the year we graduated college."

I gave him a sweet grin and then dragged Terri down the hall with me. As I typed in the passcode, I shook my head. "He really needs to change this. Anyone can figure it out. He uses this as his passcode into his office and he thinks he can run a bar."

I knew damn well Tucker would be great at running this place. My pride made me act like a bitch, but deep down I was so proud of him for following his dreams, not caving into his father's demands, but doing what he wanted to do. I actually envied him, but I'd never let him know that.

"Will you please tell me what is going on?" Terri pleaded.

The door opened, and I pushed her in, causing her to stumble.

"Oh my God, Charlie! What has gotten into you?"

My eyes scanned the room. I swore I heard angels sing when I saw it.

Rushing around his desk, I grabbed the degree off the wall. "There it is!"

Flipping it over, I showed it to Terri, who pinched her thumb and finger between her eyes and asked, "What are you doing?"

Ignoring her question, I placed the frame on the desk and started to take off the back.

"Oh my God! What are you doing? You can't take that, Charlie! What is wrong with you?"

I stopped what I was doing. *Shit. She's right. I can't just show the board a degree. I have to show them a relationship. A real relationship.*

Jesus. I was losing my mind. I think between losing my parents, *The Twilight Zone* board meeting, and now running into Tucker in his bar had finally caught up with me. I was honestly feeling as though I was going crazy.

Dropping into Tucker's chair, I turned the degree over and stared at it.

Could I do this? Could I honestly do this?

The idea of being married to a man for a year made my stomach sick. But being married to Tucker? That might work. As much as I couldn't stand being near him, I longed to be near him. He was the reason no other guy was worth the effort. Tucker was and always would be the only guy I've ever felt this way about.

Wait. That totally sounds insane.

"Holy shit. I have no choice," I mumbled as I buried my face in my hands.

"Okay, I'm really starting to get worried about you, Charlie. I think you're stressed. Really stressed, sweetie. Maybe we should go home. Have you thought about talking to someone? It's a lot to handle, with your folks and all."

I dropped my hands onto Tucker's desk and looked at her. My entire body sagged as I let out a moan that would make even Mr. Pootie proud. "I don't want to talk to anybody about my folks." Maybe that wasn't such a bad idea though.

Closing my eyes, I dragged in a deep breath. One thing at a time. "I have to get married, and I only have three months to do it. Correction. Three months and some change."

Note to self: Put a countdown clock on my phone for Doom's Day.

She sat in the chair opposite the desk. "Okay, I'll bite. Why do you have to get married, and why in three months? Holy fuck, you're pregnant, aren't you? And the baby is due in three months and you need a baby daddy?"

"Terri, be serious, this is heavy-duty shit I'm talking about here. I found out today that my dear old granddaddy had a bylaw written into the articles of incorporation that said in the event something would happen to my father before I turned forty, in order for me to take over the company, I had to be married. And not just married to any random guy, but to someone who held a business degree. I have to stay married for at least a year, it can't be arranged, and I have to be able to prove to the board that the marriage is real."

She stared at me. Then her mouth fell open.

"No. No. No." She stood and started to pace.

"I know! It's fucked up in a huge way."

Shaking her head, she faced me. "No, what I'm saying no to is I know what that mind of yours is thinking. You're thinking Tucker is the guy."

"Yes! It's perfect. We've known each other for years so it would make sense. We start dating, we fall in love, and *bam*. I can sell it to the board as two lovers who rekindled an old college flame. We get married. It's perfect. I just need to figure out how to seduce Tucker and make him fall in love with me enough to marry me. In three months and three weeks."

My best friend stared at me, her mouth gaped open.

"Please tell me you're not being serious."

"I am! I don't know what else to do!"

"So you're going to lie to Tucker and pretend you're falling in love with him?"

I gave a small shrug. I had to force myself not to say I really was in love with him, as that made me sound even more pathetic than I really was.

Good Lord, who was I kidding? I was the queen of pathetic.

"Yes. I mean, we all know I like Tucker."

"How can they even do that? Force you to marry? Charlie, you went to law school, is that even legal?"

I chewed on my lip. "I can have the board vote on it, but there are a few old codgers on there who I'm pretty sure want me gone. I'm the twenty-eight-year-old daughter of the former CEO who is only in this position because she's the heir apparent. The lawyer said if I fight it, it could be months. I don't have months. I just need to get married, then work on getting this stupid thing to go away."

"This just all seems so far-fetched. I mean, you're being forced to get married."

"I know. I sat with the stupid lawyer nearly all day trying to find a loophole. I've got nothing. But if I can get Tucker to marry me, I can buy myself more time."

She turned away from me. "Charlie, this is the most insane thing I think you've ever done. Maybe you need to go and talk to someone. Maybe you misunderstood things, with your parents' deaths it might be—"

I held up my hand, forcing her to stop talking. My eyes teared up, and I could feel the breakdown coming. You know, the one I had been putting off for the last week.

The door to Tucker's office opened. When I looked at him and saw the immediate concern in his eyes, the floodgates broke free. I stared at him, and I broke down and started to cry.

But in that moment, I wasn't sure if I was crying for the loss of my parents or the loss of Tucker.

Four

TUCKER

CHARLIE DROVE ME crazy. I wanted so badly to hate her, but every time she walked that sweet ass by me, I was transported back seven years ago. The memory of her wrapped in my arms as we swung in the hammock was one of my favorites. And the one I had jerked off to in the shower more times than I could count.

Little did I know she was going to freak out on me and leave me a fucking note saying to forget the entire weekend happened. Nash tried to warn me about Charlie. Everyone knew she put her father above everything. Her only goal in life was making her father happy. Screw her own happiness. She'd given up so many dreams for him. I wondered if he knew how much his daughter had given up.

I sighed and dropped my head back, then rolled it around to ease the stress. I'd never be able to forget the most incredible seventy-two hours of my life. Or the way she fell apart over and over while whispering my name. I wondered if she had remembered telling me she was in love with me. She had been drunk, but her confession nearly knocked me on my goddamn ass. Her leaving that fucking note proved she was lying about what that weekend meant, and it caused me to see blood red. I knew she was lying, and she knew it too.

The memory hit me right in the chest.

CHARLIE GIGGLED AS I carried her up the back steps. She'd had one too many drinks and was currently teasing me that she had a secret.

I laid her on my bed and pulled my T-shirt over my head. "What's your secret, Pumpkin?"

Her eyes lit up and tears filled those beautiful blue eyes.

"I love you," she softly said.

Every ounce of air felt like it was pulled not only from my lungs, but from the room as well.

She closed her eyes and shook her head. "I think I loved you the first moment you smiled at me. How stupid am I?"

I had planned on sleeping out on the sofa, but when the girl you've secretly loved for the last few years tells you she loves you . . . well, you have no choice but to make love to her.

"Please tell me you're not too drunk to know what you're saying, princess."

Charlie chewed on her lip, her eyes turning dark. "I'm not too drunk."

I smiled as I crawled over her body, pressed my lips to hers, and gave my heart to her. Forever.

"TUCKER? TUCKER?"

Snapping out of my memory, I smiled at Pam. One of my managers.

"Yeah, sorry. What did you need?"

She looked me over and smiled bigger. "Do you have the number to Pine Brewery? I think we're going to want to order more of their American Amber Ale. It's been one of our biggest sellers."

"That's awesome," I replied. I knew that one was going to go over well with this crowd. Craft beer was my thing; I had a passion for it.

My father still didn't get my desire for what I did. He nearly stroked out when I told him I was opening my own bar. His only response was that at least my degree would get put to use.

"It sure is. Want me to go to your office and get it?"

"Actually, Pam, I let two of my college buddies use my office. With Charlie's parents dying . . ."

Pam gasped. "Oh, your poor friend. I hope he's going to be okay. How sad."

With a nod, I replied, "Charlie is a girl."

She frowned. "A girl? Her name is *Charlie*?" When she snarled her lip, I got defensive.

"It's short for Charleston."

Then she made a face. "That poor girl. What a dreadful name."

Opening my mouth to argue with her, I quickly shut it. It wasn't worth it, and why I felt the need to defend Charlie was beyond me. I'd always done it, though. Anytime anyone said anything bad about her, I stood up for her. Even though down to her very soul, she was a cold-hearted bitch.

That was a lie.

Charlie was far from being a bitch, even though she tried to play the part of one. She didn't know any of us knew about how she volunteered at the battered women's shelter once a week. Or the pet shelter on Town Lake every Saturday morning. I'd seen her at a cancer fundraiser last year, and I overheard her asking to keep her donation anonymous. It was later I found out she had donated $300,000.

Charleston Monroe didn't have a bad bone in her body. She was perfect. Beautiful. Smart. Sexy.

Jesus, Middleton. Snap out of it.

I didn't have time to think about Charlie.

"I'll go grab the number while I'm thinking about it. We'll call them first thing Monday morning."

Pam grinned. "Back to work! It's super crazy busy in here. I'll make the rounds."

I placed my hand on her arm and gave it a friendly squeeze. "Thanks, Pam."

Her eyes lit up. "Any time, Tucker."

Turning, I headed to my office. Hopefully everything was okay with Charlie. I hated how she was going through this alone. But then again, she wanted it that way. She'd always wanted to fly solo, so why should I be concerned?

When I opened the door to my office, I froze. Charlie sat in the chair at my desk and looked as if she was about to cry. She appeared so defeated. She opened her mouth to say something, and my entire world stopped when I saw the tears streaming down her face.

I should have gone to her. Pulled her into my arms to comfort her. But I didn't. I stood there like an asshole as she buried her face in her hands while her sobs filled my office. The words in the letter she wrote me flashed before my eyes.

"It was a mistake. We need to forget this weekend ever happened. There could never be anything between us."

"Charlie!" Terri blurted out as she ran around the desk.

Pulling her up, Terri wrapped her arms around Charlie. I'd never in all the years I'd known Charleston Monroe seen her cry.

Not once.

She was the strongest woman I'd ever met. Even at her parents' funeral she didn't cry. I had snuck in at the last minute and sat off to the side where I knew she wouldn't see me, but I could see her. I watched Charlie like a hawk, ready to rush in if she needed someone. Why in the hell I thought she would want me was beyond me. Wishful thinking, maybe? Her chin had quivered so many times it actually made my own eyes water. When it was time for them to close the caskets, she stood, walked up to her parents' caskets and took in a slow, steady breath. She said something to her father, then turned to her mother and smiled. It was the saddest smile I'd ever seen in my entire life.

As soon as Charlie's crying had started in my office, though, it stopped. "I'm okay. I'm fine."

It was that quickly she pulled herself together. There was the all-business Charlie I knew. God forbid anyone see the other side of her. The side I knew she had buried deep down.

I walked into the room and headed to the file cabinet. "I'm sorry to interrupt. I needed a number."

Our eyes met, and I fought to keep the tightness down in my chest. Charlie was hurting, and I just ignored it. Just dismissed her feelings as though she'd dismissed mine all those years ago. I was a prick, and I knew it. She wiped her tears away and shot me a dirty look. So maybe the cold-hearted act I was playing was a bit much. After all, she suffered a major loss only a week ago.

"Of course you'd walk in now, wouldn't you? Go ahead, M-Middleton. Make a smart-ass comment about how I broke down. How karma is a bitch and so am I, because I know you want to go there with me."

Stopping, I slowly shook my head. "It's okay to cry, Charlie."

Her teeth sank into her lip as her chin trembled. "No, it's not." Her head dropped and her fucking chin started to quiver. "It's not ever okay."

Her last words were barely a whisper.

God, who told her she couldn't show emotion?

She started toward the door and tripped. Jesus, those fuck-me shoes she wore were going to be the death of her and me. I'd never in my life saw anyone stumble like she did.

Terri caught her as Charlie yelled out, "Son of a fucking bitch!"

"Do you kiss people with that mouth?" I blurted. I wasn't sure why I was acting like a dick. I guess it was just something we did to each other.

"Fuck you, asshole."

"Been there, done that, Charlie, remember? Oh wait, that's right. You wanted to forget it ever happened. My bad."

Terri stopped walking. "I'll be right out."

With a wave of her hand, Charlie retreated through the door and never looked back.

Terri walked up to me and threw her hands on her hips. "What in the hell is wrong with you? Her parents died, Tucker. Have you *ever* seen her cry before? Hell, I've known her since I was eighteen, and I've never even seen her cry during a sad movie. She didn't even cry at her folks' funeral."

Turning back to the files, I found the one for Pine Brewery.

Slamming the file cabinet door, I took in a deep breath. "I'm sorry. I shouldn't have kicked her when she was down."

Her brows pinched together. "That's it?"

"What do you mean?"

She shook her head. "That's all you're going to say for treating her like that, knowing what she has gone through? What is wrong with you two? Clearly you both still have feelings for each other and won't admit it, so instead you attack one another."

I threw my head back and laughed. "Yeah. Right." I pointed the file toward the door and said, "Charlie Monroe has no heart. The only thing she cares about is her job. That's all she's ever cared about. That and living up to her father's expectations. I feel terrible her parents are gone. I honestly do, but that changes nothing between us. She made her feelings for me very clear seven years ago."

Terri threw her hands up and let out a frustrated groan. "Whatever! Believe what you want to believe, Middleton. I'm done trying with both of you."

She headed toward my door but stopped and faced me again. "But just so you know, Charlie admitted to Lily that she loved you only weeks after that weekend y'all spent together. All those times she tried calling you, to explain."

A knife pierced my heart . . . or at least it felt that way. *Charlie had admitted to my sister she loved me?*

"How do you know she told Lily that?" I asked.

Terri shook her head, disappointed at my reaction to her little bomb she had just dropped.

"Lily told me. She told me the real reason Charlie ran that morning. It's a damn shame you never let her back in to tell you or answered any of those calls and texts, but then again, maybe you really didn't care about her that much. Maybe it was your fucking ego that was wounded. Whatever it is, Tucker, she cares about you, and you just treated her like shit when she needed you the most. I hope you're feeling good about the pissing contest you just won."

She slammed the door behind her and I jumped.

Walking over to my desk, I dropped into my chair and rubbed

my neck. I stared at my degree that sat on my desk. What was it doing there? Picking it up, I turned and hung it back on the wall. My eyes caught the security system I had.

A strange feeling came over me. Opening up my laptop, I pulled up the video footage for my office and went back a few minutes to where Charlie and Terri had walked in. Lifting my headphones to my ears, I hit the play button. As I sat there and listened to Charlie and Terri speak, my anger grew more and more. Pulling off my headphones, I leaned back in my seat and stared at the screen, infuriated. I'd paused it at the part when Charlie started crying. My heart ached for her, but after hearing the little plan she had concocted that involved me, whatever sympathy I had for her turned into full-on anger.

After pacing in my office for thirty minutes, I finally stopped. The corners of my mouth slowly moved up until I let out a roar of laughter.

"You want to play dirty, Charlie? Oh, I can play dirty. Game fucking on."

~

"JIM, HOW MUCH has Charlie had to drink?" I asked as I watched her talk to some douchebag.

The way he kept placing his hand on her leg was driving me up a fucking wall. Of course, what guy wouldn't want to put his hand on her leg with the way she wore that little red dress. It showed off every amazing curve of her body. I might have been pissed off at Charlie more than ever, but I didn't want to see another man hurting her when she was in such an emotional state.

Douche. What you mean is you don't want any other guys hurting her, but you'll gladly hurt her any chance you can get.

I ignored my inner thoughts. After fuming in my office about Charlie's plan to seduce me, I decided to turn the tables on her. I'd seduce her, ask her to marry me, and then do what she did to me. Leave her. It would be a dick move, but revenge was the only thing on my mind right now.

Jim shrugged. "No clue. It's girls' night, and I was banned from the table. Terri said Charlie was on the hunt for a one-night stand. I ain't standing in the way of any of that. According to Terri, it's been years since Charlie was laid. Dude, do you know what years of sexual frustration can do to a woman when she's on the prowl? That's like being in the crosshairs of a lioness on the hunt."

My face tightened and my pulse sped up at the thought of her fucking some guy tonight. "Don't you think she's a little emotionally unstable to be hooking up with someone tonight?"

Jim stared at me with a blank expression. "Since when do you care what Charlie does? Wasn't it you who practically delivered her Sam, even when you knew he had a girlfriend? He was one of the only guys I know for sure Charlie has dated since the . . . incident. Which, by the way, if Terri and Lily ever found out you did that, shit would hit the fan."

A grin moved over my face. "Karma is a bitch."

"Dude, she never cheated on you."

I shrugged. "Whatever. All I'm saying is she looks pretty toasted. Maybe y'all should take her home."

Jim let out a roar of laughter. "Right. Like Charleston Monroe would go for being told what to do."

Throwing down the dishrag, I let out a string of curse words. "Well, I'm not going to let her leave with a stranger when she got drunk in my fucking bar. I'll take her home."

"What? You're leaving?" Pam asked in a panicked voice.

I turned and smiled. "I have to take a friend home who drank too much. I won't be long. Hold the fort down for me?"

Her face beamed with pride. "Of course!"

Walking around the bar, I headed over to Charlie's table. Stopping in front of her and the dickhead, I cleared my throat. She looked up, frowned, then focused back on him. His hand slipped a little farther up her leg, and I was happy to see she had the sense to push it back down.

"Charlie, I think you've had enough to drink. Why don't you let me take you home now?"

The guy stood up. "You her boyfriend or something?"

Popping up, Charlie stumbled but grabbed the table. "No. He is most certainly *not* my girlfriend."

Flashing her a confused look, Charlie covered her mouth and laughed. "Boyfriend. He's not my boyfriend."

Without taking my gaze off of her, I added, "I'm her friend though."

Narrowing her eyes, she shot me a serious go to hell look. "Friend? Is that what you call ignoring me for the last seven years."

There was no way I was getting into this with her here. "We're friends, Charlie, and I'm worried you've drunk too much. With your declaration of wanting to get a strange dick tonight, I'm thinking that might be a bit dangerous."

Her mouth dropped open and the guy next to us said, "Well, hell yeah. I knew we had something going on, baby."

Charlie looked between the both of us. She must have done it one too many times or too fast because she started to sway.

"I'm feeling . . . funny."

The guy next to me took a step back. "Dude, you can have her. I don't do the ones who throw up."

I watched as he took off toward the bar, stopping to talk to the blonde I had been talking to earlier.

Bastard.

When I looked back at Charlie, she was really swaying. "Come on, Pumpkin. I'll get you home."

She held up her hand to stop me, but quickly dropped it. "I think . . . I may throw up."

Sweeping her up and into my arms, I headed down the hall to the back of the bar. One of the waitresses called out, "You leaving, boss?"

Calling back over my shoulder, I replied, "Just taking a friend home."

"Yeah. Right. Don't forget a condom!"

With a roll of my eyes, I pushed the back door open that led to the small parking area reserved for the managers and me.

"Hold on, Charlie."

She covered her mouth. "Oh God. Tucker. I'm going to be sick."

Stopping, I set her down just in time. She leaned over and puked everywhere. I've worked in enough bars to know how far to stand back when someone hurls. And boy was Charlie hurling. Fucking hell. She must not have eaten a damn thing today.

"Jesus. I think I'm dying," she mumbled.

Another round and she had nothing else to throw up. She stood and looked at me. Even after throwing up, the damn woman made my knees weak.

"Hey, Tucker?"

Her voice was so soft and innocent it made my stomach jump in delight.

"Yeah, Charlie?"

"Why is everything going black?"

"Huh?"

And just like that her legs gave out, and she fell right into my arms.

I stood in the parking lot behind my new bar with a passed-out woman in my arms. Glancing around, the only thing I could do was laugh. For seven years I had hoped for another chance to have Charlie in my arms, and here we were. Lifting her up, I put her over my shoulder. The short red dress she had on rode up, and her perfect tight ass was right in my face.

"Why, cruel world? Why?" I mumbled as I walked to my car.

Five

CHARLESTON

ROLLING OVER, I pulled the covers over my head and moaned.

"Oh shit," I whispered. Even my whispered words hurt my head. I hadn't drunk like that in a long time.

Note to self: Give up alcohol. Except wine. Wait. No. Never ever give up wine.

With my head still buried, I tried to think back to last night. The last thing I remembered was talking to that guy . . . Brad. No Billy. Bobby? Brady?

Who cares? I need aspirin.

I pushed the covers over my head and went to get out of bed. I froze when I saw the sheets.

Oh. My. God.

These aren't my sheets.

Turning, I looked at the bed.

This isn't my bed.

Glancing down, I gasped.

I'm not wearing any clothes.

Covering my mouth, I jumped up. "I didn't. Oh God, please tell me

I didn't. Terri! I'm going to kill her."

Frantically looking around, I saw my purse on the chair in the corner. Rushing over to it, I dug through it until I found my phone.

As I waited for that whore to answer her phone, I mumbled, "She broke the number one girlfriend code. Don't let your friend leave with a guy when they're drunk!"

"Hey, girl! So? Did you get laid like you wanted? Please tell me yes 'cause this would make a great story."

My heart jumped to my throat as a small sound came from my lips. "Wh-what? Why? How could you? You let me go off with him? What if he had killed me!"

She laughed. "Hardly. But then again, you do drive him up a wall, and he has mentioned snuffing you out a time or two."

My finger and thumb went to the bridge of my nose. "What are you talking about?"

Terri muffled the phone, then laughed. "Hello? Terri! I'm at a strange man's house, I don't remember anything, and I'm naked."

"Wait. You're naked?"

"Yes!"

"Oh, wow. Shit just got *really* interesting. Where's Tucker?"

Tucker? How in the hell would I know where Tucker was?

"I don't know! I don't care. Terri. I don't know where I am. He could come back any minute, and I'm standing here naked. Oh my God. Do you think I had sex with him?"

"Do you feel like you had sex?"

Stopping, I jumped around a bit. "No. I'd be sore if I did, right? Fuck if I know, it's been so long."

Terri sighed. "It really has been that long. You've done forgotten how it feels, huh?"

"Aww, hell, Mr. Pootie!"

"I'm sure he's fine. Let's get back to what happened between you and Tucker last night."

I shook my head as I glanced around the room for my clothes. Dropping to my knees, I looked under the bed.

"Why are we talking about Tucker? I have bigger problems."

Then I heard a male voice clear his throat.

"Oh God," I whispered. "He's in the room, Terri. I'm naked! I can't find my clothes."

Terri laughed. "Okay, well, have fun. Tell Tucker I said hey."

My brows furrowed, and I was about to say something when the line went dead.

It was then I felt the change in the room, and everything from last night came crashing back into my poor brain, causing my head to pound harder.

Slowly lifting up, I peered over the bed, only to find Tucker leaning up against the doorjamb. He wore a shit-eating grin on his face, and fuck me, he looked so gorgeous.

Oh no.

I swallowed hard. "Um . . . I can't, um. Well, it appears I am . . . you see, I can't find my, ahh . . . the dress I had on."

Jesus. Why do I act like an idiot around him? Why!

"Your clothes had throw up on them. They're almost dry."

My stomach dropped. "Did we . . . ?"

He smiled. Full on dimples and all.

God, I want him. Even in my current hungover condition, I've never wanted this man more than right now.

Wait. No. I don't!

Yes . . . yes, you do.

Crap. What if I already had him? And I don't remember. I'm going to be so pissed off if we had sex and I don't remember it.

"No, we didn't sleep together, and for the record, you got yourself undressed."

Relaxing, I let out the breath I didn't realize I held in.

He pushed off and pointed to his dresser. "Find something of mine to put on until your clothes dry. I put them in the wash last night but fell asleep and forgot to move them to the dryer. I washed them again since they sat in there for a few hours."

My heart skipped a beat. Why did I think that was so sweet? Jesus. I really did need to get laid if I thought Tucker washing my puke-covered dress, not once but twice, was sweet.

"Um, thanks."

He nodded. "I'm making omelets if your stomach feels up to eating."

"'Kay."

It was all I could say. When he shut the door behind him, I dropped my head onto his bed.

"Shit! Shit! Shit!"

I'm naked. I'm in Tucker's house. And I'm hung the hell over.

My father would be so disappointed in me. This was not the behavior of someone in control of CMI Consulting.

It was, however, perfectly normal for a twenty-eight-year-old single woman. *Wasn't it?*

Racing over to his dresser, I opened the second drawer to the top. It was filled with T-shirts. I smiled as I ran my hand over them. They were neatly folded and organized by color. God, that was sexy as hell. I was going to smuggle one of these out of his house after I sprayed his cologne on it.

I groaned. New level of pathetic I'd reached here.

Chewing on my lip, I picked out a blue one. It was my favorite color, after all.

Slipping it on, it fell mid-thigh. Smiling, I shook my head as I pulled the next drawer open. Thoughts of Tucker telling me how sexy I looked wearing only his T-shirt seven years ago filled my memory. The second drawer contained sweatpants and workout stuff. I reached in and took out a pair of black sweatpants. It would be sexy as sin if I walked out in only the T-shirt. Too bad I wasn't trying to seduce him.

With my foot up and ready to slip into the leg of the pants, I stopped.

Tucker. Business degree. Three months, six days.

The idea I had last night came rushing back as I put my foot down and held up the pants.

If I was going to have to be married to someone, why not be married to someone I knew and had feelings for? He would barely be tolerable but easy to look at every morning and night, and at least I'd get some good sex, not to mention a lot of orgasms, out of the deal since we had to stay married for a year at least.

My body shook at the idea.

Then my phone buzzed on the bed. I put the pants back in the drawer, shut it, and then dove across the bed and swiped my phone to answer it.

"Terri!"

"Charlie! Hey, I forgot to tell you. Some guy named Paul Ricker called your cell last night. You were kind of already two sheets to the wind, so I said you were helping a friend move some furniture. He asked that you return his call this afternoon."

Paul Ricker? What was that weasel doing calling me on a Friday night, then expecting me to call him on a Saturday?

"Did he say what he wanted?"

"Nope. Said it was business."

"Uh-huh. Okay, well listen, can we meet for lunch later? I really need to finish talking to you."

Flipping over, I stared up at the ceiling in Tucker's bedroom. The most amazing crown molding was on display. Sitting up, I took everything in. If I hadn't known any better, I would have sworn I was in my own home.

But I wasn't.

I'm in Tucker's bedroom. Half naked and ready to implement a plan so crazy I was sure I needed to have my head examined.

"Sure. Is everything okay, sweetie? You haven't been acting right. I mean, I know you lost your parents and that's somewhat expected, but yesterday in Tucker's office you seemed a bit . . . off. And that crazy plan to seduce Tucker?" She laughed. "You were kidding. Right?"

With an evil smile, I stood and walked to the window. The view of the river took my breath away.

"No. Everything is totally not okay, but I have to go, Terri. I have some serious flirting to do."

"Oh no, you weren't kidding."

"Nope!" I said, popping my P.

"Oh God. Let's make it an early lunch. I'm dying to hear how this turns out."

Ending the call with Terri, I rushed into the bathroom. I pulled my hair out of the sloppy ponytail and fixed it. Splashing my face and thanking God for waterproof mascara, I pinched my cheeks and set off to find Tucker.

Opening the door, I realized I was on the second floor of a house. "Tucker has a house?" I asked no one. Why did I not know this? I saw the man at least once a month, if not more.

Looking down the hall, I followed the smell of eggs. My stomach rolled, and I had to cover my mouth. The smell made me feel sick.

I walked up to a beautiful grand staircase. My fingers moved lightly down the mahogany banister while I slowly walked down the old stairs. If this had been seven years ago with Tucker, I would dare say this would be romantic.

My eyes were everywhere. Taking every single thing in. The house was for sure historical. The decorations clearly matched the time period the house was built. Until I walked into the kitchen. It was state of the art and blow-me-over amazing.

Note to self: If I make this work with Tucker, we're living in his house.

I continued to walk in as my gaze scanned every square inch. Then I saw him and froze.

Oh Lord, give me strength.

He was leaning against the sink with a smile that said he liked my outfit pick. His intense stare kicked up my libido.

Okay, don't panic. Act sexy. You can do this! You have *to do this. It is time to seduce the shit out of Tucker Middleton. Forget all about the last seven years and how much the two of you hated on one another. It's show time!*

Trying out my flirting skills, I smiled and went to tell him how sexy he looked when I walked right into the barstool and toppled over it, landing with a thud onto the tile floor. My hands stung and both knees throbbed.

"Shit Charlie, are you okay?"

I was on all fours staring at the light brown travertine floor; my cheeks burned with embarrassment.

Then an energy I hadn't felt in a long time zipped through my body when Tucker picked me up and set me on the island.

"Damn, you scraped both of your knees."

Inhaling a deep breath, his cologne swirled around in my nose. The mental and physical sensations were threatening to pull me under. Being this close to Tucker again was sensory overload, and I wasn't sure I was strong enough to be in his sphere. Right now, all I knew was he left me breathless and momentarily unable to form any coherent thoughts.

I couldn't pull my eyes off of the way his muscles flexed under his shirt. Jesus, his body was nice back in college. Now . . . now he had all tight-looking muscles with abs that appeared to be painted on.

Shaking my head, I looked down at my poor knees. Crap.

"Nah. I'm okay."

Tucker's head lifted and he frowned. "You're bleeding."

I smiled. He must have thought I hit my head on the way down with the way I ogled him.

God, he has amazing eyes. Not really hazel, not really blue. A mysterious gray.

Note to self: Take a mental snap shot of this moment for later use.

Wait. Bleeding?

Dropping my stare, I looked at both knees. They were covered in . . . in . . . blood.

"Oh God," I gasped as I grabbed onto Tucker's arms. "B-blood. Everywhere."

Tucker cupped my face with his hands. "Charlie, look at me."

The smell of it hit me like a brick wall, and I started to sway. I'd never liked blood. Ever.

"Charlie. Look. At. Me."

My gaze slowly lifted until we were staring into each other's eyes.

"Take a deep breath in through your nose, out through your mouth."

Tears threatened to build as I tried to do what he said. A sob slipped from my lips. "I hate blood."

He nodded. "I know. Just don't pass out again."

I was known for passing out at the sight of blood. I dropped face-first once when we were playing volleyball. Nash jumped up to spike the ball and hit it straight into Blake, breaking his nose. I ate sand the second I saw the blood.

"You okay, Pumpkin?"

Tucker calling me his pet name tossed me right over the ledge. One tear, then two, then the onslaught came. I never cried. Ever. I was stronger than this, but this marked two breakdowns in less than twenty-four hours.

Being here with Tucker, I was an emotional mess. All the tears I had tried to keep inside over the last week pounded on the door, demanding I let them out and show how weak I truly was.

Why did my parents leave me?

His thumbs ran across my cheeks. "Please don't cry," he whispered while leaning his forehead to mine. "Charlie, please don't cry."

Between my soft sobs, I tried to speak. "Th-this . . . has . . . b-been the worst . . . w-week of . . . my l . . . li . . . life."

"I'm so sorry. Tell me what to do to take it all away."

My breath caught in my throat as I made immediate eye contact with him. I needed this man more than I needed my next breath in this moment, and he had no idea what he asked of me. This was no longer about me trying to seduce him for a stupid setup marriage. It was about my feelings for him and how he made me feel when I was with him. Lifting my head, our eyes met. I searched his face.

Did he feel the energy between us too?

It was so strong I swore I heard the air crackling.

I hated that he brought out this silly-in-love feeling from the middle of my chest . . . yet I was so over the moon for this guy. I always had been, and I always would be. There was no changing our chemistry and attraction. That mushy phrase came to my mind, "the heart wants what the heart wants," and even though I didn't want to be that woman, I was *that* woman in this moment.

The heat caused by the trail his thumbs left was unmistakable. His mouth opened and his gaze was almost pleading, begging me to say what he wanted to hear and what I longed to say.

With a heavy breath, he pleaded, "Tell me."

Say it, Charlie. Say it!

"I . . . I need—"

My chest rose and fell with each breath.

His hand dropped to my neck and pulled my lips slightly closer to him.

"What do you need?"

Another tear slipped down my cheek as I responded with a barely audible, "You."

Pulling me to him, our lips crashed. I instinctively wrapped my legs around him, feeling the fabric of his pants rub against my throbbing, exposed clit.

When his hand pushed into my hair and grabbed a handful like I was his life preserver, I moaned into his mouth.

Oh. God. I'd missed him so much. My arms wrapped around his neck as I held on for dear life. The way he explored my mouth and nipped at my lower lip had me grinding myself into his hard-on.

His hand moved down my back and under my ass, pulling me even closer to him, causing me to gasp with the feel of his cock pressed against me.

He pulled his lips from my mouth. "Fucking hell, Charlie. You're not wearing anything."

I smiled and chewed on my lip, feigning innocence. "Easier access," I whispered before he crashed his mouth back to mine.

The knock on the door caused me to jump, and Tucker quickly stepped away from me. Both of us breathed as though we had just run a race. He looked down at his hitched-up T-shirt that showed I had nothing else on. I quickly pulled it down.

"Jesus," Tucker whispered as he scrubbed his hands down his face. The way we both got so lost in each other scared me, and I knew if he had known I wasn't wearing panties sooner, he'd have been inside me.

The door opened and we both turned to see who was walking in.

My mouth fell open when a beautiful red-haired woman appeared. She stopped dead in her tracks when she saw us. She looked familiar, and I tried to remember where I'd seen her.

"Hey," was all she said.

I instantly fiddled with the T-shirt to make sure I was covered up as much as I could be, considering the few garments I wore.

"Gina. You're late," Tucker said with an edge to his voice that hinted at anger.

My heart dropped. *Who is Gina?*

"What happened?" She gasped as she made her way over to me. "Oh my gosh. Tucker, run upstairs and get some gauze and antiseptic from the half bath."

Okay, who is this person? Why is she in Tucker's house and how in the hell does she know he has gauze and antiseptic in the half bath?

That warm, fuzzy feeling was now gone as my libido got doused with ice water. If that wasn't enough, the nausea came back when I looked at the blood.

Tucker cleared his throat and said, "Perfect timing."

My head jerked over to him. *What?* How could he say that after what happened between us? There was no way he could deny the connection we still had.

My eyes widened in horror. What if she was . . . oh, no. *Oh. Dear. God.*

"Um, I'm okay," I sputtered out. The realization I had no panties on and this woman had her face near my vagina did not sit well with me.

"No, you have two nasty cuts on your knees. What in the world happened?" the redhead asked. When I looked back up to Tucker, he was gone.

"I, ah . . . I tripped over the barstools."

She chuckled. "Tucker told me you were a bit of a klutz."

Snarling my lip, I stared at her head while she tried to dab the blood off my knees.

Anger raced through my blood. "And who exactly are you?" I asked. The unfriendly nature of my tone surprised me.

Glancing up, her eyes turned evil. "I'm Tucker's girlfriend."

Whoosh.

All the air from the room vanished.

My head spun as I lifted my fingers to my tingling lips.

Tucker came racing back into the kitchen and handed the gauze and spray to Gina. He ran his hand through his hair. "Let me check to see if your clothes are dry."

I jumped when she sprayed my knees. "Shit! Fuck! Damn! That hurts like a motherf'er."

She looked up at me. "My, what a ladylike mouth for a CEO of a billion-dollar company."

About to tell her to fuck off, she kept talking. "Looks like they are small but deep. Wow, you must have hit the stool hard."

Nothing would come out of my mouth as I watched her put the gauze on my knees and then add tape to hold it in place.

Tucker cleared his throat. "Your clothes are, um . . . they're dry."

Gina stood up and smiled. "There, all better."

With a forced smile, I started to get off the island.

"Let me help you," Tucker said.

"No!" I yelled out, causing him to freeze. The last thing I needed was to feel his hands on me again. My skin was still singed from where he had his hands before the arrival of Gina. I jumped down and then gasped when the pain shot through my kneecaps.

"Shit," I mumbled. Tears burned in my eyes again. This time it wasn't from my knees or the blood; it was knowing Tucker had been about to cheat on his girlfriend. With me. What was I more upset about? The fact that he had a girlfriend or that he was a cheater? Maybe it was because my plan was just ruined. There would be no getting Tucker to marry me and save my job. I was fucked.

"Why didn't you let me help you?" Tucker asked.

Reaching for my clothes, I glared at him while grabbing them from his hands. "Do you even have to ask? Forget it. May I use your room to change?"

He nodded while rubbing the back of his neck.

"Of course you can."

Turning back to Gina, I grinned. "Thank you so much."

She shrugged. "I'm a nurse, so it was no problem. I just got off a double shift." She looked at Tucker. "That's why I was late for breakfast."

I felt sick. I thought he was cooking breakfast for me . . . but he was cooking it for her. *I'm such an idiot.*

Feeling like a complete fool, I rushed out of the kitchen and up the stairs, ignoring the pain in my knees.

When I shut the bedroom door, I dropped back against it and covered my mouth to keep from crying.

Why am I crying so damn much?

Hell if I knew. My parents were gone, I was left with the responsibility of running a global business, and I had to find a husband with a business degree in three months.

And Tucker had a girlfriend.

My phone buzzed on the bed. Ignoring it for the moment, I ripped his T-shirt off my head. Tossing it onto the bed, I got dressed.

Paul Ricker's name flashed across my screen. Whatever the hell he wanted, it would have to wait. He was the last person I wanted to talk to right now.

The knock on the door caused me to quicken my pace getting dressed. Slipping on the red dress, I grabbed my heels that were next to the chair. Reaching for my purse, I went to open the door, but it opened for me. Tucker stood there with a confused expression on his face.

Are you fucking kidding me?

He was confused. I was the one who should have been confused after he just had his tongue down my throat and his dick pressed against my very naked vagina all the while his girlfriend was on her way over for breakfast!

Note to self: All men are scumbags.

"I have to know something."

Standing up straight, I held my breath. "What?"

"Why did you come downstairs in only my T-shirt?"

"You told me to get dressed while my clothes dried. What else was I supposed to put on, Tucker?"

He pinched his brows together and was about to say something when I asked, "Who's Gina?"

When his mouth shut, he looked taken aback by my out-of-the-blue question.

Ugh! Damn it, this week keeps getting worse.

Pushing past him, I made my way down the steps.

"Charlie, wait. How are you going to get home?"

Gina came walking out of the other room, interrupting my

not-so-nice response to Tucker. "Leaving so soon?"

If I hadn't known any better, I would say there was a bit of a bitch tone to her voice. Understandable, considering the circumstances.

"Yes. I have an appointment I need to get to."

"Oh, bummer. Well, I'm glad Tucker was able to take care of an old college friend who got a bit too drunk last night."

Great. Let's just add to my humiliation, why don't we? I didn't even bother to answer her as I kept my eyes forward.

"Gina! What in the hell?" Tucker said as I pulled the front door open and stepped outside. A cold front must have blown through because it was a breezy, cool September morning. I inhaled the much-needed air.

Hitting the only number I knew to call, I prayed Tucker wouldn't follow me outside. I needed to put as much distance between the two of us—*and his girlfriend*—as possible.

"Hey. I need a ride."

"Where are you?"

I could hardly get the words out of my mouth. "Your brother's."

She didn't even question it. "I'm around the corner. I'll be right there."

My voice cracked. "Thanks."

My shoulder burned from the contact when he touched me.

"Charlie, why don't you come back in? We really need to talk about what happened in there."

Counting to five, I put on my game face. The one I'd been wearing for the last seven years. The one that would make me a successful businesswoman for the rest of my pathetic life. Turning, I flashed him a wide grin. "Which part, Tucker? The one where we almost fucked on your kitchen island? Or the part where Gina walked in?"

His brows furrowed.

"You know what? Never mind. I'm sorry if I ruined your evening last night and clearly your morning. It's a good thing she came when she did before we did something we would *regret*."

His face was pained. "You like that word, don't you? Or maybe you just associate it with me."

My heart dropped. "What?"

With a shrug, he glanced over my shoulder. "Looks like Lily's here. I hope your knees feel better."

He turned and walked back into his house, leaving me feeling as empty as I felt that day seven years ago.

Tearing my stare away from his retreating figure, I walked to Lily's Jeep. Opening the car door, I slipped in and shut it.

One look at Lily and I let my tears fall. Again. Fuck me, this crying shit was for the birds.

She reached for my hand and squeezed it. "Oh, Charlie."

With a subtle shake of my head, I dropped it against the headrest. My head pounded, my knees hurt like hell, I missed my parents, and the only man who could save me from the mess I was in professionally had a girlfriend. And as much as I told myself I couldn't stand to be near Tucker, I knew it was far from the truth. Deep down I was more upset that he'd kissed me knowing that he had a girlfriend. Tucker never seemed to be the type of guy who would cheat. Never.

The only way I could make this marriage thing work in such a short period of time was with Tucker. What in the hell was I going to do now?

Great.

Just freaking great.

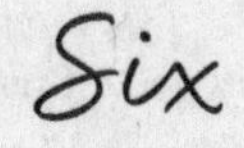

Six

CHARLESTON

LILY SET THE cup of coffee in front of me. I was on my sofa with my knees tucked under my chin and Mr. Pootie by my side. I'd gotten the silent treatment from him after coming home. His breakfast was late, and he had been pissed. He refused to eat it until he couldn't take it any longer, probably from what he thought was starvation. Now he was settled in next to me snoring.

"Terri said she was on her way."

I didn't respond as I looked out the window. The letters the lawyer had given me caught my eye. I hadn't had the strength to open and read them yet. I knew the moment I did, I'd be thrown into another fit of crying. It seemed to be my go-to reaction the last few days.

"Do you want to tell me what happened between you and my brother?"

The only person I had ever been truthful with when it came to Tucker was Lily. She knew how I felt about him and the real reason I walked away from him that morning. She also knew how miserable and pathetic I was every time I saw him with a girl.

With a deep breath in, I held it for a few seconds before exhaling.

"God, Lily. I'm such a bumbling mess when I'm around him, and I don't know why. He makes me feel like I'm walking around in a damn fog. And the worst part is, I can't stop falling whenever he's around me."

"Your knees?"

Looking back at her, I frowned. "I had this brilliant plan that I was going to seduce him this morning, and I tripped over his barstools."

Her mouth fell. "*What?* Seduce him? Why?"

I heard the worry in her voice.

The doorbell rang, and I breathed a sigh of relief.

Lily jumped up. "Stay there, I'll get it."

After Terri and Lily greeted each other, Terri practically skipped into the living room. She flopped down in a chair and looked at me. "So! What happened? Did y'all work out your stupid differences and bump uglies?"

"Gross! He *is* my brother, you know, Terri."

With a weak smile, I looked down at Mr. Pootie sleeping soundly. If only my life was such a breeze. I shook my head and answered softly, "We kissed."

They both gasped, and Mr. Pootie meowed.

"Oh. My. God. Tell me you didn't ruin it, Charlie."

My head snapped up, and I glared at Lily. "Why would you assume *I* ruined it?"

She shrugged. "He seemed a bit upset when I picked you up. Wouldn't even wave back at me when I pulled up."

I let out a sarcastic laugh. "Oh no, that was because his *girlfriend* showed up and broke up the kiss that the cheating asshole instigated."

Lily and Terri both looked at me with a confused look on their faces. "Tucker doesn't have a girlfriend," Lily stated.

"Psh. Then he doesn't keep you very informed. Gina showed up this morning for breakfast." Mr. Pootie stood and looked at me. Running my hand down his perfectly shaved back, I grinned. "I know, boy, you're the only man in my life I can trust."

He seemed pleased with this declaration of mine as he turned three times and settled back in next to me.

With her fingers rubbing her forehead, Lily responded with a sigh.

"Wait. Gina is not Tucker's girlfriend. They dated months ago and not even for that long. She was stopping by this morning to pick up some medical books she left at his house. Tucker mentioned yesterday she was stopping by after her shift."

Terri looked at Lily and then me. "Damn. Do you have a shot of whiskey I can put in my coffee? This just got juicy."

I snarled my lip at her and shot her a go-to-hell look. I knew I recognized her! I must have seen her with Tucker one night when we all went out. "Wait. When I asked her who she was, she told me she was his girlfriend."

Lily laughed. "Of course she did. She walked in, saw the two of y'all kissing, and probably got jealous."

Shaking my head, I replied, "No, she couldn't have seen us kissing. When she knocked, Tucker pulled away from me."

"You were in the kitchen?" Lily asked, her brow quirked up as though she already knew the answer.

I nodded.

"Then she saw you through the window. He never shuts the blinds."

My stomach twisted into a knot. "Oh my gosh. That little lying bitch."

Terri laughed. "Score one point for the ex."

"Wait, let's go back a few steps. What brought on the kiss?" Lily asked.

Groaning, I dropped my head back. "Oh God. It's so complicated."

"Why? Because you're secretly lusting after my brother. Doesn't seem complicated in the least bit to me."

Terri giggled then shot up. "Wait. Last night you had a grand plan to seduce Tucker. Tell me you didn't put it into action. I mean, I get you only have three months to get married."

Lily gasped. "What? Married? Holy shit, what am I missing? Okay, *you* need to do some explaining, Charlie."

Looking back at them both, I sighed. I could go the long version or the short. Terri had already heard all of this, so I decided to go with the short. "My grandfather had a bylaw written in for CMI. If I was to inherit the company before the age of forty, in order to take control, I have to be married. And not just to any man, but to someone with specific requirements."

Lily's mouth opened and she yelled, "What!"

Terri held up her hands and said, "Girl, I was just as surprised. This is not the 1950s where the women are required to have a man by their side."

I nodded. "I said pretty much the same thing."

"Charlie, you have to be able to do something," Lily replied.

With a shrug, I slowly shook my head. "If I try to take it to court, it could take months, and by then someone else will be in control, and God knows what will happen to the company. Even though I'm CEO, I can't remove the bylaw because, well, it concerns me."

Terri leaned forward. "I find it very hard to believe your father would have allowed that to be in there. I mean, look at how he pushed you and groomed you to take over that business. The last thing he wanted was for you to be tied down to a guy."

I thought of Mr. Ricker and my stomach turned. "He told the VP to take it out, turns out he never did. He claims they never got the time to do it, which is bullshit. I've been racking my brain trying to think of how to prove he lied to my father and said it was done."

"Your dad wouldn't have checked to make sure it had been done?" Lily asked.

"Not with Ricker. For some reason, my father trusted him implicitly. Even though I don't trust him as far as I can throw him."

"Okay, get back to the marriage thing. Can't you just hire someone, marry him, and then divorce him?" Lily asked.

I laughed. "No. Dear ol' granddaddy stated that I had four months—which, by the way, started the day my father died—to be married. The marriage cannot be arranged, and there needs to be proof of a relationship. His only downfall was when he enacted this stupid law, he only required I be married for one year."

"That's a weird rule to have in there," Terri stated as she took a drink of her coffee.

"I guess because back in his day divorce was so frowned upon. But it gets better. My hubby has to have a business degree and sit as a chair on the board to . . . *help me* . . . run the company."

Lily stared at me like I had dropped a bomb on her, much like Terri had last night.

"Please. For the love of all things that are good in this world, tell me you're joking with us." Lily scoffed.

With a shake of my head, I replied, "I wish. I'm chairman of the board and CEO for now, but if I'm not married by December, Paul Ricker gets the position."

They both gasped, and again Mr. Pootie put in his two cents with a drawn-out meow. Clearly he was as upset over this as we all were. "Yeah, piecing it together yet, ladies?" I watched as my cat got up and headed over to his window seat, clearly tired of this conversation. So was I, to be honest.

"That asshole!" Terri bit out.

Lily's face looked concerned. "Okay, so maybe now we need to talk about you and my brother."

"She wants to seduce Tucker and marry him."

I shot Terri a dirty look.

Closing her eyes, Lily fell back against the chair. "This is not going to turn out well."

"What are you talking about, Lil? They both like each other, yet they are too stubborn to admit it. Hey, speaking of, the kiss this morning?"

My chest squeezed as I thought back to the moment we shared together. With a smile, I bit into my lower lip, still feeling it tingle.

"Holy shit, Charlie," Lily whispered.

My eyes lifted to hers. "I have no desire to get married. My life has always been about CMI, drilled into my head that I needed to be married to that, not a man. So, when Terri mentioned Tucker and I saw his business degree last night, I got an idea." I gave a small shrug, knowing this could go one of two ways. My best friends would think it was an amazing idea, or they would tell me I was insane.

"The only man I could *ever* imagine being married to is . . . Tucker. This morning I woke up in his bed naked. Which, by the way, thanks for helping me out last night, Terri. You totally broke the girl code on that one. Never leave a friend down like that!"

Lily sighed. "Can we please get back to you being at my brother's house naked?"

I nodded. "Right. Well he was washing my clothes because I had thrown up on them. Anyway, he told me to put something of his on. I grabbed a T-shirt and then remembered how much it turned him on that weekend we were together when I wore his shirt. I thought maybe if I could win him back over . . . *seduce him* . . . we could start dating. And . . . and then . . . we could . . ."

"Get married," Terri finished.

Chewing on my finger, I nodded. "Anyway, I'm such an idiot around Tucker, always have been. I walked into the kitchen and tried to put my sexy on, but damn it all to hell, he looked sexy standing there, and it threw me all off balance. Then he smiled at me, his dimples popping out, and the next thing I knew I was on the floor in pain, then on his island while he looked at my knees. And then . . . we kissed."

"A small kiss?" Terri asked.

My cheeks heated. "No. Far from small. Big. Fire hot. Like, he was up all against me, and I swear, if that bitch hadn't showed up we would have been . . ."

"Stop! Ewww, gross. Please, I already have a visual in my head, thank you very much."

I chuckled.

"So why did he look so mad at you when I picked you up? I get why *you* were upset, you thought he had a girlfriend after he kissed you."

Terri chuckled. "You mean after they were all up in each other's business?"

Lily threw a dirty look Terri's way. "Shut. Up."

"He wanted to talk to me, but I was still reeling over what had happened and the thought that he had a girlfriend. I might have said something about regretting the kiss."

Lily and Terri both sighed. "God, Charlie. Way to break the guy's heart again," Terri said as she got up and headed into my kitchen.

"What? I thought he had a girlfriend!" I fell back onto the sofa and stared up at the ceiling. "Ugh. This whole thing sucks. How in the hell am I going to seduce a man who probably hates me even more now? It took seven years to get him to even touch me again. I only have a few months to win him over, get him to ask me to marry him, and show the board it's a real relationship."

Lily stood over me with a frown on her face. "Here's an idea. Why don't you tell Tucker the truth?"

I sat up and spun around to look at her. "The truth?"

"Yeah, Charlie. If you tell him what's going on, maybe he'll agree to it."

Laughing, I looked between them. "Where have you both been the last seven years? If I told Tucker I needed him to pretend to be my boyfriend, then we had to get married and stay married for a least a year, he would laugh in my face. He'd probably enjoy watching my pain and suffering."

Lily placed her hands on her hips. "Or . . . he would do it because deep down inside you're both crazy about each other."

My thumb came up to my mouth, and I started chewing on my nail. "I don't think I can take that risk." As I lifted my eyes up to them, they pooled with tears. "If he said no, I'd lose everything."

Terri dropped to her knees and took my hands. "Oh, honey, he's not going to say no. Deep down Tucker really cares about you."

I lifted my eyebrows. "You don't think he'll say no?"

She shook her head. "I don't think so."

Turning over her shoulder, she looked at Lily. "What about you, Lily?"

When Lily looked up from her phone, she frowned. "Um. I think being honest with him is the best thing you could do. If you're not, this could turn bad really quickly."

"Is everything okay, Lily?" I asked.

With a heavy sigh, she looked at me. "Yeah. Sorry. Um listen, I've got to run, honey. But I agree with Terri. Just tell him the truth."

Quickly walking over to me, she kissed me on the cheek. I reached up for her arm and looked at her. "Promise me you won't say a word to Tucker about this."

She rolled her eyes. "Oh God, Charlie. You're going to ask me to lie to my brother?"

I stood up. "No. I'm just asking you to not share what I shared with you this morning. Let me handle this my way."

"This is not going to end well if you keep the truth from him. I can't watch you hurt him again."

Terri agreed. "I'm with Lily on this one, Charlie."

My heart sank. I knew if I told Tucker the truth, he would turn down the idea. I'd hurt him too much for him to ever do anything for me. I had to do it this way. It was my only hope of keeping control of my father's company and following through with my promise to him. I had to seduce Tucker and make him see he could trust me again. The irony of me trying to get the man to trust me while I built our relationship on a lie wasn't lost on me. A strange pain in my chest hit me, but I pushed it away.

"I don't have any other choice," I whispered.

Lily's shoulders sank. "You do; you're just too afraid to pick the right one."

Seven

TUCKER

GINA LEANED AGAINST the kitchen counter with a smug expression on her face when I walked back into the kitchen from my room.

"You're still here?" I asked, pulling out the orange juice.

"What in the hell did you ever see in that woman?" she asked.

I ignored her.

"I mean, the way she was hanging all over you when I walked up."

"I'm pretty sure we were both hanging all over each other, Gina. What else do you need? I'm not really in the mood."

My phone buzzed in my pocket, and I took it out to see it was Lily. Traitor. She'd come and picked up the enemy.

Lily: Charlie freaked because Gina told her she was your girlfriend. Charlie thought you were about to cheat, and that's why she bolted.

What in the hell?

My angry gaze lifted from my phone and landed on Gina. She had the nerve to smile.

"You fucking told her you were my *girlfriend?*"

Her smile dropped.

"Gina! Answer me!" I shouted.

"I was kidding. When she asked me who I was, I said it in a playful way."

A playful way. Holy shit.

"Get out of my house and don't you ever come back."

"Tucker, baby, please."

Gina moved toward me, her arms reaching out, but I shook my head. I knew months ago things were over between us. Why it had taken me so long to kick her ass to the curb was beyond me. We had nothing in common.

"Get out."

She shook her head. "Let me explain. If we could only—"

Taking her elbow, I pulled her to the door and grabbed her backpack, pushing them both outside.

"Get. The. Fuck. Out! And don't ever come back or try to contact me."

Turning, I rushed up to my bedroom to get dressed. I knew what I had to do, and I wasn't about to wait a minute longer.

~

I STOOD OUTSIDE Charlie's penthouse. What in the hell was I even doing here? For the last seven years the two of us had exchanged jabs, dirty looks, and heated glares. Most of the time they were sexually heated, but we both ignored it. She walked away that weekend, never looking back. I knew why; Lily had told me, but it still didn't help with the hurt and anger that she just wasn't honest with me . . . that she didn't think I would support her and help her build her career.

Seeing her this morning brought all those feelings I'd locked down right back up to the surface. I had never wanted a woman more than I wanted Charlie and at the same time, I refused to open my heart to her again. Especially knowing she had planned to deceive me.

But here I stood, outside her place, getting ready to jump full into this little game she played. I felt like a dick, but a small part of me knew why I did it. If I could get any part of her, even if temporarily, I'd do it.

Knocking, I waited for her to open the door. I figured she would open the door and then slam it right in my face. However, when it opened, she frowned and let me in. I was surprised. Of course, she was on the phone and distracted. She was talking business. Christ, it was Saturday, and she was taking a business call. Guess she has a lot of pieces to pick up after her parents' funeral.

I rolled my eyes and looked around her place. It was cute. "Charming" would be the better word. It looked as if Charlie liked antique furniture and the colors blue and white. My eyes wandered around the room. I could tell it had been remodeled, and Charlie stayed with the charm of the original building. I couldn't help but smile . . . Seemed like we had something in common.

Feeling something at me feet, I looked down and let out a terrifying girly scream.

A pillow hit my head, causing me to look over to Charlie. She leaned against the giant windowsill looking beyond pissed off. When I glanced back down, I saw a cat. A cat that had been shaved.

Yes. I said shaved.

"What in the hell happened to you?" The cat looked up at me and if I hadn't known any better, I would have sworn the little fucker gave me a dirty look. I hated cats. Well, "hate" might have been a strong word.

No . . . I hated cats.

"Listen, Paul, it's Saturday afternoon and you and I both know this is a bullshit call of yours. This can wait until Monday, so until then, I'm through with this conversation. Unless it's an emergency, I'm off the clock. Yeah, well, that was my father. It's my company now."

My cock jumped in my pants at how she talked to this douche with authority. It was hot as hell.

She frowned at something this Paul guy said to her.

"Have a good day."

Jamming her finger against her phone, she took it and acted like she was going to throw it across the room. Instead, she held her hand up, tossed the phone onto the sofa, and dramatically let out a scream so loud I nearly jumped ten feet into the air.

"I hate that man!"

My brows lifted.

"Better him than me."

Her angry gaze snapped over to me.

Shit.

"Get out of here!"

Lifting my hands, I shook my head. "She's *not* my girlfriend, and she hasn't been for months. She said she was only kidding when she said that to you."

Charlie laughed. "Oh, yeah, right. Bullshit. She said she was your girlfriend . . . who kids about stuff like that?"

I shook my head and walked over to her, desperately wanting to pick up where we had left off. This woman drove me insane.

"She's not."

Charlie was pressed against the large window that overlooked downtown Austin. She looked sexy as hell, and I wanted to crawl back into her. She'd opened a door I thought had been closed and there was no fucking way I was going to let her slam it shut on me again. Right now, I didn't really give two shits that she was using me. I'd use her right back—and enjoy every minute of the abuse.

"We need to talk," I finally said.

She pushed off the window and headed into her kitchen. "About?"

"This morning."

"What about it?" she casually said, glancing over her shoulder at me. I saw it in her eyes though. She wanted me as much as I wanted her. Fuck any plans she had, I knew Charlie wanted me. A small part of me was glad I was the one she was trying to trick into marrying her. It meant she had feelings for me.

"If Gina hadn't walked in on us, I'm pretty sure we would have fucked."

She stilled for a moment, and I wished I had used a different word.

"I guess it's a good thing she walked in then, isn't it?"

"Is it?"

Turning toward me, she had a mixed look on her face. Half hope and half fear.

"Are you asking me if I thought it would have been a mistake to sleep together?"

"Yes. You seem to like making that accusation when it comes to us."

Her lips pressed together, and I realized I held my breath while waiting for her to answer.

"Yes and no."

My head jerked back. "What the hell kind of answer is that, Charlie?"

"An honest one."

I stared at her, waiting for someone to jump out and tell me this was all a joke. That the woman I had pined over all these years, the one who had consumed my every dream it seemed like, the one I had jacked off to more times than I wanted to admit to, was actually standing here possibly going to give us a shot. However, I knew that wasn't reality. Reality was she needed a man to marry, and that man was me. Maybe I should have been flattered. Maybe deep down inside she truly did want a relationship with me, but then the truth of seven years ago hit me.

Charlie only wanted me to help save her own ass. She needed my help in becoming a successful businesswoman and holding onto her father's company. I was a pawn in the game she played.

"Explain it to me, Charlie."

She sighed. "Can I at least make myself a drink? It's been a hell of a few days."

My heart ached for her. I couldn't imagine what it must have been like for her to lose both of her parents and then find out she had to marry some dude in order to run the company she had given up everything for. My feeling of sorrow for her quickly turned when I forced myself to remember what I had heard on the tape from my office. Charlie's plans to seduce me were for one reason only.

"Want something?" she asked, pulling me away from my thoughts.

"Bottled water, please."

She reached in, got a bottle of water out, and set it on the island while she walked over to put water on for tea.

"Why did you really come downstairs dressed like that?" I asked, stepping closer to her.

A look of pure fear covered her face the closer I got. I was positive she saw the look of hunger in my eyes. She clearly wasn't feeling as bold as she was this morning when she had walked into my kitchen with nothing on but my damn T-shirt. I liked having the tables turned.

"What are you doing?" she asked in a shaky voice. This didn't sound like the same woman who had put the asshole on the phone in his place. This sounded like the scared girl I had fallen in love with back in college. The same girl who had ripped my heart out and walked away from me without so much as a second glance because her career was more important than giving a relationship with me a try.

"I'm picking up where we left off this morning."

Her lip twitched; I knew she was hiding a smile.

"The moment is long over."

My brow lifted. "Is it? Doesn't look like it based on the hardness of your nipples."

Charlie glanced down and then folded her arms over her chest.

"We're not in your house," she stated.

"So?" I moved closer to her.

"And I'm not sitting on a kitchen island with my legs wrapped around you."

Smirking, I added, "Minor details."

"I'm not naked."

"I can fix that."

Charlie finally let a grin move over her face. "What are we doing, Tucker?"

The brave woman who tried to seduce me this morning was long gone. It was up to me to turn the tables on her and see how far I could get her to go.

"We're about to fuck, Charlie."

She rolled her eyes. "Oh, so romantic."

When I finally made it to her, I lifted my hand and placed it on the side of her face. Her eyes widened at the touch, and I tried like hell to ignore the rip of energy that raced through my body.

"Do you want me to be romantic, Charlie? Do you want me to seduce you? I'll romance the shit out of you if that's what you want."

Her throat bobbed as she swallowed hard. "You're confusing me."

"What's so confusing about what we are about to do?"

Sucking her lip between her teeth, her eyes met mine.

Finally, her chin lifted and a spark filled her baby blues. "Romance is for pussies."

That was the Charlie I knew and loved.

Loved.

Jesus, could I do this? Closing my eyes, I thought about that morning I woke up to her note. How she had acted like nothing had happened between us.

The anger rushed into my heart.

Opening my eyes, I smirked. "Then fucking it is."

Her chest heaved with each breath. I was almost afraid to move, praying like hell this wasn't a dream, and I was really about to sink into the woman of my dreams again. Literally. Scratching a seven-year itch that had been a long time in the making. She was in my dreams all the time. Even when I had been dating other women and slept next to them, Charlie always filled my dreams.

More like haunted them.

The corners of her mouth rose into a smirk. "What are you waiting for? An invitation?"

Leaning in, I brushed my lips across hers. "One would be nice."

Her tongue slid over her soft pink lips before her eyes went from my mouth to my intense gaze. She struggled with something internally.

"We should talk first," she said with a shaky voice.

"About?"

Her eyes closed and she seemed to be trying to get a hold of her emotions.

"I need . . . there's something I need to tell you. Ask you, really."

When her eyes opened, her gaze fell to my mouth.

"Tell me you don't want me, Charlie. Because I can feel this between us. Fuck, it never left. We've just been stupid and ignored it."

Her expression was unsure. I ran my tongue along my lower lip and then pulled my lip in between my teeth. Charlie's breath hitched. I remembered she told me that weekend how sexy she thought it was when I did that.

"We . . . should talk . . ."

"The only talking I want to hear from you in the next few minutes is you telling me to fuck you harder."

Her chest heaved. I placed my hands on either side of her, gripping onto the counter, caging her in.

Charlie's eyes were filled with conflict. It should have been a damn warning, but it fueled me on instead.

She slowly shook her head and whispered, "I'm . . . I'm supposed to be seducing you."

My brow lifted. "Does it really matter? Tell me right now, Charlie. Tell me what you want."

She pressed her lips tightly together before she finally whispered, "I want you, Tucker. I've never not wanted you."

Closing my eyes, I whispered, "Finally."

Eight

CHARLESTON

THE ROOM FELT like it was tilting from side to side. What in the hell was happening?

Note to self: Tucker is better at this whole seducing thing than I am.

When he lifted his hand behind him and pulled his shirt off, I nearly fell to the floor. His body had been amazing seven years ago, and I'd seen him without his shirt on since. But now, with my mind thinking only about sex, I was dying to have him inside of me. My eyes ravaged his beautiful body.

Sweet Jesus. How often did this guy work out? His muscles seemed to have muscles.

"Keep eye-fucking me like that, Charlie, and I'm going to come before I even get to pump a few times inside of you."

"Jesus," I whispered. When did he become a dirty talker? I liked it. A hell of a lot more than I should.

Lily's voice decided now would be the perfect time to enter my mind. Her telling me to be honest with Tucker. Tell him I needed to marry someone to keep the position within my company. But would he go along with it? Would he do this for me even when I hurt him so bad all those years ago?

He seemed to be over it and with the way he tried to rip my clothes off, I started to think seducing him would be easier than I had initially thought. Hell, he was the one who came over here after this morning. Clearly he wanted me as much as I wanted him.

"Christ, baby, I need to be inside of you."

When his hand slipped into my cotton pants and then my panties, my mind went blank. The only thing I could think about was his fingers slipping inside me while he held my other leg up, opening me up to him more.

I moaned when he coated his fingers and rubbed his thumb on my throbbing clit.

"You're so wet. Tell me you want me, Charlie. You have to say it or this train needs to come to a full stop."

I nodded frantically. "Yes," I gasped, my fingers digging into his bare back.

"I want you too," he breathed against my neck before placing light kisses all along my neck.

My body was beginning to tighten and I knew if he kept it up, I'd be coming any second.

"Tucker, oh God!" I cried out, my hips rolling against his hand, trying to get him to push with just the right pressure.

"That's it, baby. Let me hear you call out my name when you come."

"So . . . close!" I whimpered. When he pressed his mouth to mine and pumped his fingers faster inside of me, I lost it. I moaned into his mouth, my body shaking and climaxing from one of the best orgasms I'd had in years. Holy fucking hell . . . that was just from his fingers.

"I need to have my mouth on you," Tucker said, pulling his fingers out of me and picking me up. My body felt limp as he carried me from the kitchen to the sofa.

"Can anyone see in?" he asked.

My head was spinning, so it took me a few moments to realize he was talking about all the windows in my apartment.

"No. No . . . only at night."

Tucker set me down and steadied me before he lifted my T-shirt over my head. He growled when he saw my lace bra. Thank God I'd put on a push-up bra. Judging by the way he was staring at my breasts, I'd have to say Tucker approved.

Note to self: Buy more sexy lingerie. Tucker likes.

He dropped to his knees and pulled my favorite pair of cotton pants off of me. Then he slowly pulled off my lace boy-short panties. I stood there with nothing but my bra on.

"You're so beautiful."

His words made my chest tighten. They'd been the same whispered words seven years ago. It began to feel like a repeat of that weekend. Except this time, I couldn't afford to run away even though I started to feel a sense of panic rush through my body.

I had stronger feelings for Tucker now than I did back then, and it was very clear to me the risks of the game I was playing. But he wanted me too. After all, he was the one who came over here and started to seduce me, so it was okay. He made the move on me.

Yeah. To pick up what you started this morning. I couldn't forget that.

When he pushed me down onto my sofa, I tried to catch my breath. He was going down on me, and I almost exploded from the anticipation of that alone. Oh God. Oh God. Oh God. How long had it been?

Stop this, Charlie. Stop. This. Now.

He slowly spread my legs apart, and I sat there watching his face as he gazed at me. Not just me. Me down there. The way he swallowed hard and licked his lips had me letting out a soft moan. No man had ever studied me like this. It was like he was waging an internal war with wanting to just stare at my nether region or devour it.

I was voting on the second. I was about to come again just thinking about what he was about to do to me.

He didn't give me much time to think about it because he dove in, his tongue licking through my folds and flicking my overly sensitive clit.

"Shit!" I cried out, nearly jumping off the sofa.

Tucker's hands gripped my hips and he held me in place as he licked, sucked, and bit at my pussy. I tried like hell to pull back some, but he had me seated firmly. I did the only thing I knew to do—I gripped his hair with my hands and slowly rolled my hips against his face, drawing out every ounce of how good this felt.

Jesus, where is your self-control, Charleston? Get it together.

Another orgasm was building, and I arched my back and screamed out his name.

"Tucker! I'm coming, oh God, I'm coming."

Stars exploded in the room. My body trembled as wave after wave of pure delight rolled over me.

Before I knew it, I was turned and lying on the sofa with Tucker leaning over me.

"You fucking drive me insane, Charlie."

Gasping for air, I responded, "Ditto, Tucker."

Tucker pressed his mouth to mine, and I tasted myself on his tongue. At first, I wanted to push him away. I'd never let a guy kiss me after oral sex. But instead, I laced my fingers into his hair and pulled his mouth closer, deepening the kiss. He moaned, I moaned, and then I felt the tip of his cock at my entrance.

"Yes," I hissed. As I wrapped my legs around him, I pulled him closer to me, causing the tip of his head to push inside of me.

"Charleston," he whimpered. The sound of my name off his lips made me lift my hips. He couldn't go anywhere but deeper inside, and that's exactly where I needed him right then.

"Fuck me, Tucker. Please . . . fuck me."

He pushed the rest of the way inside of me, causing me to let out a loud yelp. When he stilled, he pulled back and looked at me. "Are you okay?"

I nodded and bit down on my lip, trying to ignore how the size of him pushing into me felt like he had just ripped me in two.

"I forgot how big you were, and it's sort of been a while since I've been with anyone."

Tucker smiled and then kissed me gently. Our pace slowed down and as he pulled out slowly and pushed back in even slower, I felt my body melt into the sofa.

"Feels. So. Damn. Good." Tucker was breathy, his mouth pressing light kisses along my jawline.

My fingers moved lightly over his chiseled back as we moved in perfect unison.

"Tucker," I whispered his name as if he was the most precious thing in the world to me. And maybe in a way he was. I denied my feelings for this man for so long; I wanted to stop denying them. I wanted him. All of him.

"Charleston, baby, I can't . . . you feel too good, and I'm fighting to not lose control. Are you almost there, baby?"

He pulled back and our eyes met. The slow pace of his lovemaking was messing with my heart. I needed him to let go; this was feeling too real. Too much like that fateful weekend.

"I am. Lose control. I need you to lose control. Please."

Tucker closed his eyes and leaned up. He grabbed my legs, moved them over his chest and shoulders, and started to do exactly what I had asked him to do.

The sounds of our bodies smacking together and our breathy moans filled my living room. It was carnal, raw, and sexy as hell.

When Tucker moved his hand between us and pressed on my clit, I came undone.

"Tucker!" I screamed, my body pulsing as my orgasm took over.

"Jesus, I'm coming, baby, hold on."

I watched as Tucker fell apart. His face showed exactly how good this felt, and I couldn't pull my eyes away from him. The expression on his face was one of pure ecstasy, and the power that gave me knowing I was the one who was putting that pleasure on his face was enough to make me come again.

The next thing I knew, Tucker was over my body, barely able to hold himself off me as we attempted to catch our breath.

"Fucking hell, Charlie."

My chest tightened. Sex with Tucker was the best sex I'd ever had. And the fact that he was the only man to ever call me by my real name during sex also played around with my heart and head.

Could I do this? Seduce this man and somehow get him to marry me, then spend the next year pretending I wanted to stay married? Putting on a show for whom? A bunch of old men who needed me to somehow prove to them I could run my own goddamn company?

The thing that scared me the most was . . . would I really be putting on a show?

"Hey," he whispered, kissing me lightly on the forehead. "Are you okay? You seem a little lost."

Pushing the stupid problem out of my head, I looked into his eyes and smiled. "I'm more than okay. I'm blissfully happy, sedated, and completely relaxed."

"Thoroughly fucked?" he asked while lifting a brow.

"Yes. You're a lot better than my vibrator."

Tucker laughed and it was then we both froze. He was still inside of me, and I could feel the warmth of his cum trickle down my thighs.

"Fuuuck!" he cried out as he jumped up and looked down. We'd forgotten a condom.

His hands grabbed at his hair, and he let out a string of curse words. "I've never in my goddamn life forgotten a condom."

I smiled. "The anticipation of being inside of me throw off your game?"

He glared at me and my smile faded. I should have been upset, and I was. I had no real idea of how many women Tucker had slept with, but a weird part of me loved how he was so lost in me he'd forgotten just like I had. It was too late now to freak out about it. So, if he was going to play that role, I'd play the other.

"Tucker, it's okay. I'm on the pill. I've only been with two guys since you, and it's been a while since Josh. I've been tested."

Tucker froze, then slowly turned and looked at me. "Two guys? That's it?"

My heart dropped. I'd seen Tucker with different women, but I had always pretended to think he didn't sleep with all them.

"Please don't tell me some crazy insane number that's going to make me feel sick to my stomach. Please."

A slight smile cracked his lips open some. "Four. And the last one was Gina, and that was a few months back. I've been to the doctor since, and I'm clean."

My brow lifted. "Four women in seven years. I guess that's not too bad; it's better than twenty, right?"

Tucker shook his head and glanced down. "Bathroom?"

"Down the hall and the third door on the right."

"Don't move, I'll come back and clean you up."

His thoughtfulness made my chest squeeze. I couldn't do this. I couldn't trick him into marrying me.

Not Tucker.

He walked back in, a towel wrapped around his waist. My mouth went dry. When he dropped down and gently cleaned me with a warm washcloth, I nearly came again.

Then he slipped his fingers inside me. "Charlie, you're soaking wet again."

"You're turning me on with the damn washcloth. I've never had a man do that before."

He lifted a brow. "Wash you after sex?"

"No," I whispered.

Then he reached down and picked me up into his arms. "Bedroom?"

"Very last door down the hall on the right."

Tucker soon had me calling out his name as he pounded into me again. He'd asked me if I wanted him to wear a condom and since neither one of us had one, we decided to go bareback again.

Jesus, it felt good. He felt good. This felt so many ways right. After I was thoroughly fucked again, he pulled me into his arms and I slowly drifted off to sleep. I'd talk to him about the marriage clause later. Right now, I wanted to relish in the feeling of being back in Tucker Middleton's arms.

Darkness filled the room and when I rolled over, the bed was empty. I sat up and looked around, but I couldn't see anything.

"Tucker?" I called out before leaning over and reaching for the lamp.

My eyes had to adjust to the brightly filled room. I stood and stretched. I ached in the most delicious ways. Lord, how many orgasms did that man pull out of me?

As I turned, the white envelope caught my eye. It was on the pillow where Tucker had been.

A sense of dread filled my chest, and I had a hard time breathing. My hands shook as I reached for the envelope, opened it, and read Tucker's note.

*

Charleston,

Do you regret it?

Tucker

*

Everything stopped and my panic morphed into pure anger. I stared at the note before standing and letting out a scream.

"You asshole!" I shouted as I ripped it in two and threw it.

I hated Tucker Middleton.

Hated. Him.

Nine

TUCKER

"YOU LOOK LIKE shit."

I lifted my eyes to look at Nash. "Thanks a lot, dude."

He held up his hand. "Speaking the truth."

With a long sigh, I dropped down on the stool next to him. "I fucked up."

"With?"

"Charlie."

His eyes widened. "Charlie? As in, Charlie Monroe? The woman who nearly destroyed you seven years ago? The woman you vowed to never let into your heart ever again? *That* Charlie?"

I nodded. "That would be the one."

He laughed. "Don't tell me you fucked her."

There was no reason to even speak; he saw it on my face.

"Dude! Fucking hell, why didn't you call me? I would have cock-blocked you. Don't you remember the months of endless drinking after she walked out on you? The vow you made me take to stop you if you were ever tempted?"

"I remember."

"Then why? Why would you do that? No woman's pussy is worth that kind of heartache."

Glaring at him, I said, "Don't talk about her that way."

Nash rolled his eyes. "Christ. What happened?"

I glanced around the bar then motioned for him to follow me back to my office.

Once I shut the door, I told him everything. How I had listened to Charlie telling Terri about her plan to seduce me and try to get me to marry her so she could keep her position at the damn company her father left her in charge of. How I'd come up with my own plan to let her attempt to seduce me and change the playing field. And worst of all, how I fucked her and then left her a note asking her if she regretted it.

"Dude. Damn, that was sort of harsh."

"Harsh? She's fucking planning on trying to trick me into marrying her!"

He lifted a brow, leaned back in his chair and smirked. "Can you honestly look me in the eyes and tell me you wouldn't marry Charlie?"

"No, I wouldn't."

He laughed. "I call bullshit. If she had come to you and told you what happened, that she was being backed into a corner and needed to have a fake marriage, you wouldn't have jumped at the chance? To spend an entire year pretending to be married to her? An entire year of fucking her whenever you wanted?"

I rubbed the back of my neck and looked down at the floor. "Maybe, if she had come to me. But she didn't. Instead she decided to fuck around with my emotions. Pretend she was into me to get what she wanted."

His head tossed back in a fit of laughter. "Oh shit, you don't get it, do you? Bro, you're both fucking crazy about each other. You're too hurt and stubborn to admit it, and she's too damn scared to admit it. She didn't ask you because she was worried you'd say no. I bet the idea of having to be married to someone for a year made Charlie feel physically sick. Married to you though, the guy she secretly pines over . . . *that* she could do."

"Secretly pines over me? How the fuck do you know that?"

Nash's smile faded some, and he cleared his throat. "It's not hard to miss, asswipe. You just gotta open your eyes."

My brow lifted as I stared at my best friend. There was something he wasn't telling me. He knew something about Charlie and her feelings for me, but he wasn't going to offer up how he knew. I let it go; I wasn't in the mood anyway.

"So, what are you going to do? I'm pretty sure Charlie isn't going to let this go. Are you going to let her know you know about the marriage clause?"

A slow smile moved over my face. "No. I'm going to make her work for it. If I hadn't watched that tape from my office, I'd have fallen right into her plan only to get my damn heart broke in a year when she tells me she wants a divorce. Payback is a bitch, and Charlie Monroe is going to have to prove to me she wants to marry me for one reason only."

Nash grinned. "And what's that reason?"

My heart ached slightly in my chest at the idea of it.

"Because she loves me."

~

A WEEK HAD passed with no word from Charlie. She hadn't been into Sedotto and neither had Terri or my sister Lily. I found it a crazy coincidence that my bar's name meant seduced. I'd gotten the idea from my grandfather. He loved Italy and said the country seduced him with her beauty. Italy made him happy. My bar made me happy.

I chuckled as I poured a shot of whiskey. I never drank when I was working, but tonight I needed it. I hadn't really slept since the morning I woke up while holding Charlie in my arms. I wanted nothing more than to stay there with her. But I was hurt and angry and scared by the way my heart pounded in my chest.

I downed the shot and closed my eyes. The image of Charlie looking into my eyes as I fucked her hit me again. It was an endless torture day after day.

Maybe I was making a mistake with this plan of mine, which was causing me to second-guess myself. I needed to tell her I knew about her little plan of seduction.

All of a sudden the air changed, and I looked toward the door. There she was. A fucking vision of beauty dressed entirely in black. My eyes did a quick sweep of her body like I always did when I saw her. Lily stood on one side of her, Terri on the other. Jim and Nash followed behind the girls. Nash leaned in and said something to Lily that made her cheeks flush as she looked at him and smiled a smile I'd never seen on her face.

What in the hell?

Jim walked up and tapped the bar. "Hey, you don't mind if we hang here tonight, do you? Charlie's with us, and Nash told me you and her were not in a good place."

I couldn't pull my eyes off of Charlie as I watched them all walk over to the large round table that had "*reserved*" marked on it. Shit. Had one of them called earlier and talked to one of the managers to let them know they'd be here? It was a standing thing; if any one of them called and requested a table, my managers knew to rope one off for them. Perks of knowing the owner.

"Nah, not at all. Charlie and I are just fine."

I finally brought my gaze to Jim. His eyes widened some and then he chuckled. "Yeah, those are words I never thought I'd hear you utter."

Jim, Terri, Nash and Charlie, along with another buddy of mine, Blake, had been friends since our freshman year of college. Lily popped into the group a year later after she started at UT. Terri and Jim hadn't been dating then; that came about a few years ago. We were inseparable even after the whole thing with Charlie and me. We were like the three musketeers times two.

After pouring another whiskey, I made my way over to the table. Charlie had her face down, looking at her phone, which was typical. I was positive it was for work. As I walked up with Jim, I said so only he could hear, "Let me sit next to her."

"You sure?" he asked in a hesitant voice. My friends knew to put themselves between Charlie and me. It was a rule I'd put into place seven years ago, more for myself than Charlie. Sure, for the first few months it was so I didn't strangle her, but after that, it was purely for me. Anytime I was close to her, it physically hurt.

"Yep," was all I said before sliding into the booth and right up next to Charlie. She stilled for a brief moment and then went back to typing away on an email.

"All work and no play makes for a dull day," I whispered against her ear.

"Fuck off, asshole."

Okay, so we were back to hating each other.

"Don't you mean 'fuck me, Tucker?' I vaguely recall you asking for that the last time we were together, right? Isn't that what you want from me, Charlie?"

Her hands dropped to her lap, and she glared at me. "No, lucky for you, I found someone else to do that for me."

My smile faltered, and I tried not to let the panic I felt in my heart show on my face. What if I pushed Charlie to that option with the note I left, and she decided to go after someone else to marry her?

I leaned back, anger pulsing through my body. There was no fucking way I'd let another man marry her. Ever.

"You're mad at me."

The heat from her angry stare made me glance her way.

"No, what in the world would make you think that?" She leaned in closer and her body heat nearly made me kiss her. "You're a dick."

"Come to my office so we can talk . . . alone."

"No."

I growled. "Charlie, get your sweet ass up now and get into my office before I throw you over my goddamn shoulder and drag you there."

Her eyes filled with heat, and my cock jumped in my pants.

Shit, did that turn her on? Me telling her what to do?

"Now!" I said, this time with more authority in my voice.

She pushed me to get out of the booth, and when I did, she slipped out and stormed off in the direction of my office.

I couldn't help the smile that spread over my face. Charlie still wanted me; I could see it in her eyes. I couldn't help but wonder how long she would play the "I'm mad at you" game before she tried to make another move on me.

Once the door shut, she spun around and threw herself into my arms, causing me to stumble back and hit the door. Her hands were everywhere. My hair, my chest, my dick, back to my hair. The plan I had come up with was to tease her some and then walk away . . . yeah, that went out the door as Charlie desperately attempted to unbuckle my pants.

"Charlie." I grunted when her hand found its way to the bulge in my underwear.

"Tucker, I need you to fuck me. Please. I can't stop thinking about you being inside of me. I want to feel your cum inside me. I want your hands on every inch of my body . . . now!"

My knees went weak. Fucking hell, this woman drove me insane.

She dropped to her knees and pulled my jeans and underwear down in one quick move. I tried to stop her from doing what I knew she had planned, but it was too late. Her tongue licked from the base of my dick to the top and then she licked the pre-cum off my head.

"Fuuuck!" I groaned.

She smiled, took me inside her mouth, and started sucking while she worked her hand over my shaft. When her other hand came up and played with my balls, I nearly grabbed her head and shoved my dick in deeper.

"Ch-Charlie . . . oh, fuck. Fuck. Fuck."

She took me deeper, and I glanced down at her. Her blonde hair was down, but she'd pushed it over her shoulder. Her eyes met mine, and I forced myself not to come. The intensity of this moment was almost too much.

"Stop," I urged. "Fuck . . . God, don't stop!"

Jesus Christ. What was wrong with me? I was telling her to stop and then a second later telling her not to stop. When she took me deeper and hit the back of her throat, I knew I had to stop her.

Reaching down, I pulled her off me. She let go with a loud pop.

"I need to come inside of you. We can save the deep throating for the next time because damn you, woman, you've made me wait too long."

She smiled and I tried like hell to ignore how her smile made me feel.

"I'm not wearing any panties."

I groaned and picked her up. Her warm pussy rubbed against my dick, and I walked her over to my desk where I pushed a few things to the side and set her on it.

Dipping my fingers inside of her, I nearly whimpered when I felt how wet she was.

"Do you want me to fuck you, Charlie?"

She nodded.

"No romance?" I asked.

She shook her head. I couldn't help the way it made my heart crack a little. I wanted to romance her. Shower her with the attention I knew she deserved. Was this all a game to her? Did all she want from me was my cock? Part of me was thrilled she wanted that much, but the bigger part of me wanted the full package with this woman. For now, I'd take what I could get.

Grabbing her hips, I pulled her to the edge of the desk, lined up my cock, and pushed hard and fast into her.

"Oh God!" she cried out.

"Are you okay?" I asked.

Her teeth dug into her bottom lip, and I felt like a fucking asshole for being so rough with her.

"I'm more than okay."

I moved slowly and our eyes met. Son of a bitch, she felt good. So damn good.

"Tucker," she gasped.

My mouth crashed to hers and we lost ourselves in the kiss. When I pulled back, I still moved slowly. Leaning my forehead toward hers, I asked, "Tell me what you want from me, Charlie."

I wasn't asking about sex. I was asking her about us. What did she want from us? If she told me right now about the stupid-ass marriage thing, I'd tell her I'd marry her tomorrow.

But she didn't.

Instead, a dark mask covered her face, and she smirked as she purred, "Sex. Lots and lots of sex."

I smiled as I pulled out and pushed back into her—hard and fast. "I definitely can help with that."

After fucking Charlie like she asked, and a few orgasms in the process, I lowered us both onto the ground and dragged in a few deep breaths.

"Shit, what in the hell was that?" Charlie asked between sucks of air.

"Sex. Lots and lots of sex."

We both laughed.

"That was the best sex of my life," Charlie said as she turned and looked at me.

All I could do was smile. I couldn't admit the same thing to her. That would mean opening my heart to her again, and there was no way I was doing that. Not until she came clean with me.

"You look beautiful," I whispered.

Her eyes softened. "Thank you."

I stood and reached my hand out for her, helping her up. We both searched my office for our clothes and silently got dressed. We'd been in here for thirty minutes. I had fucked her on my desk, then up against the door, and finally made it to the floor where I slowed things down and brought out another orgasm from her before I finally lost my own control.

"What do we say we were doing in here?" she asked as she threw her hair up into a ponytail.

"I think the only thing they would believe is if we told them we were fighting."

She grinned.

"So, what is this, Charlie? What are we doing?" I asked, hoping like hell she'd fess up and drop this stupid-ass plan of hers.

"We're having fun, that's all."

My brow lifted. "Having fun?"

She nodded and her eyes looked pained. Even with her job title on the line, she still had a hard time admitting what was happening between us.

"Are you sure that's it? Nothing more?"

Chewing on her lip, she asked, "Do you want something more?"

I leaned against my desk. "I think you're the one who needs to answer that question."

"Um . . . can we just go slow and see where this takes us? I mean, I, well, I have this problem."

My heart started to hammer in my chest. Yes! Finally! She's going to be honest with me.

"A problem?"

I'd never seen Charlie Monroe look so nervous in my entire life.

"Is it a problem I can help you with?"

She nodded. "I hope."

Fucking finally. I didn't really want to play this damn game.

"Then tell me what it is, and I'll see what I can do."

Her mouth opened and closed at least four times before she sighed and turned back to the mirror. She pulled out a tube of lipstick and smoothed it over her lips.

"I'm addicted to your cock and can't seem to get enough of it."

My stomach fell. I forced a smile when she turned back to face me.

"I know you feel the attraction too."

All I could do was nod and ask, "So, what do we do about it?"

She was walking back over toward me, trying her best to act as seductive as she could. When she tripped on the area rug, I couldn't help but laugh. Little did she know she didn't have to try and seduce me. She did that simply by smiling at me. The more she tried, the more she made herself into a klutz.

"I guess we fuck like rabbits and as often as possible."

"Are you trying to get me addicted to you?"

She winked. "That's the plan."

Thud. And there it went. Charlie Monroe wasn't interested in me as anything other than a solution to the problem she faced.

"I have a date tonight."

The words were out of my mouth before I even thought it through.

Her eyes widened. "What?"

With a small shrug, I said, "I have a date tonight. It was planned before you and I . . . did this." I motioned between us. "Whatever the fuck this is."

My voice was now laced with anger. I was pissed at myself for being such a dick.

"You're not going on it, are you?" she asked.

"Why shouldn't I? You just made it clear that we are nothing but fuck buddies. Are we exclusive fuck buddies?"

Her mouth fell as I saw the hurt in her eyes. I knew deep down in her heart we were much more than just the sex, but she wouldn't admit it.

The hurt was replaced with anger. "You just fucked me into oblivion, and you have the nerve to tell me you want to go on a date tonight?"

I pushed off my desk, anger now present in my own eyes. "Why not? You made it damn clear this was just about sex. *Lots and lots of sex.* So why shouldn't I date. Maybe I need something more than just sex, Charlie. You ever think of that?"

Her throat bobbed as she swallowed hard. "I . . . I don't know if I can . . . I need more time."

"Time? Honey, you don't have much time." I let her read the double meaning behind that statement all she wanted.

And with that, I walked past her and out of my office. I wasn't sure if I was going to be able to play this game much longer. The music started to pound against my body as I walked out into the bar area. One full sweep around the bar and I found the one person I was looking for.

Ten

CHARLIE

THE SOUNDS OF Mr. Pootie snoring next to me only served as a reminder of how pathetic I was. Here I sat with ice cream in one hand and a remote in the other as I flicked through the channels and talked to myself. My parents' letters sat on the coffee table, staring at me. I still hadn't had the courage to open them.

"We already watched that movie last night. Nope. Saw that episode of *Cupcake Wars.* Ugh, romance movie. No, thank you."

Hitting the off button, I dropped the remote on the cushion next to me.

"Do you think he's with her tonight?" I asked, glancing down at my sleeping cat. I poked him to wake him up. I needed to talk, and he wasn't being cooperative. He looked up at me and shot me the dirtiest look.

"I said, do you think he's with her tonight?"

I got a meow in response before he laid his head back down, clearly not amused.

"Yeah, I know I'm a stupid ass, but if I open up to him I know what will happen. I can't fall for him because I have to keep a clear head. After all, I may need to marry him, but falling back in love with him is out of the question."

Mr. Pootie didn't even bother to open his eyes when he responded with a drawn-out meow. If I didn't know any better, I could have sworn he told me to shut up.

"Yes, I know I haven't fallen out of love with him, but I've learned to control that feeling."

Another spoonful of ice cream went into my mouth.

"What a crock of bullshit," I mumbled.

I thought back to the other night at Sedotto's when I walked out of Tucker's office and saw him talking to the brunette. She laughed at something he said and then when he wrapped his arm around her waist and led her to the door to leave, I almost burst into tears. We'd just finished having sex not even ten minutes before he walked out the door with another woman.

How could he be such a dick?

I closed my eyes and groaned. He'd given me the chance to tell him what we had going on was something more, and I didn't take that chance. I practically pushed him into her arms. Since then, I'd found out through Lily and Terri that Tucker had been out with this girl at least once more this past week.

Were they having sex? The thought alone made me feel ill.

Maybe I needed to cut my losses with Tucker and find someone else. I didn't have much time left. I pulled up my contacts and started to go through them. When I landed on Nash's name, I paused. My finger lingered over the button to push, but I backed out and pulled up Tucker's name. The racing of my heart should have been my first clue it would be a mistake to call him. What if he was with someone? I didn't think I could bear the thought. I finally groaned and tossed the phone back down.

"What in the hell am I doing?" The thought of even kissing Nash made me want to gag, yet breaking down and calling Tucker was not an option.

I settled in for a movie and soon found I fought to keep my eyes open. Falling down across my sofa, I grabbed a pillow and closed my eyes for just a few minutes.

The knocking on my door had me jumping up. I spun around a few times and tried to figure out where I was.

My living room.

I'd fallen asleep.

I felt like it'd been thirty seconds, but it could have been three hours for all I knew.

Another knock had me letting out a small scream.

Who in the hell was at my door? If it was my crazy neighbor asking me again for sugar or something, I was going to kick him in the balls.

Throwing open the door, I started to talk. "What do you need now? It's late and—"

The words faded away when I saw him standing there, his eyes roaming over me, causing me to shiver.

"Tucker? How did you get up here?"

He shrugged. "Your doorman remembered me from the other day."

"So, he let you up here like he let you up the other day?" I made a mental note to talk to the night doorman about letting men come up to my apartment.

"Yes. Turns out he's an old softy. Especially after I told him how we were college sweethearts and I was trying to win you back."

My stomach jumped. "What?"

He laughed and made his way into my place. "Don't worry, he believed the lie."

It felt like someone kicked me in the stomach. Tucker wasn't trying to win me back. Maybe all this was for him was sex. I couldn't blame him, really. There was no denying the sexual tension between us all these years.

"Why are you here?" I asked, my pain morphing into anger.

"I missed you."

The softness in his voice almost melted my cold heart.

Almost.

Note to self: Don't let Tucker into my heart ever again. It's dangerous.

"What's wrong? Your date didn't go well tonight?"

He frowned. "I wasn't on a date, and even if I was, that was your fault."

"My fault!" I cried out. "How in the hell is it my fault that you're dating some . . . some . . ."

His eyes widened, and he waited to see what I was going to call the woman I'd seen him leaving the bar with.

"Some fake Barbie."

He laughed. "Fake Barbie?"

Dropping onto my sofa, I was hit with the memory of Tucker inside me. I pushed it away.

"Go away, Tucker. I'm not in the mood to deal with you."

"If you didn't want me here, why did you call me?"

My head snapped up and I laughed. "Huh? I didn't call you. Seriously, was the date that bad you have to make up excuses to come see me? That's really sort of sad."

He smirked. "You called me about an hour ago. I kept calling out your name, and you didn't answer. I got worried and came over to make sure you were okay."

The stupid, warm, fuzzy feeling in my chest made me swallow hard. Damn him for being sweet.

"I didn't call you. I think I'd remember if I called you."

Tucker glanced down next to me and saw my phone. My eyes landed on it, and I picked it up. Pulling up my call log, I saw I had indeed called Tucker about an hour ago.

Shit. Why cruel world, why?

"Oh, I laid down on the sofa and must have accidentally called you."

The grin that moved over his face made me want to stand up and slap it off him.

He folded his arms across his thick chest, making those pecs appear even bigger.

Look away from his massive chest, Charlie.

Thick, stocky chests were my weakness. Correction: Tucker's thick, stocky, sexy-as-hell chest was my weakness.

"So, did you have my number pulled up or something?"

"What?" I asked, a nervous chuckle slipping from my lips. "No!"

Good night, nurse. Even I thought that sounded like a lie.

He sat down on the leather chair across from my sofa and stared at me with a look of something akin to sadness appearing on his face.

"I only went out with her twice and nothing happened."

Please don't let the relief show on my face. Please.

"What do I care? What you do on your dates is your business."

Leaning back, he put his foot over his leg, and I couldn't help but use that as an excuse to eye him up.

Damn it. Why does he have to be so good looking? He looked amazing in that tight black T-shirt. Every time he moved it showed the definition of his muscles.

Ugh. I hate him.

"You don't care?"

I wanted to reply that I really didn't give two flying fucks, but instead, my stupid heart won out over my brain.

"Maybe a little. Did you sleep with her?"

"No. I already said nothing happened," he answered.

"Kiss her?"

"Yes."

My chest squeezed with a strange pain.

That's jealousy, you stupid bitch.

"Oh," I whispered.

"I kissed her on the cheek the first night when the date was over. The second date, which was another setup date, she kissed me first. On the lips."

Chewing on the corner of my lip, I asked, "Did you kiss her back?"

"No."

"Why not?" I asked, hoping his answer had something to do with me. Actually, I hoped it had everything to do with me. It was wishful thinking, but I still held out hope.

He looked me in the eyes and said what I had been silently praying he'd say. "Because all I could think about was how much I wanted to be kissing you instead of her."

Pressing my lips together, I tried not to smile but lost.

I softly asked, "Really?"

When he smiled and his dimples went on full display, I moaned internally. This love-hate relationship thing we had going on was going to get emotionally exhausting.

"Really-really."

Mr. Pootie jumped next to Tucker and he jumped back some, letting out a girly scream that made me chuckle.

"What in the hell is this thing? That's twice now he's scared the piss out of me."

Crinkling my nose, I replied, "*That* is Mr. Pootie, my cat."

Mr. Pootie had jumped up next to Tucker and was currently giving him the stare down. I forced myself not to laugh as I watched the two of them face off. Poor Tucker. I already knew Mr. Pootie would win.

"What the fuck is wrong with him?"

My mouth fell open. "What do you mean? He's a perfectly beautiful baby boy!"

Turning to look at me, Mr. Pootie meowed and glared back at Tucker. It was almost as if he was trying to tell me to throw Tucker out of our place.

"He looks like someone was drunk and went at him with some buzz cutters."

"Tucker! He's been groomed to look that way. What is the matter with you?"

Lifting his paw, Mr. Pootie gave Tucker a go-to-hell look before he began cleaning himself.

With a glance between my cat and me, Tucker asked, "You did this on purpose? I mean, you had him cut like this *intentionally*?"

Rolling my eyes, I sighed. "Yes. I had him cut like that."

"Why? He looks like a pussy."

With a smirk, I said, "He is a pussy."

"You do realize if any other cat saw him like this, he'd be made fun of."

"He would not!" I argued. "He would be the envy of all the other cats. He loves getting his hair cut."

Tucker looked like he might actually get sick.

"No cat of mine would *ever* be allowed to get his hair cut like this. Hell. No."

I couldn't imagine Tucker with a cat. A dog was a different story. Tucker was the type of guy who would have a boxer or some sort of dog like that. Something athletic and bulky, like he was.

My eyes roamed over his toned body again. I hated the way it made my insides shake. The warmth that pooled in my lower stomach was hard to ignore, especially when the bastard would smile at me like he knew exactly what I was thinking.

"Charlie, if you keep looking at me like that, I'm going to bend you over the couch and fuck you from behind."

I gulped for air and felt my entire body heat.

"You think I'd let you fuck me after you just insulted my cat?"

Tucker smirked. "I seriously doubt he knows I insulted him."

Mr. Pootie jumped onto Tucker's lap and started to knead his paws right on his junk.

"Hey! What in the hell! He's trying to claw my dick!"

I didn't even attempt to hide my laughter.

"He's not trying to claw at your dick. He's kneading because he wants to snuggle with you."

Tucker's mouth dropped open. "Snuggle with me?"

I nodded.

"I'm not snuggling with your goofy-looking cat."

With a shrug, I stood and made my way over to Mr. Pootie. Picking him up, I gave him a kiss before looking down at Tucker.

"That's a shame. My pussy was really looking forward to a little one-on-one."

Tucker's throat bobbed as he narrowed his eyes at me.

"Are you trying to say you want me, Charlie?"

I scoffed. "Hardly."

Lies! All lies.

I wanted him more than I could stand. I was beginning to wonder who in the hell seduced whom.

He stood and took a step closer to me, causing me to hold Mr. Pootie tighter.

"You're lying."

"I am not!" I stated in a childlike voice.

Christ, I'm a grown woman for fuck's sake.

"Look me in the eyes and tell me you don't want me . . . right here, right now."

Ugh. I could lie my ass off in a boardroom, but to Tucker, I was finding it very difficult. My mouth went dry as I struggled to swallow.

"You should go," I finally managed to get out.

Tucker raised his brows as he slipped his hands into his jeans pocket. He slowly nodded and then moved around me and headed to the door.

Closing my eyes, I fought the urge to call out for him. I needed to keep the ball in my court. I needed to make Tucker want me like he'd never wanted me before. He couldn't be the one doing the seducing. It had to be me, and I had to make this more about sex and not about the feelings I knew we both had for one another. Or was I going about this all wrong?

"Tucker?" I asked, turning to face him. His smug grin begged to be smacked right off his unshaven face.

"Change your mind?"

"No. I was going to see if you wanted to go to a movie."

His smile dropped and he stared at me like I'd asked him to solve world hunger. "Like, as in a date?"

I gave a small shrug. "What's the matter? Do you only think of me as someone you can fuck and then leave? Oh wait, that's what you did the other day in your office."

Holding up his hand, Tucker's eyes went nearly black. "Now hold on a second, I asked you then about this being something more. You're the one who said . . ."

"I know what I said then," I blurted out, cutting him off. "I'm changing my mind."

The left side of his face twitched with the threat of a smile.

"You want to date?" he asked.

"Maybe. I don't know. I'd like to give it a try."

The way he looked at me for the longest time had me dying to know what he thought.

Finally, he frowned and gave me a cautioned look. "Why now, Charlie?"

My heart started to pound at his question. If only he'd known how hard it was to walk away from him all those years ago . . . how it nearly tore my heart in two. Just a few days ago my only reason for going after Tucker was to save my position as CEO of my father's company, the company that was now mine. Now it was completely different. The thought of him dating any other woman made me nearly mad. I wanted back what we shared that weekend, and I wanted it back for longer than a damn year.

I chewed on my lip, knowing I should be honest with him. If I came clean now, he'd probably walk out of here and never look back. He'd think I was playing him, and I couldn't risk that.

"Well, if I'm being honest, maybe my intentions at the beginning were purely selfish reasons."

His brow lifted. "And now?"

Wringing my hands together, I answered him honestly. "It killed me knowing you left with that woman and went out on a date with her more than once. I didn't like it."

The corner of his mouth rose into a small smirk. God, it was sexy as sin.

Note to self: Make Tucker smirk more.

"You didn't like me being out with her?"

I shook my head then lifted my chin some. "No, and I'm not afraid to admit it. I sat here and pouted about it if we're going to be truthful."

He made his way closer to me. "Truthfully? The whole time I was with her, I couldn't stop thinking about you."

I grinned. "What were you thinking about?"

"Being inside of you."

My breath hitched and I felt the room tilt.

"Touching you and liking how wet and ready you always are for me. Hearing your little whispers begging me to fuck you harder."

"Tucker."

My voice sounded heavy and deep. I didn't remember this version of Tucker all those years ago. The dirty talker. I liked this version very much. Very. Very. Much.

Stepping up to me, he laced his fingers through my hair. "You scare the fuck out of me, Charleston."

Widening my eyes, I fought to breathe. "I don't mean to."

He closed his eyes and whispered, "Don't hurt me again. Do you hear me?"

With my knees shaking, I reached for him and held onto his arms before I dropped to the floor. His admission to me hurting him all those years ago played havoc with my heart.

Tell him the truth, Charlie. Tell. Him. The. Truth.

When my mouth opened, I had every intention of telling him my stupid plan to seduce him into marrying me because I needed his help in staying CEO of CMI, but a whole other set of words slipped from my lips instead. Words that were more pressing on my body. I'd let my mind sort it all out later.

"Make love to me, Tucker."

He smiled, pulled my hair back and rubbed his soft lips across mine as he whispered, "Anything for you, Charlie. You're my fucking weakness. Always have been, always will be."

He deepened the kiss. I was lost in him. He was my safety, my escape from everything else. He was the world I dreamed of.

"Tucker," I whispered against his lips. "I need you."

Eleven

TUCKER

FUCK. I WANTED her to admit the stupid plan she had come up with, and she almost did.

Goddamn it.

I wanted to walk away tonight. Leave her wanting me, begging for me. When she asked me to make love to her, there was no way I could leave. Not when my dick was ready to burst. I needed inside of her.

My fingers moved along her sides, making her entire body shake. I grabbed at her shirt and pulled it over her head, breaking our kiss only long enough to get her shirt over her head.

I moaned when I saw the little white lace bra she had on. My hands cupped her breasts, making her drop her head back and let out a whimper that made my cock press harder against my jeans.

Dropping to my knees, I pulled her cotton pants off and stared at the white boy shorts she had on.

Christ Almighty. This woman could be dressed in a brown sack and I'd still think she was gorgeous.

"So damn beautiful," I softly said while placing kisses along her stomach.

Her hands pushed into my hair and she tugged softly at first, then harder as I kissed through the cotton and finally blew my hot breath onto her pussy.

"T-Tucker," she groaned, grinding her pussy into my face.

Looking up at her, I nearly lost my load when I saw her rubbing her nipples through her bra.

Fucking hell.

"We're going slow tonight, Charleston."

She nodded and dropped her gaze down to me. Her chest heaved with each breath. I hoped like hell I was the only man who had ever made her feel like this. The thought of someone else touching her nearly had me wanting to pound my fists on my chest and claim her as mine.

Slipping her panties off her, I kissed up her thigh and moved to her stomach. Charlie groaned in protest and I smiled. My girl was hungry tonight.

My girl. There was no other way I could think of her, and she had to know how I felt.

I stood and picked her up, grabbing her by the ass. Her legs wrapped around my body, and I walked us to her room.

"I'm going to explore every inch of your body," I said as I slowly placed her on the floor. She only wore her bra, which looked hot as hell. Making quick time, I stripped out of my boots, jeans and T-shirt, tossing them all to the side.

"Turn around, Charleston."

Her mouth parted slightly and her tongue made a quick sweep over those plump, pink lips. Her eyes moved over my body in a such a greedy way I had to grab onto my cock and squeeze it, making sure he knew who in the fuck was in control here.

"Turn. Around."

She did as I asked, but as she glanced over her shoulder at me, I caught sight of the young, innocent girl I had made love to over seven years ago.

I made her mine then, and I was taking back what was mine tonight. I was done fucking around with her about where we stood.

It only took one move with my fingers to get her bra unclasped.

Pushing it off her shoulders, I placed a kiss on one shoulder, moving over to the other.

"You're so beautiful. The most beautiful woman I've ever seen."

Her head dropped back against my chest as I cupped her tits from behind. Massaging them, I softly kissed along her neck.

"You're mine, Charleston. Do you hear me? No one else's . . . mine."

Her arm lifted and her hand landed on the back of my neck, drawing me closer to her mouth.

"I'm yours, Tucker."

There was something deeper and more meaningful about both of our admissions. There was no doubt in my mind Charlie was the one and only woman I'd ever let myself fall in love with. I'd tried to fall in love with someone else—hell, I even dated women for long periods of time—but none of them were Charleston Monroe. None of them could hold a candle to her.

Our bodies were pressed together, and I wanted to bend her over and fuck her fast and hard. However, that wasn't what either of us needed right now.

"Lay on the bed, Pumpkin."

She gave my hair a simple tug and then crawled onto her bed, giving me the perfect view of her amazing ass. I wanted that ass someday and I'd take it. For now, though, I needed to be patient.

Charlie rolled over, her blonde hair now down and laying over the pillow. Her legs slid up and down, as if she was shy and not sure what she should do while I watched her.

Dropping my knee onto the bed, I smiled. "Spread your legs for me, baby. I'm going to taste you."

Her eyes closed as she followed my command. My heart hammered in my chest as I drew closer to her. I could smell her desire for me. I snapped. I'd make love to her slowly, but right now I needed to feast on her.

"Oh God!" she cried out when I pressed my tongue inside of her with purpose.

I licked and then sucked on her as fast as I could. Her head thrashed back and forth and she grabbed at her sheets.

"Wait! Tucker! Oh my God. I'm going to come! Tucker!"

She cried out my name and moved her hips against my face, moaning sounds of pleasure and simultaneously moving in time with my fingers that pumped in and out of her. Her entire body went ridged, yet shook with her orgasm. Her screams filled the air. Charlie was still moaning when I asked about a condom. We'd gone without the other night, but I wasn't going to assume.

"Do you want me to put a condom on, Pumpkin?"

Her eyes met mine. "I want to only be with you, Tucker, just you. No one else."

My chest nearly fucking exploded.

"Okay," I said, dropping a kiss to her perfect mouth.

"I've had you bare, Tucker. I don't want anything between us ever again. I don't think I could take something between us."

Her honesty did something to my heart as I fell for her more. Leaning down, I took a nipple into my mouth and rolled my tongue over it.

"Jesus, Tucker."

Smiling, I moved to the other one while reaching my hand between her legs. She jerked, and I knew her clit was still sensitive.

"Please, more. I want more," she begged while trying to guide my cock into her.

"Patience, baby. I want to kiss you until I make you come again."

Her back arched while I gently bit onto her nipple.

"Oh God. I'm dying a slow, glorious death thanks to you!"

Laughing, I moved my lips to her neck where I dropped light kisses all the way to her ear. I knew how much she loved me breathing into that ear of hers. As I slipped my fingers inside her, I tugged on her earlobe before moving my mouth to her ear.

"Hold on, baby, I'm going to make you come many times before I'm done with you."

And like a switch I had turned on, Charlie moaned out my name again, her hips bucking against my hand.

I lined up my dick and slowly slid inside of her. The warmth of her body and the greedy way her pussy sucked me in nearly had me coming.

Moving slowly, I kissed her lips. Her fingers lazily explored my back before moving to my ass where she grabbed a handful and squeezed, making me drop my face into her neck while groaning.

"I want to go slow, Charleston, and you are going to make me fuck you. Don't make me fuck you when I want to take my time with your body."

"Tucker, what are you doing to me? Please don't stop doing what you're doing to me."

When I pulled my head back, our eyes met. My chest pulled tight and my voice tried to crack, but by some miracle I held it together. "I'm making love to you, baby."

She smiled, as tears formed in her eyes. "Don't stop. Please don't ever stop."

I wanted to ask her what she meant when she issued that command. Don't stop making love to her or don't stop loving her. Either way, I was on board with both.

STARING AT THE clock, I watched as it slowly ticked to three thirty in the morning. My arm was wrapped around Charlie as I lay spooning with her. I wanted like hell for her to tell me the truth last night, but I could also see the internal struggle in her eyes. She wanted to tell me, but was afraid I'd run. To be honest, I really didn't know what I would do when she finally told me the truth because I knew eventually she would. It was a matter of time.

A slight sigh from her lips had me holding my breath for a moment to see if she was awake. When I heard her slow, steady breathing, I carefully rolled back over and stared up at the ceiling.

What in the fuck are you doing, Tucker?

At first, I simply wanted to get back at Charlie. Fuck her a few times and leave. Give her a little taste of payback and the awfulness of having a broken heart. I needed to be honest with myself, though. I never had any intentions of leaving her. I'd follow through with this game she played. Hell, I'd even marry her and hope like hell I could convince her to stay married to me. There was never any doubt about the way I felt for Charleston. I was in love with her, and I was almost sure she felt the same way about me.

Glancing her way, I let out a breath and closed my eyes. I needed Charlie to come clean with me, even if I acted like I didn't know what she had planned. If she didn't fess up, I'd never truly know how she felt about me.

Charlie rolled over and snuggled up against me, letting out a contented sigh when I wrapped my arm around her.

I kissed her head as I dragged in a slow, hesitant breath and closed my eyes. If Charlie wanted to play this dating game, then so be it. I'd just have to be the better player and play by my rules . . . and win. Although for me, it was no longer a game of payback. It was a game that involved my heart, and I wasn't about to lose like I had before.

Game on, Charlie. We'll see who seduces whom when this shit is all said and done.

~

NASH STARED AT me, his mouth agape. I silently urged him to say something and when he finally did, I let out the breath I had been holding in.

"Have you lost your damn mind, Middleton?"

I sighed. "No, just hear me out."

"Hear you out? Tucker, this is a dangerous game you're both playing, and you're digging yourself in deeper. Dude, just tell her you know and then work something out like two grown-ass adults."

I shook my head. "I can't, I'm already too deep into this. If she found out I knew about 'Operation Seduce Tucker,' she'd be pissed, storm away, and find some other jerk to play the part. We've really reconnected, and I'm enjoying spending time with her and I think she is too. It was her idea to date, man. That has to mean something, right?"

Nash rolled his eyes. "Because she needs to make it look like a real relationship to her board of directors. Come on, you're not that stupid. Don't be her pawn in this game of chess, man. You're smarter than that."

The door to the bar opened, and we both turned to look.

"Holy shit, look what the damn cat dragged in!" Nash shouted as he jumped up and walked over to Blake. It had been a number of years since we had seen him. He left town a couple of years after graduation and went to work for some fancy design firm in New York City.

"Blake Grant, what in the hell brings you back to Austin?" I said, jumping over the bar and making my way over to one of my best friends.

"I'm back for good," he said, reaching out and pulling me in for a quick hug.

"No shit?" Nash asked. "You're moving back to Austin?"

Blake nodded. "I am. Got an offer from an architectural design company. They work mostly residential, but I'm ready for a change."

I laughed. "Tired of designing skyscrapers?"

He rolled his eyes. "Something like that. I co-designed the latest one here in Austin, the Bryan Building."

Nash and I looked at each other. "You designed that?" I asked.

He nodded. "Yeah, it's not a big deal. Listen, I'm in town for a few days looking for a place to stay. I really could use a night out on the town with you guys."

Before I had a chance to answer, the sound of Charlie's voice came from behind us, causing all three of us to turn around.

"Holy shit. Charlie Monroe."

When Blake rushed over and lifted Charlie into a hug, I balled my fists. He'd always had a crush on her, even knowing my feelings for her, so him holding her nearly drove me to punch that fucker.

What happened next, though, had me wanting to kick the ass of one of my best friends, one I hadn't seen in more than three years.

Twelve

CHARLIE

BLAKE HAD ME wrapped up in his arms, and the only thing I could focus on was the jealous rage building in Tucker's face. I'd always known Blake had a thing for me; Tucker had told me that weekend up at the lake house. I'd used it to my advantage a time or two to get a dig into Tucker, but nothing really ever happened between us. Not that Blake hadn't tried on more than one occasion.

"What are you doing here?" I asked, motioning for him to put me down.

"I'm moving back to Austin."

My eyes widened, and I couldn't help but notice the hopeful look on his face.

"Tell me you're still married to that damn job of yours, Charlie, and that you aren't seeing anyone."

Okay, so I wasn't really ready to come out into the open with this, but here it went.

"Sorry, Blake. I'm seeing someone."

His brows pulled in tight. "You're dating someone? Who?"

My gaze drifted past him and landed on the man who still looked enraged. I walked over to Tucker and rested my hand on his chest, slightly giving him a tap to snap him out of whatever the hell craze he was in.

"Hey, you okay?" I said softly. My voice brought his eyes to mine and he relaxed. I had to admit I liked that Tucker was about to go all caveman on one of his best friends over me. It made my chest tighten and a strange feeling settle into the pit of my stomach. It wasn't desire. It was more like . . .

Holy shit.

Oh shit. Oh shit. Oh shit.

I was head over heels in love with Tucker, and I had no idea what to do with this revelation.

It was Tucker who surprised me even more. Leaning in, he placed his hand on my lower back and pulled me closer. He kissed me so softly, yet passionately, on the lips. I had to steady myself when he pulled it away. It hadn't even been that long of a kiss. More like a *hey, I missed you today* kind of kiss. Yet, it left me damn near breathless.

And it was him totally owning me in front of Blake, that much I was sure of.

"No fucking way. Y'all are together? You and Charlie? The woman you vowed to hate for all of eternity?"

I raised a brow and looked at him. "For all eternity, huh?"

Tucker grinned. "Don't even play that card. Lily told me you said the same thing, and she told me all about the names you called me over the years. There was even mention about the little curse you tried to put on me one night while in New Orleans, if my memory serves me correctly."

My face burned with embarrassment. "Hmm, maybe I should call that particular curse off of you." I reached up on my tippy toes and whispered against his ear, "I rather like your dick these days, and it involved it falling off and shriveling up in front of your eyes."

"You put a curse on my dick?" Tucker asked with a chuckle.

I nodded. "Yep."

He pulled me in closer, and I could feel Blake's eyes on us.

"I can't believe the two of you are together. I thought that weekend was just a fluke."

Tucker tensed in my arms, so I knew it was up to me to alter the course of this train wreck.

"Guess who is playing in Austin this weekend?" I asked, looking around to each of them.

"Who?" Nash asked, obviously grateful for the change of subject.

Blake continued to stare at me. He hadn't changed much since the last time I saw him. Dark hair, same mysterious brown eyes, fit body. The only difference was the hint of the small tattoo peeking from under his shirt collar. I didn't dare ask him about it. The less attention I gave him, the better it would be for everyone involved.

"The Foo Fighters," I said with a wide grin. We'd gone and seen that band so many times during college.

"We've got to go see them!" Nash declared with a roar of laughter.

"I'm down for it," Blake said.

"Sorry, y'all. You'll have to go without us. I've made plans this weekend for Charlie and me."

Facing him, I smiled. "You have?"

The way his face lit up had the butterflies taking flight in my stomach.

"I wanted to make sure you didn't have work or anything first before I told you about my plans."

The desire to tell him he came before my job was strong, but I kept it to myself. "No, and if anything comes up, I can always handle it over the phone."

The way his mouth turned up into the most beautiful smile made my breath catch.

He leaned down to whisper in my ear, causing goosebumps to form in anticipation of his mouth so close to my body and to the revelation of the plans he'd made for us. "Good. I made plans to go to the lake house, just you and me."

His smile was brilliant as he beamed at me with happiness. I returned the smile, thinking about how exciting it would be to go back to where we had first made love.

Jesus, Tucker was so goddamn handsome and it made me wonder

how he had managed to not settle down before now. I was glad, of course, but I still felt the urge to pinch my arm to make sure I wasn't dreaming.

We're dating . . . actually dating.

Guilt ripped through me, making me sway a little as a wave of sickness rolled through me.

This all started with a lie. A plan to seduce him back into my life and then get him to marry me before the deadline all to save my position within the company.

I covered my mouth and turned away.

"Charlie? Are you okay?" Tucker asked me.

Shaking my head, I rushed to the ladies' restroom. Once inside, I ran to a stall, opened it, and threw up my breakfast.

Tears streamed down my face as the reality of what I was capable of and what I had done had set in.

I lied to Tucker. I loved this man and I was lying to him.

The knock on the stall door startled me.

"Hey, are you okay?"

"I . . . I must have ate something that didn't agree with me."

"Do you need anything?"

The concern in Tucker's voice nearly made me blurt out my confession right then and there.

"N-no . . . just a few moments."

"Charlie?"

Placing my hand over my mouth, I silently cried harder. Over the years, Tucker and I had said some pretty mean and hateful things to each other, but I never meant a word and I knew he hadn't either. I wanted—no, needed—this weekend more than anything to make up for what I had done to him in the past and what I'd almost done to him now.

"Baby, are you sure you're okay? Let me get you a warm cloth to wipe your face."

Tears fell harder as I forced myself to speak.

"Th-thank . . . y-you."

I listened to him walk toward the door and leave. Standing, I rushed out of the stall and to a sink. I cupped my hands and rinsed my mouth out at least ten times before he came back into the restroom.

"Here, take this."

With shaking hands, I took the cloth and placed it over my face. My makeup was already ruined, so this would only be an improvement.

"You don't think you're getting sick, do you? We don't have to go to the lake this weekend."

I could hear the disappointment in his voice.

"What? No! No, I'm fine. I really think I just ate something that didn't sit well, that's all. I feel totally fine now."

The corner of his mouth rose in a slight smile. He pushed a piece of hair behind my ear that had fallen out from my neatly styled bun.

"You look beautiful today."

My heart raced in my chest. How could he say that after he just heard me throwing up?

I scoffed. "I'm dressed in a skirt and blouse, and I may or may not have vomit on them somewhere. You're not a very good liar, Tucker."

He slowly shook his head. "It's not the clothes that make you beautiful, Charlie. It's the person wearing them."

The pounding in my ears sounded like I was standing in the middle of a gun range and people were shooting on both sides. No matter where I turned, I couldn't escape the onslaught of emotions and sounds threatening to make me surrender all of my dirty secrets to this man.

"Tucker," I managed to get out in a breathy whisper.

I needed to tell him the truth. Now.

"I have something I need to tell you."

The knock on the bathroom door and the immediate opening of the door as one of Tucker's employees peeked her head in had me halting my words.

"Tucker, there's a problem out here we need your help with."

He rubbed the back of his neck and sighed. "Okay, I'll be right there. I was making sure Charlie was okay."

I let out the breath I had been holding in when the girl looked my way and gave me a sad smile.

"Go on ahead. I'm fine now, Tucker. Honestly."

He looked at me, almost with pleading eyes as he said, "What were you about to say?"

Chewing on my lip, I waved my hand in the air. "Nothing. It was nothing at all. I, um . . . I need to take off."

He looked crestfallen by my response.

"Were you wanting to grab lunch together? Is that why you stopped by the bar?" he asked, reaching down and kissing me on the forehead. I wouldn't expect him to kiss me on the lips after what I'd done in that stall.

"I was, but now I'm not sure I'm up for it. Besides, I didn't have much time and I need to get back to the office."

He frowned. "Okay, maybe another day then."

Smiling, I nodded and moved around him toward the door. I exited the ladies' room and continued to walk down the hall and out into the bar.

"Hey, you okay?" Nash asked as Blake gave me a once-over.

"Fine. Must have eaten something sketchy. I'm heading back to the office."

Glancing to Blake, I forced a smile. "Nice seeing you, glad you're back."

He winked. "Glad to be back."

Walking out of the bar, I rushed to my car parked out front. My hands shook as I started it and pulled out. Taking in one deep breath after another, I forced myself not to cry again. I'd need to get my shit together before the board meeting this afternoon.

The last thing I wanted was for Paul Ricker to see any weakness in me. It was becoming more and more apparent I had to figure out a way to stay as the CEO besides getting married.

There had to be another way. I was finished with this game I had started. I was going to be with Tucker because that was what I wanted. What I needed.

Not because my job depended on it. That was no way to start a relationship with the man I love. I'd find another way to stay in control of CMI. I had no other choice.

Thirteen

TUCKER

"TUCKER? TUCKER?"

Someone grabbed my arm. "Tucker!"

Turning, I saw Frank, one of my bartenders. "Hey dude, I've been calling out your name for the last few minutes. Where are you tonight?"

I let out a frustrated groan. "Sorry man, I've got a lot on my mind."

He laughed. "I'd say so. You're a million miles away. I said I've got this if you want to take off."

Glancing around the bar, I smiled. We were busy, for a Wednesday night. "Nah, it's okay. I do think I'm going to head back to my office and work on some paperwork, though. Call me if it gets too busy."

"Will do, boss."

Once I sat at my desk, I attempted to get what happened this afternoon out of my head. What in the world had made Charlie get sick? I knew she was crying on the other side of that bathroom stall. And what was she about to tell me? Hell, I knew what she was going to tell me. I could see it in her eyes. She was about to tell me about the marriage deal and then we got interrupted.

"Fuck!" I shouted. My hand jerking through my hair. I needed to come clean to her. Let her know I knew about the stupid plan of hers. Even though I was pretty damn sure we'd moved past her trying to seduce me and me wanting revenge. What we had going was the real thing. I knew it the moment she got jealous over that date and when she said she wanted something more than just fucking.

Interrupting my thoughts, my phone buzzed on my desk, and I groaned when I saw who it was.

"Hello?"

"Tucker, it's your father speaking."

I rolled my eyes. Like I really wouldn't know it was him calling. I had caller ID and he knew that.

"Hey, Dad. How's things going?"

"Your mother and I are having a party for some business associates of mine, and we'd like for you and your sister to join us."

Why he couldn't fucking treat me like a son was beyond me. He completely ignored my question.

"When is it?"

"This weekend, Saturday to be exact, at The W downtown. It's a black-tie event so I expect you to come dressed as such, that is, if you even own anything other than jeans and T-shirts."

Asshole. .

"Sorry, I can't make it. I have other plans for this weekend."

He laughed. "What, managing the bar?"

"I happen to own the bar, Dad. I think at least that would garner a little bit of respect from you."

"Respect? You want respect, son? Then come get a real job and work with me. If it's good enough for your sister, why isn't it good enough for you?"

Sighing, I waited a good five seconds before launching into the same old shit. "Because I am not the least bit interested in marketing, and I don't want to sit behind a desk my whole life and ignore my family."

"Is that what you think I've done? Ignore you? I gave you everything, including paying for a college education that has done nothing for me."

"For you!" I laughed. "So, is that it? You sent me to school so I'd come work for you. Sorry to disappoint you, Dad. I would have never come to work for you."

"Care to enlighten me as to why?"

"I have, Dad. Time and time again and you refuse to listen. That is not the life I want for myself. I love what I do. I love owning my own place, and I'm not ashamed of that. But apparently you are, so let's end this conversation before it goes any further."

"It's a bar, for fuck's sake, Tucker!"

"One of the fastest growing bars in Austin. You'd know that if you ever let me talk about my success, but in your eyes, the only way to succeed is to have a giant office on the top floor and fuck your secretary with your loads of money that can't buy you or your family happiness. You think Mom doesn't know? Doesn't smell that skank on you when you get home? You're fucking insane if you believe that."

The silence on the other end of the line was deafening. I hadn't meant for that last part to come out, and it was obvious that today was not the day to take a phone call from him. All these memories flooded my mind in the silence. Beginning of my sophomore year of college I found out I was going to intern at the state capitol. I had been so excited I rushed to my father's office in an unannounced visit. Much to my surprise, his always present secretary was not at her desk, so I let myself into my father's office. I found his secretary, and she wasn't taking a memo of any sort. She was laid over the conference table, my father fucking her from behind. They never saw me, and I never said a word to anyone about it. It was that day I knew I *could never* work alongside my father. Knew I *would never* work alongside him.

I did the only thing I knew to do to piss him off. I started working in a bar and saving up my own money to someday open my own place.

"What did you say?" my father finally said, breaking the silence.

"I saw you with her. Back in college I stopped by your office one day, and you stupidly left your door unlocked."

"Tucker, I can . . ."

"Don't, Dad. I don't want to hear your fucking excuses. You cheated on Mom, and that was the day I decided I would *never* work for you or with you. So, you might as well accept that I'm doing what I'm doing and will never be a suit like you."

He exhaled. "We need to talk about this, Tucker."

I laughed. "Don't worry, Dad. Your dirty little secret is safe with me. I tried to tell Mom so many times, but I couldn't bring myself to break her heart. I couldn't destroy her world like that. Are you still fucking your secretary or have you moved on to someone else? Maybe your friends' wives?"

"Tucker, you will hear what I have to say. I'm not cheating on your mother. I need to explain what you saw."

"What I saw? I know damn well what I saw, Dad. You fucking a woman my age in your office. Nothing you can say will change how I think about that."

"You're going to come to the party, and then you and I are going to talk about this. It was a moment of weakness, and your mother and I were going through a rough patch."

"No, Dad. I won't be at your party. You're a dirty, rotten, fucking cheater and I hate you."

I hit *end*, dropped my phone, and buried my hands in my face. I hadn't even heard anyone come into my office, but I felt her there the minute I caught my breath.

"How long have you been there?" I asked, my chair turned away from my office door.

"Long enough," she said softly, moving to stand in front of me. My eyes lifted to see her sad expression. I let my eyes wander over her. She wore a long black dress coat with black high heels. I frowned because earlier she was in a pantsuit, at least I thought she was.

"You said you were going to call me," she purred with a small smile.

I was grateful she wasn't trying to get more information out of me about the conversation she had overheard with my dad.

"I was about to call you."

Her hands moved up and she untied the belt on her coat, allowing it to open. My stomach dropped and my chest squeezed with a feeling I was starting to get used to when it came to Charlie.

"Fucking hell," I whispered as I took in the sight before me. She had on a black corset, a garter belt that held up two black stockings, black heels, and nothing else.

In that moment, I knew I'd died and gone to heaven. That was the only explanation for the angel who stood before me.

And holy shit. She isn't wearing panties.

She moved slowly toward me, never breaking eye contact with me as she proceeded to straddle my chair and press her pussy against my jeans.

"Seems to me you need to let off some steam, Mr. Middleton."

Reaching around her, I grabbed her bare ass and lifted my hard cock into her.

Her brow arched. "Up already?"

My hand laced into her long blonde hair that was now down and flowing over her shoulders. "The moment you walked into the room, I was up. Happens every damn time."

She smiled. "Good to know."

Her hands went to my jeans where she quickly worked at getting my cock out and in her hands.

"Can I at least take off my jeans?" I asked.

She shook her head. "No. I need you inside of me. Now. I've had a fucked-up, shitty day and I need you."

"Need me or my cock because needing one over the other means two different things . . ." I asked as I pushed her hand away from me.

"Both. I need you both."

The idea that Charlie had come to me after a long, hard day made me feel good. I'd gladly be the one to make her come over and over again to help her and me forget this shitty day.

"Fuck me, Charlie," I said, positioning her pussy over my now rock-hard dick.

She closed her eyes and sighed before sinking slowly down on me.

"Oh God," she whispered. "You're so deep like this. So. Damn. Deep."

My hands grabbed her hips and I pushed farther into her, causing her to gasp.

"Tucker!" she cried out, grabbing my shoulders. "No matter what happened today, all I could think about was coming here like this to be with you. Only you, Tucker, only you."

My chest fluttered. "That's it, Pumpkin, keep doing what you're doing. God . . . that feels so good."

Charlie moved over my cock painfully, yet deliciously slow. She twisted and rolled her hips, and I nearly came twice but held off through gritted teeth. I needed her to come first, and it needed to be fast.

Reaching between us, I pressed her clit and kissed her mouth. She moved faster, so I circled her faster.

"Yes, yes, that's it," she gasped against my mouth.

"Do you like fucking me like this, Charlie? I sure as hell loved you showing up like this. So damn hot, baby."

She groaned and kissed me harder. I pressed a bit more on her clit and she exploded. Her body shook, her pussy squeezed down on me, and I was soon moaning right along with her. Our mouths pressed together, our bodies shaking. I didn't know how it was possible, but each time we were together it only got better. Hotter. Each time something was growing stronger inside of me and it made me wonder if she was feeling the same way.

When she finally stilled, she didn't attempt to move. She stayed on me, my dick still inside her, owning her, and I fucking loved it.

Her forehead pressed against mine, and she let out an almost inaudible contented sigh that said she had just gotten thoroughly fucked. I wanted to puff my chest out knowing I was the one who made her feel that way, only me and no one else.

"I don't want to move. Actually, I'm not sure I can move, but I wish we could just stay like this forever," I softly said. It was true. I didn't want to leave.

Her fingers played with my hair as she replied, "Me too. You make me forget about everything except what we feel like together."

Wrapping my arms around her, I stood as she wrapped her legs around me. I was still inside her, and I felt my cock jumping back to life. Pushing her against the wall, I moved in and out of her slowly as I grew hard again.

Holy shit. I couldn't believe I was already up for round two.

"Tucker. Oh God, Tucker," she whispered. "More. I'll never be able to get enough of you."

And more was exactly what I gave her. And more was exactly what I took.

~

I'D LEFT THE bar early with Charlie. We went to her place and made love again. Actually, we hardly made it through her front door before I was stripping out of my clothes and fucking her on her sofa again. That damn cat of hers sat on the sofa table and stared at me the whole time. I felt like I was being judged, especially when at integral moments that hairless bastard would look at me and meow, like it was offering a critique or some shit. After the last meow, I couldn't stand it any longer.

"He's staring at me!" I growled.

Laughing, she wrapped her legs around me and drew me deeper inside of her.

"He's not staring at you! Just fuck me already, Tucker!"

Somehow I was able to finish—probably because I simply closed my eyes and tuned the cat out—and then we dragged our exhausted bodies to her bedroom where Charlie quickly drifted off.

Charlie's sleeping body was snuggled up against mine. My arm draped over her side as I stared out over the night sky of downtown Austin.

There were so many things running through my mind. My father, our conversation. The idea that he thought he could explain his cheating-ass ways to me. Charlie's little plan to seduce me, the feelings I had for her. My head was in a fucking fog, and I didn't know what to do about any of it.

"Tucker," Charlie said above a whisper.

"Yeah?"

Silence.

When I leaned in closer, Charlie let out a muffled groan. "Please . . . don't . . . don't go!"

I swallowed hard, my heart beating faster. *What in the fuck?*

"Don't leave . . . I'm sorry! I'm so sorry!"

Frozen, I tried to say something, but nothing would come out of my mouth. My body couldn't move, and I dreaded what was going to come out of her mouth next.

"Tucker."

My name was barely a whisper. If I hadn't been tuned into her, I would have missed it.

"Charlie," I softly said when I placed my hand on her shoulder. "Baby, wake up."

Sitting up quickly, Charlie grabbed the sheet and wrapped it around her chest. She was breathing heavy when she turned and looked at me.

"Tucker?"

Placing my hand on her cheek, I asked, "Hey, are you okay? Were you dreaming?"

She looked confused, her gaze darting from me to the bed, back to me again.

"I guess. I, um . . . I had a bad dream."

Her eyes looked full of fear, her face filled with a boatload of regret.

"Want to tell me about it?"

When her expression turned solemn, I knew my answer.

"No," she said sharply before getting out of the bed and making her way to the bathroom.

I sat there, trying to decide if I should follow her or not. With a heavy sigh, I got out of the bed and went after her.

The door creaked open, and I watched as Charlie splashed her face with cold water. Her eyes finally met mine in the mirror.

My breath caught in my throat at the look she gave me.

Goddamn it, Charlie. Just tell me. Please just tell me.

She slowly turned to face me. Her chin quivered and her mouth opened.

Come on, baby. Come. On.

The look of pain on her face nearly killed me. I rushed over to her, cupped her face in my hands, and brushed my lips over hers.

"Talk to me, Charleston."

A sob slipped from her lips. "I . . . I . . . I want to so badly, but I'm so afraid."

My mouth crushed to hers and when she opened to me, I practically exploded when our tongues touched. The kiss was slow, deep, and full of something so much more than passion.

Her hands landed on my chest, causing a burning feeling to hit me.

I loved this woman more than I ever dreamed I could. I needed her to tell me about her stupid-ass plan. She needed to spill it, so we could move past the wall that she'd been hiding behind.

It was so fucked up, but right now all I wanted to do was make love to her. I wanted to coax it out of her, but I knew it had to be on her terms. Picking Charlie up, I walked us back to her bed. Gently placing her down on the soft covers, I crawled over her. Slipping my hand between her legs, I groaned. She was ready for me.

I pushed inside of her and we both groaned.

Lacing my fingers with hers, I pushed her hands above her head and looked into her eyes.

"Listen to me, Charleston."

Her blue eyes stared into my gray.

"There is nothing you could do or say that will make me run or push me away ever again."

Her eyes filled with tears.

"Th-that's not true."

I pulled out and pushed slowly back in, causing her to close her eyes and moan. More tears spilled out onto her cheeks.

"We were meant to be together, Charleston. We're *meant* to be together. You know that and I know that, and there's nothing that could ever divide us again. Nothing."

I believed it with all of my heart. I have never felt this way before about any other woman. Charlie made me want things and those things only involved her.

Marriage. Kids. All of it and she didn't have to fucking trick me into it.

When her eyes snapped open. My heart skipped a beat. There was hope dancing in them.

"Tucker," she gasped.

"Say it."

Her body arched when I pushed deeper inside of her.

"Goddamn it, say it!" I urged, pulling out and pounding back inside of her.

She gasped for the breath she needed to speak. "We're meant to be together."

Smiling, I leaned down and kissed her tear-soaked cheeks.

"Fuck yes we are."

I wanted to tell her I loved her, but I didn't. I would, though.

Soon.

And with that, I slowly made love to the woman I had fallen in love seven years ago and continued making love to the woman who'd owned my body and soul for those entire seven years.

Fourteen

CHARLIE

MARGE SAT AT the large table looking awkward as her gaze bounced between me and Mitchell Landing.

"What did you find out?" I asked, the nervous edge evident in my voice.

Mitchell cleared his throat, "All but three of the other board members support you, Ms. Monroe."

Marge smiled a brilliant smile.

I held mine back. "What I need to know is if there is a legal way you can get me out of this marriage clause."

Looking away, I could see he was hiding something from me.

"What do you know that you're not telling me?" I demanded.

Mitchell looked at Marge and then turned his gaze towards me. "Ricker is having you followed."

My mouth dropped open. "What in the fuck?"

"Charleston!" Marge gasped.

"Oh, for the love of all that's good and holy, Marge. It's just the three of us." Turning back to Mitchell, I opened and closed my hands a number of times before placing them flat on the table.

"Why is he having me followed?"

His brow lifted. "Why do you think? He's reported back to a few on the board that you're dating someone you've known for a number of years and that things seem to be . . . serious."

I stood. "He's crossed both a personal and a professional line, and I will not allow this man to invade my privacy."

I was fuming. How dare that son of a bitch think he can get away with this. But right then a lightbulb went off.

"Wait a minute, what if we could use this against him?" I asked.

"We could probably find some legal reason for letting Ricker go, if you want to take it that far."

An evil grin spread over my face. "Fire Ricker? That would make my world, but that still doesn't take care of my dear granddaddy's little twist he has for me. Unless we can find some sort of legal loophole around the bylaws, I still need to get married and the months are ticking away."

Marge's watch went off with a reminder. She stood and made her way out of the room.

Sighing, I stood and walked over to the large window.

"Mitchell, I need the truth from you."

I could feel his eyes on me. "We can fight, Charleston, but it will take longer than you have. You'll be removed as CEO while the legal proceedings go on. You still have majority stock and a say-so. Just not in the day-to-day operations."

Tears pricked at the back of my eyes. The last few weeks I'd spent with Tucker had only shown me that this wasn't the life I thought I wanted. Hell, a part of me deep inside always knew that I wasn't this person, wasn't the head of a huge company. I wanted more out of my life and Tucker made me realize that with every minute I spent in his arms.

But I'd made a promise to my father that I'd run the company, and I was damn good at it.

"I'm sure I want to do this."

I heard him stand and soon felt him next to me.

"You could step down as CEO and appoint someone else. You'll still be a very rich woman and retain your stock portion and your vote in the company."

The breath I blew out hit the window. "The company wouldn't go in the direction it should though. I had so many plans, so many places I wanted to take this company. Yet . . ."

My arms wrapped around my stomach, and for the first time in my life I felt like I was going to lose my composure in a boardroom.

"Yet, this isn't what you want?"

I chewed on my lip for a moment before looking back at one of my father's best friends.

"Do you see your family much, Mitchell?"

Sadness swept over his face.

"Not like I want to but, Charleston, you can still have a family. You can still run this company and be a wife and mother. Women do it all the time."

"I'm not worried that I couldn't do it. I could, but at what price? You already see what's happened by me taking the weekends for myself. Do you honestly think I could drop my kids off in the morning, come to work, and be off in time to pick them up and take them to soccer practice each day?"

His gaze drifted down to the floor. "Maybe not all the time, but some days you could."

"I don't think I want some days."

Turning back to the window, I cursed under my breath. "Damn my grandfather for doing this to me. Why did he have to be such a prick?"

A low rumbled laugh came from next to me. "That prick built this company with his cutthroat mentality."

"And almost lost it, if you remember. If it hadn't been for my father, CMI Consulting would have been broken up into a few other companies."

I dropped my head back and sighed in frustration. "I'm not the person I wanted to be. I'm lying to the one person I should be able to tell everything to. I'm scheming to keep a position I'm not sure I even want anymore."

His hand on my shoulder made me jump.

"I wish I could do something more, Charleston. I really do."

Turning to the man who was like a second father to me, I let him pull me into his arms. I didn't show weakness when it came to CMI, but in this moment, I was really missing both my father and mother. Each for different reasons.

The door to the room opened and Paul Ricker and Mr. Potts both walked in. Their eyes widened when they saw me in the arms of Mitchell. I took a step back and smoothed out my pencil skirt.

"What's going on here?" Ricker asked, casting an accusing glance at me and then Mitchell.

"Nothing that concerns you," I stated.

He cleared his throat. "I think it does if there is an affair going on between the two of you."

Potts's head snapped over to look at me so fast I thought for sure he broke his damn neck.

"What!" Mitchell boomed.

I was not in the mood for this asshole's games today. "Oh, for fuck's sake, Ricker. Stow the accusation, will you? I was upset and my father's best friend, who also happens to be my friend, was comforting me. In case you forgot, I did lose both of my parents not too long ago. Contrary to what you think," I said as I walked up to the rotten scumbag, "I'm not entirely made of stone. I have some heart left."

Ricker sneered at me. "Good to hear that. By the way, how're things going with the marriage?"

A smirk moved my lips up some. "You should know; you're having me followed."

Mr. Potts sucked in a breath of air. "What? You're having her followed?"

I wasn't surprised when Ricker didn't deny it. "The board needs to make sure this isn't an arranged situation."

My head fell back and laughed. "The board or you? Maybe you get off reading the reports you get back. I can leave a window open so that your flunky detective can video me if that would help convince the board."

Mitchell cleared his throat, and I knew I'd gone too far. My father was probably rolling over in his grave right about now.

"If you keep this up, my personal lawyer will have a field day with you, and you'll be the one looking for another job, Ricker. I'd tread very lightly with this situation if I were you."

Paul Ricker reached up and messed with his tie some. His face turned red, and it appeared he was having a hard time breathing.

Marge appeared in the door just in the nick of time.

Plastering on a smile, I said, "If you'll excuse me, gentlemen, I have a meeting I'm running late for."

I followed Marge out of the room and down the hall. It felt like someone was squeezing my chest, making it harder and harder for me to breathe.

Please God, please let Marge have had success.

"Did you find anything out?" I asked in a hushed tone.

She nodded and then replied, "I did, and trust me when I say you'll be happy to hear it."

With a smile, I lifted my chin a little higher and walked into my office, the same office that used to be my father's. Marge shut the door behind her and held up a large envelope.

"What's that?" I asked, making my way to my chair and sitting. Marge took a seat in one of the large leather chairs on the other side of my desk. I'd kept all of my father's office furniture. At the time, it had felt like the right thing to do. One of these days I would change it . . . well, that was if I stayed on as CEO.

"I was right. The cameras I found in here are indeed working and recording everything."

I let out the breath I held. "Thank God." Since the first day I set foot in this office, I swore someone was watching me. Marge waved off my concern at first, thinking I was feeling the presence of my dead father instead.

"He's here guiding you, sweetheart," she would say every time I mentioned it. Then she stumbled upon one of the cameras and showed me. It didn't take us long to find three more. I had a strange feeling there might even be more.

Marge smiled. "Once I figured out who your father would have trusted with the videos, it didn't take me long to track them down. His name is Dustin Greene."

I was momentarily stunned when I heard the name. "Did you say . . . Dustin Greene?"

She nodded. "Yes, his father owned the security company monitoring the cameras and he recently retired, giving control over to his eldest son."

I could feel my body begin to sweat. Blake's brother owned the company who had the security tapes from my father's office. Holy hell. Did my father know?

"Do they do the security for the rest of the office?" I asked.

Marge frowned. "No, that's why it took me so long to figure out who was monitoring it. The bill came across your desk in your father's name about a week ago. The moment I saw it, I remembered it was the one piece of mail your father never let me open."

"Why was my father having his office . . ."

My voice trailed off, and I looked around. "Is it still recording everything?" I asked in a hushed voice.

She chuckled. "Yes."

"Well, shit." I dropped back into my oversized, leather office chair and sighed. "I need to figure out if I still want that."

Marge lifted a brow. As if telling me there was a reason my father had to have recording devices in his office.

Note to self: Don't ever have sex in this office with Tucker. Or pick my nose. Or do anything else I don't want people to see.

My mind quickly went back to all the times I sat in this office on this side of the desk and on the opposite side. Why wouldn't my father have told me about the cameras? Why wouldn't he have told anyone? Even Marge.

"I'm not understanding why my father felt the need to have his conversations recorded and then kept private."

Her brow lifted. "Maybe he knew something you didn't. But I'm not surprised. You grandfather had them in his office as well."

A slow smile spread over my face. "Maybe. But if we can find the conversation where he told Ricker to change that ridiculous marriage clause, maybe I can get this moving along faster than we had thought."

"Do you still want to keep this between us?"

Leaning back in the chair, I nodded. "Yes. Not even Mitchell needs to know this bit of information."

Marge nodded.

My eyes traveled to the envelope again. "What's in there?" I asked.

"The cameras were installed seven years ago, recently updated right before your parents were killed."

My mouth dropped open. "What!"

She nodded. "I went back and looked at the board meeting notes and noted when Mr. Ricker said he spoke to your father about the clause. I asked Mr. Greene for that entire year, six before and six months after."

"Looks like we have some videos to watch," I grumbled.

"I have two copies. I'm not sure if it is wise for me to watch them here, so I'll do it while I'm at home."

Damn, this was why my father kept this woman around. Not only was she the best executive administrator in the state of Texas, but she was street smart too.

"Smart thinking. We shouldn't use the office server."

Marge handed me a thumb drive. "I'll take the first half; you take the second."

"I know what I'll be doing this weekend," I said with a jutted-out lower lip.

~

THE KNOCK ON my office door had me looking at the clock on the wall. It was after six.

"Come in," I called out.

The entire room came to life when Tucker walked in. The smile on his face made the ache between my legs grow.

"Hey, you ready to go?"

I gave him a confused look. "Go?"

"This weekend, the lake house."

Dropping my mouth open, I groaned while closing my eyes. "Shit! Tucker, I completely forgot about the plans you made."

I felt like a complete jerk. The look on his face went from excited to disappointed.

I stood. "No! I mean, I can still go, but I would have been packed up and ready to go if I had remembered. Sorry, just a hella long day today."

He'd shut the door to my office when he walked in. He made his way around my desk and pulled me closer to his body.

"Baby, you don't need a bag because I plan on keeping you naked the entire time."

I smiled and kissed him. His hands moved over my silk blouse, leaving a wake of tingles in his path.

"As amazing as being naked all weekend sounds, I think I'll at least want to bring something a little more comfortable for the drive up there."

"Lily packed you a bag. I sort of figured with the crazy week you've had, you might have forgotten."

My heart jumped, and my stomach did a few flips. The fact that Tucker was so understanding about my job made my eyes fill with the threat of tears. I held them off and pushed them away.

"I'm so sorry. I'm working on a merger with another telecommunications company, one much smaller than ours. Trying to convince them they'd be better off joining us now rather than us taking them over in two to five years."

He widened his eyes. "Damn, woman, it's fucking hot as hell hearing about you taking over companies and shit."

With a smirk, I went to cup his junk when I remembered the cameras. My hand jerked away like I was about to do something terribly wrong. Tucker frowned.

"What's wrong?"

I looked around the office and whispered, "Cameras."

His brow lifted. "Pictures?"

"Huh?"

Tucker shrugged. "I don't know. I figured we were playing a word game."

Hitting his shoulder, I replied, "I'll tell you later. Let me finish up one thing and then we can leave."

It was then I noticed Tucker had a small bag in one hand. "I brought you a change of clothes. Your other bag is in my car."

I kissed him then pointed over to the other side of the room to the large conference table and sofa. "You can either have a seat there or over here."

He looked at the large leather seats at my desk and then over to the sofas. "I'll pick the sofa."

Tucker made his way over to the sofa, and I couldn't help but watch him as he walked off. Damn, he had a nice ass. A really nice ass.

"Stop staring at my ass. It's creepy." He never even turned around to say that to me; he knew that's where my eyes had strayed.

I chuckled. "You like it."

"Maybe we could role play. You're the boss, and I'm your hot assistant you take advantage of with your dominatrix ways."

I quirked my brow. "You wish."

He moaned. "Fuck yeah, I do. I'll look up costumes on the internet while you finish up."

Laughing, I took a seat in my chair and finished looking at the reports Marge had sent for my once-over and approval.

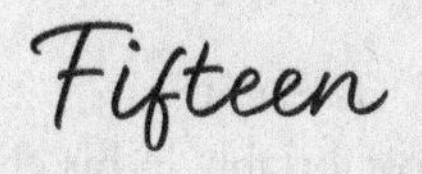

TUCKER

I SAT BACK on the sofa and watched as Charlie went over paperwork. She frowned, picked up the phone, and dialed a number. Glancing at my watch, I wondered if she knew how late in the day it was. No one would still be here.

"Philip? I need you in my office right now."

My eyes widened in surprise, and I wasn't sure if it was from her demanding tone or the fact that this Philip guy was still here.

Ten minutes later, there was a knock on her office door.

"Come in." Charlie's voice reminded me of the days when we exchanged jabs. There was a coldness in it that actually made me feel sorry for this Philip dude.

"Ms. Monroe, you're here late."

Her eyes narrowed, and I couldn't help but smirk. The asshole sauntered over to her desk as if he expected something other than what was fixin' to come out of my girl's mouth.

"B and G shipping."

It was all she said as she pointed to the chair and motioned for the guy to take a seat.

"Yes, I'm over that account."

"You were tasked with helping to get them on a course of sustainability. You've recommended an organizational redesign."

He nodded.

Charlie's brows lifted. "Is that it?"

The guy shifted uncomfortably in his chair. "Well, no. They have some unclear responsibilities, other issues that are hampering the effectiveness and efficiency of the company, but I think we can get them running smoother with the redesign."

"What about changes in management? How about changing up their cycles? Where are the diagnostic analysis that you've worked up?"

He let out a chuckle. "Ms. Monroe, I know my job. It's why you pay me what you do. I'm sure you have a lot of accounts you have to look over, and I'm sure you are inundated by the learning curve required to get up to speed on all of the accounts."

Oh hell. Dude did not just say that.

Charlie flashed this jerk a smile and stood. I could see the way he looked her body over and it made me fist up my hands. Smoothing her dress, Charlie walked around her desk, leaned on it next to this dick and folded her arms over her chest.

Jesus Christ, she looked fucking hot as hell towering over this dick.

"A learning curve?" she asked.

The guy licked his lips. "I'm sure I can . . . help you . . . if you'd liked to have dinner and discuss this a bit more."

Now her hands were to her sides, gripping her desk.

"Philip, I have more knowledge of this shipping company in my right pinkie finger than you do in that brain of yours. Do you honestly think I wouldn't notice you've been pushing this company to the side? What I want to know is why we don't have a solid plan in place to deliver to them next Wednesday when we sit down with them."

He smiled, as if that would smooth things over.

"I'll have the plan in place, Charleston."

She pushed off the desk and walked closer to him. Leaning down, she placed her hands on the edge of the chair.

"It's Ms. Monroe to you, and if you ever suggest again I don't know how to run a company I've been groomed to take over since I was ten years old, your ass will be out on the street faster than you can say CMI. Do we understand each other?"

He swallowed hard and nodded.

"I want these reports by Sunday, six p.m."

"What?" He stood and was about to argue with her. Even though he was taller than Charlie, she stood up straight, her chin lifted high, and a defiant look took over her face.

"Do you have a problem working on this? After all, it should have been finished by noon today."

He took a step back when Charlie stared at him.

"No, I'll have it done by Sunday."

She grinned. "Good."

Spinning on her expensive-ass high heels, she rounded her desk and stood there, staring at him. It was a silent dismissal, and one he heeded.

He turned to leave, finally catching a glimpse of me sitting on the sidelines. His face turned white as a ghost.

That's right, asshole, I just heard everything.

"Philip, one more thing."

He pulled his gaze from me and turned to face her. Charlie now sat, her eyes back on the pile of papers in front of her.

"If you ever so much as look at me the wrong way or think to ask me out again . . ." Her gaze lifted. "You'll be fired. That goes for any female employee here at CMI. Do I make myself clear?"

He didn't answer her right away. It wasn't until she lifted a brow and tilted her head to give him a stern look that he replied.

Philip nodded. "Yes, ma'am. It was a simple misunderstanding."

"Good, don't let it happen again."

The guy hurried out of the office, shutting the door a little harder than necessary.

I glanced from the door to Charlie, back to the door, and back to Charlie.

"Holy fucking shit, that was the hottest thing I think I've ever seen."

She looked up at me. "What?"

Standing, I made my way over to her. "You putting that asshole in his place. Christ, Charlie, that was sexy as hell. I really want to role play now."

Her cheeks turned a beautiful pink.

"Please tell me you're almost done because we really need to get out of your office, and soon."

Digging her teeth into her lip, she gathered up the papers, an envelope, and a few other files and pushed them into her briefcase.

"I'm ready. I can go over the rest of these on the drive up to the lake house."

I frowned.

"I'm sorry; it won't be but maybe thirty minutes more of work."

If there was one thing I was going to have to get used to, it was Charlie being married to her job. I wanted to chuckle. Fuck . . . I was already making plans to share her with this damn company.

"Let's go," she said, grabbing her purse and rounding her desk.

~

CHARLIE WAS RIGHT; she only had about thirty minutes left of work to do, and she knocked it out on the drive up. She also made five phone calls and chewed out three of the people for not having their jobs done or not having something done right. She talked about shipping companies, telecommunications, biopharmaceuticals, as well as growth and low-cost expansion in some automotive plant in fucking Germany. To say I was impressed was an understatement.

When she finally threw her work into the backseat and let out a sigh, I turned to face her.

"How in the hell do you know about all of that shit?"

She laughed. "It's my job to know it all. I don't know everything about all of it, just the things that matter. I pay people who know the important things. We have former FBI agents, Nobel Prize recipients, Ivy League professors, and economists, just to name a few, working for us. They're the ones who are supposed to know their jobs."

"Yeah, but how do you know when they're falling short on the job?"

Charlie shrugged. "I learn what I need to know about the companies, what we need to do for them, and when that's not being done, I have to play the hard ass."

"And that means making people work all weekend?" I asked.

"If that's what needs to be done. It's not my fault they've jacked around all week and didn't get their shit done. I manage to take the weekends off."

I smiled.

"You're making my cock hard hearing you say the words 'jacked around' and listening to you talk like that. And how you stood up to that prick earlier. Christ, I almost whipped out my dick and jacked something around right then and there."

"Tucker!" she exclaimed, hitting me on the shoulder as I let out a laugh.

The closer we got to the lake house, the more the memory of that weekend came back to me. It was an amazing weekend, but one that ended not so great. I was hell bent to make sure there wasn't a repeat.

"I forgot how beautiful it was up here," Charlie softly said when we pulled up and parked. The lake was behind the house, and you could see it driving down the driveway.

"How often do you come up here?" she asked.

"Not often."

I wasn't about to tell her I had only been here three times since that weekend she walked away from me. That each of those times I was forced by my parents to be there.

When we got out of the car, she lifted her arms in the air and let out a moan while she stretched. Dropping her arms to her sides, she walked toward the lake.

"If this was mine, I'd be here every weekend." Without taking her eyes off of the lake, she kept talking. "Did I ever tell you I bought a hundred acres of land?"

My head jerked back. "You did? When? Where?"

Her arms wrapped around her body. "Last year. It has a little cabin and a small lake on it." Charlie glanced over my shoulder. "Near Marble

Falls. You and Nash would die of if you saw the deer at this place."

My heart sped up at the thought. "I could use another head on my wall."

She rolled her eyes and made her way back to my truck where she got the bag that Lily had packed for her and her work stuff.

We walked through the large foyer and living area and down the hall to the master bedroom. It was the same room where we'd made love for the first time. I chanced a peek at Charlie when we walked into the room. Her smile was evidence that those same memories hit her as well.

"Sure had a lot of fun in this room," she whispered.

"Sure did," I replied, trying to ignore the hurt I'd felt in this room as well.

I'd wait until Sunday morning. If she didn't tell me about her little plan to seduce me and marry her, I'd tell her I knew about it. That she didn't have to trick me. I'd marry her to help her keep her company . . . and more importantly, because I loved her. The second reason being the most important.

Charlie gasped when she opened the bag Lily had packed her.

"What's wrong?" I asked.

Her eyes lifted to mine. "Did your sister pack this . . . or you?"

Frowning, I answered. "Lily did. Why?"

She laughed. "Well, let's see. There is nothing but lingerie in here, a couple of bathing suits and dresses. Does she know how cold it is outside?"

I chuckled. "Hot tub."

Charlie's eyes blazed with fire.

"She also only packed me skimpy clothes." Pulling out a T-shirt, she frowned. "I'm pretty sure she cut this to make it a crop top."

Making my way over to her, I pulled the shirt out of her hands and drew her body against mine. "It doesn't matter. I told you I plan on keeping you naked all weekend."

Her arms wrapped around my neck. "I like that plan."

Leaning down, I kissed her gently on the lips. "I want you, Charlie."

Her hand slipped under my shirt where she dug her fingertips gently into my chest.

"Then take me, Tucker."

~

I WOKE WITH a jolt. My heart pounded, and I couldn't catch my breath. Glancing around the room, I remembered we were at the lake house. Glancing to my left, I panicked when I saw the empty bed next to me. Memories of the morning Charlie left me hit me like a brick wall.

"Charlie?" I called out as I pushed the sheets off of me. Glancing down at the floor, I saw a pair of sweats I'd shed when Charlie and I had made our way into the room last night. Each of us ripped each other's clothes off as we made our way to the bed. We'd made love after we got here, went for a late dinner, then watched a movie. When Charlie had looked at me with nothing but desire in her eyes, I dragged her off the couch and to the room where we messed around like two teenagers who couldn't get enough of each other.

Now my damn heart was pounding, and I prayed this wasn't a repeat of seven-plus years ago.

The sound of the front door opening and closing had me rushing out to the main living area.

Charlie was making her way into the kitchen. Her hair in a ponytail, her body dressed in running pants and a T-shirt. A jacket was tied around her waist.

"Good morning," I said, trying not to let the sound of my relief sound in my voice. I'd thought she ran away, and here she'd simply gone out for a run.

"Morning! I would have woken you up to let you know I was going for a run, but you looked too peaceful sleeping."

Making my way over to her, I grabbed her hips and leaned down to kiss her.

"Have a good run?"

She nodded. "I did. I needed it. I'm going to have to make an effort when I get back to run each morning. It clears my head and helps get me focused."

"I can think of other ways to help get you focused if you want to try those out each morning." The devilish smirk I gave her caused her to burst out laughing.

"You're awful, Tucker Middleton, simply incorrigible."

"I never said I wasn't a sex fiend, now did I?" With a smile on my face, I went to work on getting some coffee made as Charlie took out some fruit and started to cut it up. "Want a fruit smoothie?"

I scrunched my nose. "Pass. I want French toast and eggs."

One call from my mother to Linda, the woman who takes care of this place, had the place stocked with food. Of course, when my mother found out I was bringing a woman here, she was all too happy to have me skip Dad's little bullshit dinner he had tonight. She'd asked me to call him, though. Said he was upset about our fight and mentioned to her how we all needed to sit down and talk.

I had no idea what he planned on talking about. Surely he wasn't about to admit to my mother he cheated.

"Hey, you're in deep thought. Everything okay?"

My gaze drifted over to Charlie. Damn did she even have a clue as to how stunning she was?

Not wanting her to know I was thinking of my cheating father, I forced a smile. "Yeah, I was thinking about Sedotto."

She lifted her finger and waved it back and forth. "Nope, no thinking of work today. I declare today a work-free zone. I've already silenced my phone and hid it away in my bag. Today is just about us."

My dick twitched in my sweats. "I like the way you think, Ms. Monroe."

I saw my phone sitting on the counter. After sending a text to the managers, I put it on silent. "Anything happens, they can handle it. That's what I pay them for."

Her smile was brilliant. "We're letting go this weekend."

"That means no fucking fruit smoothie. It's French toast."

"With fruit on top!" she added with a sexy grin.

Rolling my eyes, I gave in. "Fine, with fruit on top."

After breakfast, we both changed and headed into town. It was a short twenty-minute drive, but we spent the entire day walking around all the shops. I'd forgotten how into antiques Charlie was and her love for old houses. She'd spent nearly an hour talking to a woman who had been outside her house watering her flowers. They talked about the old house the woman had bought with her husband and how they did all the remodeling themselves. After a tour of the whole house, we walked back to my truck, our fingers laced together and Charlie looking the most relaxed I'd seen her in years.

"Are you happy?" I asked.

She stopped and faced me. "Yes. I'm very happy. Thank you for bringing me here, I needed this."

"Do you still want to buy old places and flip them? I remember you talking about that in college. Your grandfather did it before it was the cool thing to do."

She giggled and gave a small shrug. "Pappy, my mother's father. He made a fortune doing it. It's something I'd still love to do, but with my job . . ."

Her beautiful smile faded and something else moved over her face. Regret? Sadness? Maybe even a bit of anger was there.

"Um, with my job it's just hard to find the extra time."

I wanted to press her for more.

"What about marriage and a family someday? Do you want those things?"

She stopped walking and turned to me. "W-what?"

The way her voice sounded so innocent, almost vulnerable.

"A family and a husband. Do you want that someday?"

Her chin quivered, and she dropped her gaze from mine when she answered. "Yes. I want both of those things." Lifting her eyes, our gaze locked. "Very much so."

This wasn't a part of her little plan. I could see as clear as day that Charlie spoke from her heart.

"Do you . . . want those things?" she asked in a shy voice that surprised me. Charlie had always been so sure of everything. Vulnerability was not something she showed often, if ever.

Smiling, I took her hands in mine and squeezed them. "Yes, I want them both."

I was expecting to see relief in her eyes, but it was the opposite. Her eyes filled with tears, and she pulled away from me. Her arms wrapped around her body as she turned away.

"Charlie, what's wrong?"

Her hand came up to her mouth, and I knew she was fighting to hold it in. I wanted to pull her into my arms and beg her to be honest with me. Tell her I'd marry her in a fucking heartbeat if it meant she'd be happy. If it meant she'd stay married to me and plan a future together, we'd go to the justice of the peace if this town had one.

Fuck it. I couldn't do this anymore.

"Charlie, I know."

Her head tilted and she gave me a dazed look.

"You know what?"

It was now or never. We were going to get this out in the open and deal with it so we could focus on us.

I went to speak but a woman's voice called out for me.

"Tucker! Tucker!"

Charlie turned and frowned.

"Who is that?" she asked, looking over my shoulder.

When I turned around, I saw Linda rushing toward us.

"That's Linda. She takes care of the lake house. She probably just wants to make sure we have everything."

I smiled and started making my way over to her. When she didn't return the smile but gave me a sad look instead, my heart nearly dropped to my stomach.

Something's wrong.

"Linda, is everything okay?" I asked as we stopped directly in front of one another.

Her eyes darted from me to Charlie and back to me.

"Your sister has been trying to get a hold of you. She said she's been calling your cell phone for the last three hours."

"I left it at the house. What's wrong? Is she okay?"

Charlie grabbed my hand tightly.

Linda dropped her gaze and looked like she was trying to figure out how to tell me something.

"Please, Linda, what's going on?" I asked, the fear in my voice coming across.

"It's your father, Tucker. He's had a heart attack, and you need to get back to Austin right away."

Sixteen

TUCKER

I WAS SURROUNDED by darkness. The only sound I heard was my heart slowly beating and the ice hitting the side of the glass as I emptied my drink. Again.

Standing, I made my way over to the bottle of whiskey and poured another drink.

The sound of my phone ringing made me close my eyes, spilling some of the whiskey onto the floor, but I didn't give a shit. I actually thought about dropping to the ground and licking it up.

After a few minutes, I hit the button on my phone that had been alerting me to a voicemail. Charlie's voice filled the air.

"Tucker, please call me back. Please."

The sound of sadness in her voice is nothing compared to the sadness I was drowning in.

Dropping onto my sofa, I closed my eyes.

My mother's voice played over and over in my head. *"I'm so sorry, Tucker. Your father died ten minutes ago."*

He was dead. Gone. And the last fucking words I said to him was that I hated him. I threw the glass across the room; the sound of it hitting the wall didn't even faze me. The bottle of whiskey sat in my other hand, so I lifted it and took a long drink instead.

"Why!" I screamed out at the air. "Why did you fucking have to die!"

My phone rang again and I dropped my head, damn near between my legs. I was drunk out of my mind but not drunk enough to erase the pain and guilt. Hell, it hadn't even dulled.

The sound of my front door swinging open had me glancing up. The light from outside lit up the doorway, and I had to shield my eyes. It took me a few seconds with the bright light and my drunken haze to see who was standing there.

"Charlie," I whispered as she walked into the dark room.

"Tucker," she replied, her voice filled with worry. "Oh God. Tucker."

She dropped to her knees and placed her hands on my legs. "Your mother and Lily are worried sick about you."

I let out a gruff laugh. "Ha, I'm sure they are."

Her brows pulled in tightly. "You don't think they're not in pain, as well? Tucker, you need to get your ass sobered up and get over to your mother's. She's trying to plan your dad's funeral and needs—"

"They're fine without me there."

Charlie shook her head. "What is going on with you? Why are you drowning in a bottle of Jack?"

I laughed. "Why? Because the last words I told my father were that I hated him, Charlie. That's fucking why."

Her eyes filled with sadness, and it pissed me off. "Don't sit there and feel sorry for me."

My chest ached with a pain I'd never experienced before, and for some reason, I needed someone else to feel that pain too.

She stood. "I'm not feeling sorry for you, but if you happen to remember, I know what it's like when you lose a parent."

I laughed and she jerked back as if I had slapped her.

"That's right. You lost your mom and dad, so you can relate."

Her arms folded across her chest. "Yes."

Standing, I stumbled and she reached out for me, but I pushed her hands away, making her jerk back again.

"You know what's wrong with this fucked-up picture?"

Charlie's chin lifted. "No, tell me."

"Secrets. We all keep secrets, don't we?"

When her shoulders fell, I let out a roar of drunken laughter.

"Yeah, you know all about about secrets, don't you Charlie? Like the little secret of you trying to seduce me into marrying you so you can keep the precious little title of CEO of the company your fucked-up grandfather started."

Her mouth dropped open, and a look of shock moved over her face. I lifted the whiskey bottle to my mouth and dragged in another few gulps of the burning liquid.

"Yeah, I know all about your little plan. I came up with my own little plan for us as well."

"You . . . you knew?" she asked, her voice shaking.

"Yeah, I knew."

Her hands balled up to fists. "Were you playing me this entire time, Tucker?"

"Me? Me playing you? Fucking hell, Charlie, you made a plan to trick me into marrying you!"

She shook her head. "No . . . I mean . . . at first it . . . but now."

"Now?" I asked, trying to keep my balance. "What? Did you change your mind? Did you even fucking plan on ever telling me we got together because of some fucking twisted mind game of yours? Hell, maybe you planned on keeping up the charade. We'd get married, and what, you'd have your guys on the side? How many times have you fucked guys at your job?"

Her hand came up and slapped me across the face so hard I saw stars.

"Fuck you, Tucker! I wanted to tell you, I was going to tell you! I almost told you several times, and the last was right before Linda found you."

Forcing an evil smile, I replied, "Yeah, I was about to tell you what it was that I knew. Saved by my father dying. Classic. Well, fuck you,

Charlie. Fuck you and your little games. But listen, I tell ya what, I'll keep going along with this little game of yours. I'll marry you, and you can sit at the head of your daddy's company and play God. That's what you want, right? You get off telling all those old men what to do?"

The moment I saw the tears slip from her eyes, it felt like I sobered up. I closed my eyes and shook my head. Before I could tell her I was sorry and that I didn't mean any of it, Charlie spoke first.

"Shut up. I've never in my life hated anyone like I hate you right now. And to think I was going to tell you I loved you this weekend. Tell you everything and how I even thought about walking away from CMI for you!"

That got my attention. "What?" I asked, her words rattled around in my head. Love me? Leave CMI?

"Talk about a hypocrite. How long have you known?"

More guilt hit me. Charlie was better off without me. She deserved someone who would be honest and up front with her.

"The night you told Terri in my office. I have cameras in my office and heard the whole conversation."

A loud gasp caused me to look her in the eyes. My chest squeezed in the most painful way as I watched more tears spill from her eyes.

"Oh my God. You've known the whole time? Was this your way of getting back at me? What were you going to do? Make it all the way to the wedding and what? Leave me?"

I didn't answer her because that had been my first thought, but I would never hurt her like that. Ever.

Her hands covered her mouth. My silence was her answer.

"No, I wasn't going to do that. I'd never do that to you."

Holding up her hand, she shook her head, her other hand still covering her mouth. Charlie turned and walked toward the front door. She stopped and looked back at me.

"Wait, baby, wait."

"Don't ever call me that again. I'm nothing to you. Nothing!"

Her voice screamed the last word before she slammed the door shut.

I wasn't sure how long I stood there staring at the door before I dropped the bottle of Jack and grabbed my phone. Everything was blurry, and my shaking hands couldn't figure out how to pull up her name.

"Siri, call Charlie." My words were so slurred that I was surprised my phone understood my ass.

The phone rang once before I heard her voicemail. Stumbling back to the sofa, I kept calling her, and she kept sending me to voicemail. I wasn't sure when my phone died, but when it did, I buried my face in my hands and cried for the first time in seven years. In a way I felt like I'd died right along with my phone . . . and my father.

THE POUNDING SOUND sent a jolt of pain through my head. Slowly sitting up, I saw I was on the floor of my living room.

"Jesus Christ. Look at you."

The sound of Nash's voice filled the air.

"Oh my God. Tucker!"

Lily was down on the floor next to me, pushing my hair back and looking at me.

"What are you doing? Why are you doing this?"

My mouth felt like it was packed with cotton. The only thing I could do was stare at my sister. What in the hell was happening?

Then it all hit me.

Dad's dead.

Closing my eyes, I dropped my head and went to lie back down on the floor. A pair of hands pulled me up and gave me a shake.

"Fuck this, man, this isn't you. Get your ass into the shower now." Nash pulled me down the hall, my sister right on his heels.

"Nash, Nash! Don't do that to him."

"Do what, Lily? Sober his ass up? Get his head clear so he can see how bad he's fucked things up?"

"It's too late," I mumbled. "He's dead and I can't take back what I said."

"What?" Lily said, trying to grab me before my best friend pushed me into the shower and turned on what I was pretty sure was the cold water.

"Fucking hell!" I shouted, coming alive when the frigid water hit my face.

"Get yourself washed up. You fucking stink!" Nash shouted. He grabbed Lily and pulled her out of the bathroom, her face stricken with pain.

When the door shut, I stood there, the water running over my fully clothed body. I closed my eyes, rested my hands on the tile wall and sighed.

My father was dead. I'd never be able to have that conversation with him. Know what he wanted to tell me. Was he sorry? Was it the one time? Were there other women?

Stripping out of my soaking wet clothes, I turned the water to hot and stood there for the longest time. My head was pounding, and the ache in my chest grew stronger by the second.

A light knock on the bathroom had me clearing my throat. "I'll be out in a minute."

"Okay."

The soft voice was my sister's.

What an asshole I was. I just left my mother and sister to deal with my father's death while I drank myself into a fucking stupor.

Reaching for the water, I turned it off, grabbed a towel and dried myself off. Wrapping another towel around my body, I brushed my teeth and headed out into the kitchen. Nash and Lily were talking in hushed voices. I was still in my bare feet, so they didn't hear me coming down the hall. When I saw Nash standing there, holding my sister in his arms, I felt another kick in the gut. That should be me consoling her, not my best friend.

"It's going to all be okay, baby."

He kissed the top of her head, and I pulled my brows together. Did he just call my sister baby?

Clearing my throat, they broke apart quickly.

"Interrupting something?" I asked, looking between the two of them.

"No!" Lily nearly shouted before rushing over to me. "Are you okay?"

"I guess. How's Mom?"

My sister gave me an incredulous look. "How do you think she's doing? Dad died. You took off and got drunk. She's a mess. I'm a mess. And to top it off, you destroyed Charlie. What in the hell is wrong with you?"

I felt a stabbing pain in my chest; guilt ripped through my body like I'd never experienced before. Then her words settled into my brain.

"Charlie? What do you mean I destroyed Charlie?" I asked.

"I told you he was drunk out of his mind and wouldn't remember," Nash stated, his arms folded across his chest. The look he gave me was one of disappointment.

"What are you talking about?" I asked my sister.

"You really don't remember, Tucker? You don't remember telling Charlie that you knew all about her plan and how she needed to get married? About how you had a plan of your own?"

My hands scrubbed down my face. "Holy shit. Please, God. No. I didn't."

"Yes, you did. No one has been able to get a hold of her since she left here yesterday. She called me, told me you were drunk out of your mind, and that you told her you had a plan of revenge on her."

"I didn't have a plan of revenge. I was going to tell her this weekend that I knew. I was hoping she'd tell me first, though. She came so fucking close so many times. Then . . . then Dad died and . . . *fuck*!" I shouted.

"Dude, you need to get over to your mom's house. She needs you," Nash said.

"Charlie?" I said, looking at my sister.

"She's not at her house, and if she is, she's not answering. Terri is trying to track her down, but right now Tucker, right now, you need to focus on our mother. She's falling apart, and I can't do this on my own. We both need you."

My heart was torn. I'd do anything for my family, but I needed to talk to Charlie.

"Where's my phone?" I asked, frantically looking for it.

Nash handed it to me. "Here, go get dressed."

I swallowed hard and took the phone before turning and heading to my room. After changing into jeans, a long-sleeve shirt, and a baseball cap, I called Charlie's number.

The ringing brought back the memory of last night. Bits and pieces were slowly coming together. I'd tried calling her. I fell asleep crying. She told me she was nothing to me.

She said she hated me.

Her voicemail picked up after about seven rings. At least she didn't have her phone turned off.

"Charlie, it's me. Please call me back. *Please.* I was going to tell you this weekend, I was . . . I . . . fuck I was just hoping you'd tell me first. Baby, I'd do anything for you. You didn't have to come up with some fucking plan. Charlie, I'd marry you in a heartbeat. I . . . I love you, Charleston. Please call me back."

I hit *end* and dropped my head in defeat.

"That's how you're going to tell her you love her? On a voicemail begging her to forgive your stupid ass?"

My sister's voice sounded far off. I heard her, but I didn't hear her. Everything was fucked up. So fucked up.

"Let's go. Mom needs us."

Slowly standing, I pushed my phone into my pocket and pulled in a deep breath. My entire world had changed in a matter of days, and none of it was for the better.

Seventeen

CHARLIE

MY FINGER PRESSED the button for voicemail, and I held my breath.

"Charlie, it's me. Please call me back. Please. I was going to tell you this weekend, I was . . . I . . . fuck I was just hoping you'd tell me first. Baby, I'd do anything for you. You didn't have to come up with some fucking plan. Charlie, I'd marry you in a heartbeat. I . . . I love you, Charleston. Please call me back."

Tears streamed down my face the moment I heard his voice. I could hear the sadness, but was it because of what he'd said to me or because of his father? He hadn't said it, but I knew he was thinking of the last conversation he'd had with his father a few days back. I'd overheard it, and I knew it ate him alive.

Then he said the words that stopped my heart.

"I . . . I love you, Charleston. Please call me back."

I covered my mouth and dropped my phone next to me. Burying my hands in my face, I cried harder. The hateful words from last night played over and over in my head.

He was hoping I'd tell him first? What was this . . . a game to see who would break first? He'd been playing me the entire time. How could I be sure any of this was real? And now he decides to tell me he loves me? Over the phone in a message? When he's guilt stricken with his father's death weighing so heavily on him?

No. He's looking for a way to make himself feel better. He couldn't redeem himself with his father, so he thinks he can do it with me.

Well, fuck that.

Note to self: I'm giving up on men. Every last one of them.

My phone buzzed next to me, causing me to cautiously glance down at it.

Marge.

With shaking hands, I answered it. Seeing her name made me remember the thumb drive with the videos on it that I hadn't looked through yet.

"H-hello?" I said, my voice much weaker than I wanted it to be. Marge didn't notice though.

"I found it! Charleston . . . I mean . . . Charlie! I found it!"

Leaping up, I clutched my chest. "You did? Can you meet me at the office in thirty minutes?"

Hell, I wasn't even sure where Marge lived. She might not live that close. "Or just get there whenever you can." I added.

"I'll be there in fifteen."

I rushed into my bedroom. "Great! See you then."

Throwing on jeans, a light sweater and my hair in a ponytail, I ran to my bathroom and attempted to put a little bit of makeup on. I looked like hell, and it was obvious I'd been crying.

On the way down in the elevator, I pulled up two names on my phone. I called them both and told them to get to the office and meet me in the boardroom in two hours.

Slipping into a taxi, I dragged in a shaking breath. My heart was firmly on Tucker, but my head needed to be in the game. I needed this to work. If it didn't, I had no idea what I was going to do. No idea at all.

I NEARLY RAN to my office after getting off the elevator. Marge was sitting at her desk. It was the first time I'd ever seen her in regular clothes. She looked younger. Her hair was half up and half down. Usually she wore it up in a tight bun. She had on jeans and a sweater. Unlike me who threw on sneakers, she had on a pair of black flats.

Damn. Why didn't I think of that?

She must have seen me looking at her shoes and then mine because she said, "You've got a pair of Jimmy Choo black flats in your office in the closet."

I did have a pair in there!

"You're a lifesaver, Marge, remind me to give you a big-ass raise." Kissing her on the cheek, I rushed into my office with Marge on my heels.

Kicking my sneakers off, I pulled off my socks next and slipped into the flats. "Mr. Knots and Mitchell Landing will be here in an hour and a half. Let's take a look at the tape and get a game plan together before they get here."

Marge was already on the other side of the room, getting her laptop connected to the large TV on the wall at the end of the board table. When I mentioned Knots's name, she looked up and frowned. I knew she didn't like the man; he was one of those lawyers who were part of the good ol' boy system. He started working at CMI when my grandfather was still CEO.

"This is a copy. The original is in a locked safety deposit box at my house."

My head jerked over to look at her. "O-okay," I replied, my brows pulled in tightly as I looked at my executive assistant. Did she think someone would try and break in for it? No one even knew we had tapes from my father's office.

When she was finished, she looked at me; sadness swept over her face. "Charlie, this video was taken two weeks before your father's death. Your father had found out that your grandfather tried to sneak the bylaw in without any votes on it because he knew it would never pass. It has absolutely no merit. He told Ricker to remove it."

"What?" I gasped. "Ricker made it sound like Dad knew for a while."

She nodded. "Come on, sit down," she said, grabbing my hand and pulling me into a chair.

A video started up. It was my father and Paul Ricker, who was sitting in one of the large, leather chairs in front of Dad's desk.

My chest ached at the sight of my father. Tears filled my eyes, and I had to work hard at keeping them back. I missed my parents so much.

"Paul, you and I both know this won't hold up. It's ridiculous and will never stand up in any courts nor get any votes. Get Knots on this before Charleston hears about it from someone."

My heart dropped. Had all of this been a waste of time if my father didn't think it would hold up? Knots said it would take months to work through the court system. They lied to me.

"I never did think that would hold up and so did a number of the board members," Marge tossed out. "Scuttlebutt was going around about when the bylaw was put into place because no one had voted on it."

"Why didn't anyone say anything?" I asked, my brows pulled in tightly. I assumed this had been done months, if not years ago!"

Marge nodded. "So did the rest of the board, Charlie, or they assumed your grandfather pulled some of the old-timers aside and did it in secret."

I focused back on the tape.

"Sir, your father had the companies best interest at heart."

The way my father shot daggers at Ricker had me smiling. "Listen, you and I are friends. I know deep down you think you should run this company if anything should happen to me, but I know my daughter will do the job and do it better than any of us. So, I'll say this again, get it out of there. Even if it stayed, it wouldn't hold up. You and I both know it. Charleston could take it to court and contest it. Any judge in their rightful mind would throw it out, and I'm pretty sure my father knew that. He was bitter that Sally and I never tried for a boy. This was more of a jab at me than directed toward Charleston."

Paul moved around in his chair. "Mike, we've been friends for a while now. You know I'll do whatever you want, but do you honestly believe your daughter is the right person for the job of CEO in the event that, God forbid, anything should happen to you?"

My father looked angry. "Do you honestly think I'd put my entire life's work, and that of my father's, in the hands of someone who wouldn't know what to do with it? I've been grooming that girl since she was in the single digits to take over."

Pride filled my chest.

My father went on. "CMI is her entire life. She's dedicated and smart as hell, and I've taught her everything I know."

Paul nodded. "She is very much all those things. But she is also young and hasn't even been out of school but a few years."

My father laughed. "Do you think I'm going anywhere soon?"

Shaking his head, Ricker had the decency to look embarrassed at his choice of words.

"Hell, I've gone out of my way to make sure my daughter stays away from men, and you want my father to force her to marry one. No. She doesn't need a man by her side to do this job. No woman needs a man by her side to do *any* job. Besides, by the time she's ready to take over as CEO, she'll be older and wiser. You and I will long be retired."

Paul Ricker tensed some but let out a laugh along with my father. My chest ached knowing my father would be gone weeks after this was taped.

Paul finally stood. A fake-as-hell smile grew over his face. "I'll get it taken care of as soon as possible."

"Get it done today, Ricker. We have a shit ton of lawyers I pay a pretty penny to. Get them to handle my father's little joke before someone tells my daughter about it."

"Yes, Mr. Monroe."

We watched as Ricker walked out of my father's office. There was a break in the video and another one started up.

"Found this one a few days later."

Marge's voice says over the video.

Then I heard Marge's voice again, this time coming from the TV. "Mr. Monroe, Mr. Ricker is here to see you. He said it is in regards to the situation you asked him to take care of last week."

Hitting a button, my father answered. "Send him in."

The door opened and Ricker walked in. "Paul, tell me you got that taken care of?"

Ricker cleared his throat and sat down in the chair. "Yes. It's all been taken care of. Nothing to worry about."

Lifting his head, my father lifted a brow. "It's done?"

"Yes, just like you asked me to do. I talked to Mr. Knots about it, and we handled it. He took it to one of the judges he knows who simply laughed. Said it would never hold up in court. You could, of course, move to have the board vote that Charlie would need to be of a certain age before becoming CEO."

"No," my father retorted.

"Then the subject is dropped."

Marge and I looked at each other.

My father's voice made me jump.

"Good. Good. Now let's just forget this whole little nasty thing and move on."

Marge's voice once again comes over the TV. "Mr. Monroe, you asked me to remind you when it was one."

Standing, my father smiled. "Stay here, Ricker. I need to go wish my daughter a happy birthday."

My hand covered my mouth, and I forced the tears back. Marge reached over and squeezed my knee. She kept her hand there and turned back to the TV like she was waiting for a bomb to drop.

Ricker stood, walked around the desk and sat in my father's chair.

"That bastard," I hissed.

He hit a few numbers and smiled as he leaned back in the chair. "Knots, it's me. I'm calling from Mike's office. I told him it was taken care of. If he asks to see it, show him the fake one you drew up and then destroy it."

I gasped. "Holy fuck."

For the first time since I became acting CEO of CMI, Marge didn't scold me for swearing.

"I doubt he'll ask to see it, but if he does, we're covered. There is no way in hell I'm letting some goddamn wet-behind-the-ears young girl take over this company. I've lost two wives for that bastard and this company . . . he owes this to me."

Standing, I balled up my fists.

"That dirty, rotten, motherfucking, son-of-a-bitch bastard!" I screamed. "He and Knots both betrayed my father!"

"If I had known you were calling in Knots, I would have warned you not to."

I paced back and forth, trying to think of what to do.

"There are eleven very educated men and women on the board, and not one of them thought this sounded wrong?" I asked, my hands flying up to my hips.

Marge looked at me and said, "You believed it."

I stood there, staring at Marge.

"He thinks he's going to steal this company right out from underneath me? Well, he has another thing coming."

Walking back over to my desk, I reached for my phone and then back to Marge. "I'm calling an emergency board meeting. I want all those bastards here in an hour, and I don't give two shits what they have to do to get here."

Marge smiled. I could see the pride on her face.

The good thing about this shitstorm was that Tucker was the last thing on my mind right now.

GLANCING OVER TO the church, I watched as Lily, Tucker and their mother, Patty, forced smiles on their faces as they stood outside the doors and spoke to people. I'd wait until they went inside before I slipped in.

My phone buzzed.

Terri: Stop sitting in your car and please come in. Lily will want to see you.

Tucker wasn't the only reason I was stalling. Memories of my own parents' funeral came slamming back to the forefront of my mind this morning. Dressing in black with that heavy feeling in my stomach, knowing people will glance my direction and think how sad it was I lost both of my parents not very long ago.

Me: I'm trying. It's hard for more than one reason.

Terri's reply was instant.

Terri: I know, Charlie. I know.

Her words, although simple and direct, seemed to be what I needed. I swallowed hard and stepped out of my silver BMW. The closer I walked to the church, the more my heart pounded in my chest. The closer I got to Tucker, the more my feelings mixed together. I hated him. I hated what he did to me, but I was doing the same thing to him. I had gotten together with him under the umbrella of a lie. A trick. A plan to get him into my bed and show him how much he needed to be with me so that he would surely pop the question before my deadline.

Lily had sworn to me that Tucker was not planning any sort of revenge. He swore it to her. A part of me wanted to believe him, but I kept thinking back to that first night we spent together and the note he left asking if I regretted it. Maybe that had been his only plan of vengeance.

Anger boiled up inside of me, waging a war over the grief I also felt.

Grief won out as I walked up to Patty, who stood closest to me.

"Patty," I whispered. I could feel Tucker's eyes on me, but I focused on the woman standing before me. Her eyes were so bloodshot from crying. All I wanted to do was pull her to me, so I did. Her arms wrapped around me, holding me tight.

"I'm so sorry, Patty. I'm so very sorry."

The strong woman I'd seen smiling and saying hello to people cracked for a brief moment and sobbed; then she sucked in a breath of air.

"Thank you, sweet girl."

I went to pull away from her, but she held me tighter and moved her mouth to my ear. "He loves you, Charleston. Let him love you because he feels like he has no one right now."

My intake of sharp air was evident to both Lily and Tucker, I was positive. Patty let me go and turned to the person who was walking up behind me. I stared at her. My mind spinning.

Lily gently touched my arm and moved me closer to her. I tried to give her a smile, but I knew I was failing.

"Thank you, Charlie, for being here. I know this has to be so hard with your recent loss as well."

I wanted to ask her if she meant my parents or her brother but decided I was reading too much into this because she had to mean my parents.

With a quick hug, I stepped to her side and looked up into Tucker's gray eyes. The sadness in them left me breathless.

"I'm sorry about your father. I know how hard this is on you."

His eyes held nothing in them. No emotion whatsoever. He waited for what seemed like forever when he finally said, "Thank you."

He made no attempt at hugging me—hell, he actually took a step away from me. Our eyes lingered on each other for a few more moments before he looked away and stared blankly at the person talking to Lily.

I turned and walked into the church, the threat of tears pricking the back of my eyes. I quickly found Terri sitting in the second row with Nash, Blake, and Jim. She took my hand in hers and gave it a slight squeeze.

"You okay?" she asked, her eyes filled with sympathy.

My words caught in my throat. I was far from okay. I missed my parents. My heart hurt for Tucker with the way things were left between him and his father, yet I was angry as hell at him. Maybe I wasn't angry, but rather hurt that he would play me for a fool.

Pot calling kettle black.

Maybe my feelings were hurt at the hateful things he said to me in his drunken haze; they were hateful but also true. Truer words were always spoken when liquid courage was your shield, I guessed.

"I'm fine," I finally got out. My voice betrayed me, though. I was far from fine.

Another few minutes passed by, and then the family came in. I watched Lily and Tucker as they walked on either side of their mother. Tucker looked to be helping her stand up. When they sat down in the front, I heard soft cries and sniffles and nearly jumped up and bolted out of the church. Memories of my parents' funeral came rushing back. I focused on Tucker, watching his every move.

"Tucker is not doing well at all," I heard Nash whisper to Blake.

"Yeah, I know. I stopped by last night, and he was trashed out of his mind."

I frowned. That might have explained the blank expression on his face.

Tucker placed his arm around his mother and lightly brushed his fingers over Lily's shoulder. It was a silent show of strength. I couldn't be angry with him, not right now. Not knowing how he was feeling and the guilt that had to be eating away at him.

Tucker's mother laid her head on her son's shoulder. I could see her body shaking as she silently cried. I continued to watch him, willing him to stay strong for his family. For himself.

He did just that.

~

WE ALL SAT around a giant table in Tucker and Lily's parents' backyard. After the graveside service, family and friends were asked to come back for a celebration of Roger's life.

I had mostly been zoned out of the conversation until something Nash said snapped me back to reality.

"He's talking about leaving town."

My head jerked over to Nash and Jim.

"For how long?" Jim asked, taking a drink of his beer.

Nash shrugged. "Not sure, said he needed to get away for a while. Talked about taking a backpacking trip in Europe."

This news left me feeling sick to my stomach.

"What about the bar?" Blake asked.

"I don't know. He's not thinking clearly at all. He's really fucked up, in more ways than one."

When Nash's gaze looked to mine, I drew in a deep breath.

We stared at one another for a few moments before Nash pulled his eyes away.

What in the hell was that supposed to mean? Like it was my fault Tucker's father died? It was my fault Tucker knew about me needing to get married and was planning on playing some cruel joke on me?

Well, fuck that. The sad part about all of this was I no longer needed to get married. Once I got the board all together and showed them the tapes, it didn't take long to get both Knots and Ricker fired. I was CEO of CMI . . . no marriage was needed. I should have felt relieved, but all I felt was sadness mixed with anger that my father did this to me. He left me with *his dream* and the longer I filled his shoes, the more I hated it.

"What's wrong?" Terri asked, placing her hand on my leg. "You all of sudden seem really angry."

I turned to her and spoke so only she could hear. "Do you think it's wrong for me to be upset at Tucker for admitting he knew about the whole marriage thing?"

Terri chewed on her lip. "I mean, it's sort of hard, Charlie. You started off planning on tricking him into marrying you."

"I wasn't tricking him," I stated in a soft yet firm voice.

"Okay well, you for sure weren't honest with him. It's sort of like the pot calling the kettle black."

Frowning, I couldn't help but notice how I had mentally used that analogy earlier.

"Whatever. He could have said something, but he didn't."

"Lily and I both told you to be upfront with him. You had to know this wasn't going to turn out well."

I stood, my hands balled in fists. "So, it's my fault?"

Her eyes filled with worry, and she looked around as she stood and grabbed me by the arm. We walked further out into the giant backyard, away from everyone.

"It's both of your faults. You went into the relationship knowing you only needed one thing from Tucker, a wedding ring. He went into it angry because you were using him. Neither one of you is right, but you're both right for each other, and I know you both see that. We've all known that and have seen it for years. And while I'm being honest, let me just say, we were all glad you both got your heads out of your asses and followed your hearts. You belong together."

I scoffed.

Terri shook her head. "You can act like you're not in love with him, Charlie, but you are. The sooner you accept it, the sooner you can both be there for each other. Jim said something happened between Tucker and his father a few days before his death. It's what's tearing Tucker up inside. Then the whole thing that happened between y'all has just added to it. He's in a really bad place right now, and I know he needs you."

I chewed on my lip and glanced over to the house. Tucker was talking to an older woman and a younger woman, maybe Lily's age. They both hugged him, and I couldn't help but notice how the younger woman held Tucker a little longer than necessary.

My eyes burned a hole into her, and I was pretty sure if looks could kill, she'd be on the ground.

"That's Noelle Douglas. She's one of Lily's work friends. Her mother and their parents are pretty tight from what Lily has told me. I've gone out with them both a couple times for girls' night out."

My brows lifted. "Why didn't I go?"

Terri chuckled next to me. "Seriously? Because every time we asked you out, you were too busy working. Once Noelle and Tucker started dating, we stopped asking you on the nights we went out with her. Lily thought it might upset you to hear her talking about Tucker."

Folding my arms over my chest, I watched the exchange. Jealousy slowly built while I attempted to push it away. I did a piss-poor job of it.

"They dated?"

I could feel Terri's eyes on Tucker and Noelle. "Yep."

The sick feeling in my stomach had me dropping my arms. Tucker looked down at Noelle and smiled. It was the first smile I'd seen on his face since his father's death.

Noelle's hand went to Tucker's arm and stayed there while they talked. "How long did they date?" I asked, swallowing the bile that was now sitting at the base of my throat. I may be pissed at Tucker, but he was still mine.

Wasn't he?

"I'm not sure. Lily knows, you can ask her."

"No, thanks," I said, turning and walking more out into the yard and away from the sight in front of me.

Note to self: Take the name Noelle off my short list of baby names. Damn it, I really liked that name too.

Terri must have sensed my need to be alone for a few minutes because she didn't follow me. I made my way down into the vast garden and started walking on the trails. A few turns left and right and I was soon lost. I needed it, though. My head was clearing, and I knew Terri was right. How could Tucker and I come back from this? I needed to find out, but not right now. Now he needed to deal with his father's death.

"Shit," I hissed. How in the hell did I not notice how big this garden was? I could barely hear the sounds of voices. Closing my eyes, I tried to listen to the direction they were coming. Once I got what I thought was my bearings, I headed back down a familiar path that I knew I had walked on not only a few minutes ago.

Emerging from the garden and back into the large backyard, I saw my group of friends. Only this time, Tucker sat there between Nash and Blake. No, wait, Blake was standing and Noelle was sitting next to Tucker. As I got closer, I tensed when I saw her hand on his leg. Tucker sat back in the chair, a beer in his hand and a far-off look on his face. Did he even know she was attempting to feel him up at his own father's wake?

Lily saw me walking up and smiled. "Hey, there you are," she said softly, giving me a kiss on the cheek. I tried not to look over to Tucker. "Where did you go?"

"For a walk."

Lily smiled a bit more. "I wish I had known; I'd have gone with you. I could use a few minutes away."

My heart pulled with hurt, and I wanted to draw my friend into my arms and tell her the pain gets better. Not a whole lot better, but each day it eased some.

Right then, I could feel his eyes on me, so I refused to look his way. The sound of Noelle's voice filled my head and right then I decided I didn't like her voice. It was high pitched and grated my nerves.

Then I heard Tucker chuckle. Knowing this woman had made him smile and laugh did something to me. I was the stupid one who had walked away from him the other night. I'd told him I hated him, and at the time, I had. I was hurt, but deep down I knew I was just as much to blame for this mess.

Stealing a peek in their direction, she was resting her hand on Tucker's shoulder, whispering something into his ear. Tucker's eyes looked my way, and a smirk tugged at the corners of his mouth.

Asshole.

I guess he enjoyed his ex hanging all over him. Fine. Let him move on. I didn't have to stand there and watch it.

When I turned back to Lily, she was staring off, but not in the direction of her brother—at Nash.

"I'm sorry Lily, I'm going to have to run."

My best friend's face fell. "You do?"

I nodded and before I could stop myself, I looked at Tucker again. He stared at me, a beer in his hand and Noelle at his side. She was saying something to him, but it didn't look like he was paying any attention. Then he dropped his gaze in her direction. When her hand lifted and pushed a piece of his dark hair from his eyes, I knew I needed to leave. Tucker looked emotionless though, and that was the only thing keeping me from losing my shit.

"If you need anything," I started to say to Lily while reaching for my purse, "you let me know. Okay?"

Her eyes darted from me to Tucker, then to Noelle, and back to me again.

"Charlie, it's not what it looks like," she whispered.

I played like I had no idea what she was talking about. "What? I'm just feeling a little sentimental about my folks."

Which was half the truth.

"And I've got a fire burning at work I need to take care of."

Lily's face screwed up in a look of disappointment. "Of course you do."

My eyes widened. "What's that supposed to mean?"

She sighed. "It means it's always about work with you." Her voice raised, causing our small group to all turn their attention on both of us.

"What?" I asked, surprised and a little hurt by her sudden outburst.

"It's always about that damn job of yours. You've walked away from *everything* and ruined things with you and Tucker because of that stupid job of yours. Well, I hope it's worth it when you're all alone in life with no one there to love you. Oh, wait. CMI will be there for you."

I took a step back, my hand coming up to my throat. It felt like I couldn't breathe. I knew the signs of grief, and Lily was in the pissed-off-at-the-world stage. It still hurt that she lashed out at me.

Nash stood and walked up to Lily. "Lil, now is not the time to bring this up."

Snapping my head over to him, I gave him an incredulous look. Was this something Lily had felt for a long time? Did she honestly think I put my job before her? Before our friendship?

Lily let out a defeated sigh and looked from Nash to Tucker, and finally back to me. "Just go, Charlie. It's better for you to not be here anyway."

I sucked in a sharp breath, then turned to look at Tucker. I didn't know why I thought he would stop his sister from spewing out hurtful words. All he did was lift his beer and finish it off while he ignored me.

"Lily!" Terri said, standing at my side.

"It's okay," I forced out. My voice sounded weak, and I hated that. Taking in a deep breath to settle myself, I spoke in a steady voice while trying to remain compassionate. "I'll go so I don't upset Lily. Call me if you need anything, okay?"

For some reason, my response pissed off my best friend. She shook her head slowly and scoffed. She then quietly said, "Always the cool and calm one, aren't you? You're not in a goddamn boardroom, Charlie! For once in your life, can you show emotion? Tell Tucker how you're feeling!"

My eyes darted toward him. He didn't move; he just sat there. Now Noelle looked at me with a smug expression.

Lily wasn't finished with me though. She got in one more jab and went for the kill. "You didn't even cry at your own parents' funeral,

Charlie. That says a lot about what's important to you in your life."

Terri stepped up to Lily. "That's enough," she said sharply.

Anger pulsed through my veins. She was angry and filled with grief, but that didn't give her the right to take it out on me or mention my parents. My eyes burned, and I was too emotionally exhausted to fight it anymore.

A single tear slipped from my eye and trailed down my cheek. Blake stood and walked over to me.

"Charlie," he whispered. The tenderness in his voice moved me, but again it made Lily angry.

She opened her mouth to say something but was cut off by a deep voice.

"Knock it off, Lily," Tucker finally said. When I turned to him, his eyes grew watery and he stood. He took a step toward me, and for a moment I thought he was going to walk up to me. Instead he stopped when Blake cupped my face in his hands.

"Are you okay?"

I nodded and took a step back, breaking his contact.

Swallowing hard, I pulled my eyes from him and landed my gaze onto Lily, who now wore a look of regret on her face.

Clearing my throat the best I could, I spoke softly. "I'm glad to know how you feel, Lily."

Her eyes closed. "Charlie, I didn't mean any of that. Don't leave."

I didn't give her a chance to finish. I stepped around her, wiped my face clear of any tears, and walked over to their mother as I forced my voice to stay steady.

"Mrs. Middleton, I'm so sorry for your loss. If there's anything you need, or if you'd like to talk, I'm here."

Patty smiled at me and then pulled me in for a hug. She didn't say anything, but when she pushed me at arm's length to look at me, she opened her mouth to speak. She then closed her eyes for a few moments before looking back at me.

"Charleston, thank you sweetie. I know how hard this has also been for you."

Forcing a small grin, I remained quiet. If I spoke, I knew I would break down into tears. I needed to get out of here.

Patty's eyes moved to the group outside and she frowned. "Please don't be angry with him. He cares very much about you and you've both lost . . . you've lost. . . ."

Before she could finish, she covered her mouth, turned on her heels and walked off.

I can't deal with this shit.

When I reached my car, I jumped in and dropped my head down onto the steering wheel. Everything was spiraling out of my control, and there was nothing I could do to stop it.

Well, not everything. My father's company was still very much in my control.

Too bad that didn't make me even one ounce happy.

Eighteen

CHARLIE

THREE WEEKS HAD passed since the funeral. Lily had called me three times. Each time, I sent it to voicemail and buried myself in work. I'd worked every Saturday and Sunday. When I wasn't at work, I was home with Mr. Pootie. He was the only man in my life now, and I planned on keeping it that way. Especially after I'd gone out for a run and had seen Tucker and Noelle walking out of a restaurant just a block from my place. She'd reached up and kissed him on the cheek. I'd nearly stumbled over a poor man who had stopped to tie his shoe. I jumped him like a damn hurdle and screamed in the process. Of course that made Tucker and Noelle look my way. The guy jumped up and asked me if I was okay. We both chuckled about my impressive jump, but I felt Tucker's stare. Felt it in the very core of my being. When my eyes met his, I said my goodbyes to the stranger and practically sprinted home, ignoring Tucker, who called out for me. A small part of me hoped by seeing him that day, he'd text me. But he didn't, and neither had I. My pride wouldn't allow it.

My phone buzzed with an incoming text on my desk, and I flipped it over to see it was Nash.

Nash: Feel like grabbing a beer tonight? We'll all be at Sedotto tonight.

I flipped it over and went back to work. An hour passed when it buzzed again.

Nash: Charlie, please. Lily's depressed as fuck, Tucker has been drinking nearly non-stop since y'all broke up, and I'm pretty sure Terri's planning on killing Blake soon. We need you!

A small chuckle slipped from between my lips at the mention of Terri wanting to kill Blake. My heart hurt for Lily, and I was back to being angry at Tucker. He had Noelle now to comfort his ass. Nash expected me to show up and be the salve to their wounds. Yeah, I was made of strong stuff but not strong enough to put myself in their crosshairs again.

Me: Let Terri kill Blake. I'm sorry about Lily, but she made her feelings pretty clear at the wake. And call AA for Tucker's problems. Nothing I can do to fix what's broken.

His reply was almost instant.

Nash: So that's it? You're walking away from all of us? She was angry and hurt and confused, Charlie. You know that; you've been there. And what about Tucker? Did you ever even care about him, or was it really all a game?

My body shook with anger.

Me: It was never a game. The only man I could ever see myself with was Tucker. I'm at work, Nash. I can't talk. But then, that shouldn't surprise y'all, right?

Nash: No, I guess not.

I stared at his last text, my teeth digging into my lip so hard I tasted blood. His next text made me jump.

Nash: Just so you know, Tucker is really fucked up. I know something happened with his dad, but the other night when he was wasted, he kept saying how he hurt you. He can't move on and he needs to. He can't apologize to his father, so for fuck's sake, can you at least let him apologize to you so he can get his shit together and move on if you don't intend on being a part of his life?

The fact that he was trying to guilt me only made my decision to not go tonight the right one. They all thought I worked too much and my job owned me. Well screw them . . . Every last one of them.

Nash: I'll take your silence as a no. That's fucked up, Charlie. I really thought you cared about him.

"Fuck you, Nash."

Pulling out my drawer, I threw my phone into it and slammed it.

The rest of the day I was useless. I couldn't stop thinking about Nash's text messages. I worked until seven and then changed and headed to the gym. After an hour of working out, I made my way home. Mr. Pootie was pissed off and ignoring me as I walked through my living room and into the kitchen.

"If you keep acting like a dick, I won't feed you."

The damn cat actually sat with his back to me. When I pulled back the lid on his moist food, he simply glanced back at me and gave me a disgusted meow.

"Are all the men in my life going to be like this?" I mumbled as I dropped the food into Mr. Pootie's bowl.

After a hot shower, I settled on the sofa and stared out at the night lights of Austin for what seemed like forever. A part of me wished I was staring up at a night sky filled with stars like when I went camping with my father. He loved being in the woods, and whenever he got the chance to get away from work, he always took me and my mom somewhere fun. It was camping, the beach, or a trip to one of the national parks. However, once he became CEO of CMI, everything changed. We went on less and less trips, and I had gotten to the age where I did more things with my friends' families than I did with my own.

The heaviness in my chest felt like a brick. Heading out to the balcony, I sat down on the chair, my knees pulled up and tucked under my chin as I let out a long sigh.

"I really hate the city," I whispered to myself. There were a lot of things I really hated. These last few weeks alone had made me open my eyes to all the things I had been using as fillers to make myself think I was living the life I wanted. It was the opposite. Nothing about my life was what *I* wanted. It was what my father wanted.

My cell phone started ringing, and I jumped up. I knew it was late, at least after ten. If it was work, I was going to beat someone's ass.

The name stared up at me.

Lily.

Turning away, I walked into the kitchen. I was being childish and pouting because my best friend spoke the truth.

Mr. Pootie went in between my legs, letting out a loud cry for either attention or a snack.

"Do you think I'm being a baby?" I asked, picking him up and snuggling him against my chest.

He didn't respond.

"I'll take your silence as a yes. This is why my father didn't want me falling in love, Mr. Pootie. It's a distraction, and one I can't really afford to have. I have a company to run."

Using his front paws to push me away, my cat fought to get out of my arms.

"You too, huh? Well I don't have a choice. My father trusted me with his company, and I'm going to do what I was raised to do. Run it and make it even better than it was before."

Licking his paw, he rubbed it over his ears and face. He had no interest in my declaration. None at all.

Note to self: Get out of the house more. You're losing your damn mind.

After digging through the freezer, I settled on a pint of Blue Bell chocolate ice cream and headed into the living room to find something to watch on Netflix.

Mr. Pootie jumped up onto his cat condo and peered out over the city lights. Sedotto wasn't far from my place, and my mind kept drifting off and wondering if the whole gang was out tonight. What was Tucker doing? Working or hanging all over Noelle. I picked up my phone and saw I had a voicemail from Lily. Swallowing hard, I hit the little sideways triangle and listened to it.

"Hey, I'm sorry we haven't had a chance to talk. It's been a rough few weeks. Mom is finally not crying every hour of the day."

A long pause came. I heard music pulsing in the distance. She must have been in Tucker's office.

"I'm sorry for what I said that day. I didn't mean any of it. Well, I do think you work too much, but you already know that. I didn't want you to

leave. A part of me saw the hurt in your eyes when you saw Tucker, and the stress of the situation was too much to handle. It was easier for me if you weren't there. That sounds like such a bitch thing to say, and I'm so sorry. Have you tried calling Tucker? He misses you, and I think he was really hoping you'd be here tonight."

I frowned. If he missed me so much and wanted to say how sorry he was, he sure had a funny way of showing it. I hadn't received one phone call or text from him.

Why in the hell am I hiding out here in my place? I'm young, single, and free to date anyone I chose.

"Fuck it!" I said as I jumped up and rushed to my bedroom. "Everyone is so desperate to see me, then they are going to see me."

I had never changed and put makeup on so fast in my life. Forty minutes later I walked into Tucker's bar. My eyes widened in shock. It was packed with people. Turning to the left, I spotted my friends. Nash sat between Lily and Terri. Jim was next to Terri and next to him sat someone I didn't know. It was a woman with dark hair. My heart pounded in my chest. It had to be Noelle. She turned, and sure enough, it was her.

Fucking great. This was a stupid idea.

Turning to get the hell away from this place, I ran into someone.

"Excuse me," I mumbled.

"Charleston?"

Startled, I took a step back and looked up at a gorgeous guy smiling down at me. His blond hair looked like he had been pushing his fingers through it all night. His bright blue eyes seemed to sparkle as he gazed down at me. He looked familiar, but damn if I could place him.

"Do we know each other?" I asked, forcing myself to smile politely.

He placed his hand over his heart as if I had wounded him. "I'm hurt you don't remember me. I must not have left a very good impression. Darrell Adams. Your father and mine were good friends. We played a few rounds of golf together and talked about how we both wanted to sail around the world and leave work behind."

The memory hit me.

"Oh my gosh! Yes! You had dark hair, though."

He laughed. "I did. Went for a change."

"How are you?" I asked. Darrell and I had spent hours on and off the golf course talking about life in general. He was in the same situation as me. He had a father with his own business who was hell bent on the heir apparent taking it over.

"CMI is doing some work for us; I was hoping I'd get to see you."

My eyes lit up. "Yes, we're helping y'all redesign your call center. George doing a good job so far?"

"Very much so." He nodded. "Were you leaving?" he asked, turning to the two guys he had walked in with. "I'll catch up with y'all in a bit."

I glanced back over to the table and chewed on my lip.

"Let me guess, ex-boyfriend here with a new girl?"

My head turned back to Darrell and I laughed. "Something like that. Ex owns this bar, we all hung together in college, and it was stupid of me to come here tonight."

He lifted a brow. "Because of the ex?" Darrell turned in the direction I had been looking.

"Because of the little dark-haired beauty sitting in that large booth at the very end. I think they're dating now."

Darrell smiled. "Then let's go say hi."

He placed his hand on my lower back and guided me toward my small group of friends. I frantically searched for Tucker but didn't see him.

"No . . . honestly, I'd rather just . . ."

"Charlie!"

My body sank. "Damn," I whispered as Darrell wrapped his arm around my waist and pulled me to him.

What in the hell was he doing?

"Hey . . . Terri."

God, my voice sounded weak and unsure.

All eyes went to Darrell. Terri and Lily gave him a once-over, Nash looked like he wanted to rip off Darrell's head, Jim showed no emotion, and Blake . . . Well, Blake looked like he wanted to punch the living shit out of poor Darrell. This guy had no idea what he'd just walked into.

"How are you doing, Lily?" I asked.

Pulling her eyes off Darrell, she forced a smile. "I'm doing okay. You got my message?"

I nodded. "Yes."

She sat back and stared at Darrell, giving him a look like she wanted him to explode on the spot.

"Who's this? A new friend of yours?" Nash asked, his voice thick with sarcasm.

I froze, which was so not like me. At all.

When I finally found my voice, I replied, "Darrell Adams, he's a friend of mine."

With a huge grin on his face, Darrell reached out his hand to Nash. "Our fathers were good friends. Charlie and I are . . ." He trailed off and looked at me. "Hanging out."

I groaned internally. Darrell had made it seem like we were doing more than hanging out. Before I knew it, Darrell shook each person's hands and introduced himself. Then he got to Noelle.

"I'm Noelle, it's a pleasure to meet you."

I snarled my lip at the way she openly flirted with Darrell. What a bitch.

Lily looked pissed, as did the rest of the table. The only person who seemed happy was Noelle. Lily's eyes darted to her and then back to me as she spoke in a gruff voice. "It's not what you think."

I shrugged. "Not my business."

"Charlie mentioned y'all would be here tonight, so we just stopped in to say hello. So if you'll excuse us."

My eyes widened in shock. Darrell wasn't messing around.

"Wait, you're not going to sit here with us? We haven't seen you in weeks, Charlie," Terri said, her eyes sad and hurt.

I let my eyes drift over to Noelle. They lingered on her for a few seconds since she was busy typing something out on her phone. Focusing back on Terri, I replied, "Not tonight, table seems crowded already."

"Nice meeting y'all," Darrell said and we went to turn. Oh my God, I felt him before I even realized where he was.

As I turned around to join Darrell, there he was.

Gasping, I threw my hand over my chest. "You scared me to death, Tucker."

Darrell stood taller when he realized this was the ex.

Tucker stared at me with a hard look. "Finally decide to hang out with your friends?"

I lifted my chin. "Actually, I only came over to say hello. Looks like you've got a full house at your friends' table."

Tucker's eyes looked past me and to Noelle. His eyes were back on mine and he smirked.

"Jealous?"

Darrell's fingers pressed into my hip.

"Hardly. You always were the type to jump from one to the next."

Tucker's smirk slid off his face. "Same old Charlie. Runs when the shit gets real."

The smell of booze practically dripped off Tucker.

Darrell cleared his throat. "Okay, I'm not sure what happened between you two, but we're going to be leaving now."

Poor Darrell. I really should have warned him what he was getting himself into. Tucker faced him.

"Who are you? The new flunky she tricked into falling for her? Y'all getting married? Dude, you better watch out with this one. She likes to play games."

"Me?" I shouted, taking a step closer to Tucker. "What about you? You knew from the very beginning, and you never said a word. How long were you going to play me, Tucker? Maybe your intentions were to leave me at the altar. Ultimate payback, right?"

His jaw was locked tight, and I barely understood the words that came from his mouth. "It wasn't a game."

"It never was for me either."

Tucker tossed his head back and laughed. "That's classic, Charlie. How much time you got left? A month? You pay this guy or something?"

Darrell took a step closer to Tucker. "Listen here. I don't know what in the fuck is going on, but Charlie is a friend of mine, and I don't like how you're talking to her."

Tucker smiled wide now. Normally his smiles made my lower stomach pull, but this one did the opposite. It frightened me. A look of evil moved into his eyes.

"Friends with benefits. Is that the type of arrangement you got with him? Is that what we had Charlie? Because I thought it was a hell of a lot more than that."

"Stop it," I hissed, glancing around the bar. "You're drunk and you need to stop now."

"Why? Truth hurt? Is that all we were, Charlie?"

Burning in the back of my eyes had me blinking fast. I took a step closer to Tucker. "I'm not the one who hooked up with an ex at my father's funeral."

His smile dropped, and he looked at Noelle and then back to me. He didn't say a word at first, which only led me to believe my suspicions were right.

He's with Noelle.

My heart felt like someone had stabbed me right in the middle of it.

"Think what you want. I don't care anymore. Enjoy your fake marriage. I hope you get everything you've ever wanted, Charlie."

And with that, he turned and walked off toward his office.

Lily appeared in front of me. "Charlie, you've got things all wrong." Her eyes looked at me, pleading.

I scoffed. "No, for the first time in my life, I think I'm actually thinking clearly. It was good seeing you, Lily."

Darrell took my cue and guided me away.

"Holy shit Charleston, what was that about?" he asked, his mouth against my ear.

My breaths came fast and shallow.

"I need to get out of here."

With a nod, Darrell gave a quick chin up to his friends who flashed him a smile that suggested they were happy he was about to hook up.

"Your friends," I started to say.

"Are fine without me. Come on, let's go grab some coffee."

For the first time in weeks, I actually felt myself relax and smile while in Darrell's presence. We sat at a coffee shop for almost two hours talking. I told him everything. The whole stupid plan to get Tucker to marry me, how I felt about Tucker, and how he knew about the plan from the very beginning. How lost I felt with my father gone. My doubts about my future. And he was equally open with me. He'd just broken off an engagement his parents forced him into, and things weren't so great on the home front right now.

Looking at my empty coffee cup, I sighed. "I should get home. It's late."

"Let me take you home."

"I drove, but if you want to walk me to my car, I won't argue."

Darrell smiled and it made my chest flutter. Not like how it did with Tucker, but in a different way. A nice, comfortable way. A way that said I needed a friend.

We stopped at my car, and I took in a deep breath. "Thanks for tonight and letting me spill my guts to you."

He laughed. "No worries. That's some crazy shit with your grandfather."

I rolled my eyes. "Yes, it is. So, I guess I'll be seeing you on the golf course?"

Darrell grinned wider. "I have a better idea. There's a dinner that my father's company is hosting. It's to help raise money to build a school in Africa. It's really my mother's passion, but Dad's sponsoring the trip. I'm sure if your . . . well . . ."

He looked away.

"If my parents were here?"

When he glanced back at me, I could see the regret in his eyes. "I'm sorry, that's what I was going to say. If your parents were here, I know he'd invite them."

"I already RSVP'd to the invite a few weeks back."

He quirked a brow. "With a plus-one?"

With a pout, I shook my head, causing him to chuckle again. I was beginning to really like the sound of his laughter. It eased the ache in my chest.

"Go with me? Friends only. I'm honestly not interested in going down the relationship road anytime soon."

"I'd like that. I think it will make the evening better for both of us."

Darrell nodded, then leaned down and kissed my cheek. "So do I. I'll give you a call in a few days. Maybe we can grab coffee again."

"Sounds good," I said as I opened the door to my car and slid in.

Darrell pushed his hands into his jeans pocket and looked down at me. I couldn't help but give him a once-over.

Damn, he was nice looking, that was for sure. His body was built, shoulders broad. Nice smile. Good just-fucked hair and eyes that held a certain mystery to them.

I lifted my hand and waved goodbye as I drove off.

Too bad I wasn't the least bit attracted to him in any way whatsoever.

Nineteen

TUCKER

THE LIGHT POURING into my bedroom caused me to moan.

Shit. My head pounded and my mouth was dry.

Pushing the covers off me, I glanced down to see I was dressed in what I had walked out of my apartment in yesterday morning.

I rubbed the back of my neck and made my way into the bathroom. Mindlessly, I washed my face, brushed my teeth, and then stripped out of my clothes. I took a hot shower and wrapped the towel around my waist before making my way to the kitchen. I needed coffee in a serious way. Almost a life-or-death situation, if I was being honest with myself.

As I made my way through the living room, I searched for my phone. Damn it. If I lost it, I'd be pissed at myself.

Glancing up, I came to a stop when I saw her. She leaned against the kitchen island wearing one of my T-shirts.

Oh. Fuck. What did I do?

With a seductive look in her eyes, she asked, "Good morning. How do you feel?"

My eyes swept over the kitchen. Noelle had made a pot of coffee, and it looked like she was about to make eggs.

"Fine. What are you doing here?"

Her head jerked back. "I'm the one who brought your drunk ass home. You couldn't drive, so I drove your truck here. Took everything out of me to get you in here and to your bedroom."

The only thing that made me let out the breath I held was the fact that I had woken up fully dressed.

"Where did you sleep?" She caught my eyes sweeping over her body.

"In your guest bedroom. Borrowed one of your shirts, hope you don't mind."

I shrugged as though I couldn't care less. But I did mind. The only woman I wanted to see standing in my kitchen dressed in my clothes was Charlie.

"Thanks for bringing me home, but why didn't Nash?"

"He and Lily got into some big fight. He left. Said something about not playing second fiddle. No idea what that was about."

My brows furrowed. I'd suspected something was going on with those two but just hadn't wanted to admit that my best friend was most likely sleeping with my baby sister. I shuddered thinking about it.

"I don't care to know."

Noelle moved and leaned against the other counter. All I could think about was the day Charlie came down in my shirt and we'd come close to fucking.

"Did you have to go to Sedotto today? I was thinking maybe we could spend the day together."

My head jerked over to her. I moaned as the room spun a little. "Excuse me?"

Her face scrunched up and I wanted to think it looked cute, but I felt nothing toward Noelle anymore. Nothing at all.

"I thought maybe we could hang out."

"Sorry, Noelle, I'm not interested in . . . hanging out . . . or anything else."

Her smile faded. I caught the look of disappointment in her eyes before I turned and poured myself a cup of the coffee she had made.

After a few awkward minutes in silence, she broke it. "Do you still like her?"

"By her, do you mean Charlie?"

"Yes," she said softly. I turned and leaned against the counter opposite of her.

"I love her."

Her eyes dropped, and I couldn't help but notice how her shoulders sagged. It only took her a heartbeat to look at me again.

"She was with another guy last night. They left together. It looks to me like she's moved on. You should too."

A sickness rolled through my body as I thought about it. I needed to talk to Charlie, and not when I was drunk out of my mind.

I pushed off of the counter and held up the coffee mug. "Thank you for making this, bringing me home, and making sure all was good. I'll get dressed so I can take you back to your car."

Disappointment washed over her face.

"I'll meet you back out here in a few minutes," I called over my shoulder.

She nodded. As I walked down the hallway to my bedroom, the doorbell rang.

"I'll get it!" Noelle said as I kept walking. I didn't give two fucks who was at my door. I knew it wasn't Charlie, so no one else mattered.

As I walked into my bedroom, I heard my phone going off. It was on top of my dresser. A text from Lily.

Lily: Charlie called me. Said she tried to call you this morning. Are you home? She's headed that way.

Fear instantly hit me. Holy shit.

Racing out of my room, I ran down the hall, through my living room and to the front door.

I sighed when I saw Nash at the door. He looked at Noelle and then to me.

"Are you fucking crazy?" he shouted, pushing past Noelle.

"Nothing happened. She drove me home last night because I was drunk. Since she didn't have her car, she stayed in the guest room."

My best friend stood there, his hands balled up in fists.

Leaning in closer to me, he asked, "Are you sure nothing happened?"

"Positive. I woke up fully clothed. Even my boots were still on."

He looked relieved and then pissed again. "You're lucky it was me who showed up here this morning. Charlie was on her way over here."

The rock in my stomach grew heavier. "What the fuck do you mean 'was'? Why?"

"You called her last night apparently drunk out of your mind, said some crazy shit to her, and then hung up. She's been trying to call you. Said she was worried. When she mentioned she was going to come to your place to check on you, I got a weird feeling that wasn't a good idea. I'm sure as shit glad I talked her out of it."

My entire body relaxed, and I let out the breath I hadn't realized I was holding in.

"Yeah, me too."

Noelle came back out into the living room, fully dressed. "I put your T-shirt on the guest bed. You might want to wash it if your . . . if Charlie will be coming over. It smells like my perfume."

I made a mental note to throw out the T-shirt, while also noting the hint of a smirk grow at the corners of her mouth. Nash noticed it too.

"Do you need a ride home?" Nash angrily asked.

"No, I got an Uber." Facing me, she flashed me a toothy grin. "Hang out another day maybe?"

My hand went to the back of my neck where I attempted to rub the tension away.

"I don't think so, Noelle."

When she tried to kiss me goodbye on the cheek, I took a step back. The last thing I wanted to do was send her the wrong signal. I was in this mess because I let her paw me at my own father's wake.

The moment she walked out the door, Nash faced me.

"Dude, you've got to drop whatever it is you have going on with Noelle. Charlie already thinks y'all are an item."

My brows pulled in. "How do you know that?"

He looked guilty. "I sent her a text yesterday asking her to come hang out with us at the bar."

The curiosity got the better of me. "What did she say?"

Nash shrugged. "I don't know. She made some short remark about you having Noelle now."

"Why in the hell does she think that?" I asked. He knew more than what he was leading on. "Why does she think that, Nash?"

The way his hand pushed through his hair, I was aware he knew more.

"Tell me!" I said between gritted teeth.

"I tried telling her this morning y'all weren't a thing because she mentioned it in the text. She told me I wasn't keeping up with your love life very well because she saw y'all leaving a restaurant together."

I rolled my eyes. "I ran into Noelle there. I met Lily and my mother there."

The mention of my sister's name caused Nash to jerk. Narrowing my eyes, I looked at him hard.

"Speaking of my sister, what's going on with the two of you?"

Nash shifted from one foot to the other, a forlorn look etched on his face.

"Nothing."

I let out a gruff laugh. "Nothing? I'm not fucking blind. You've been with her, am I right?"

My best friend had the good sense not to lie to me.

He shoved his hands into the pockets of his jeans and sighed. "Yes. I wanted more, she clearly didn't."

My brows shot up. "Did she only want to be fuck buddies?"

Just saying that made my skin crawl and my body shudder.

"Listen, I wanted to tell you. Lily wouldn't let me. In the beginning she said we were just having a good time and no one needed to know. I pushed her for more, for a commitment. She didn't want that. After your dad passed away, she started hooking up with some guy from work. I found out about it last night when I saw his text message come over her phone. She left it when she went to the restroom."

My chest squeezed. I actually felt bad for my best friend.

"Fuck," I said, not sure I wanted to even believe what I was hearing. "She cheated on you?"

He shrugged. "I guess. I mean, we never made our relationship public knowledge, but I was faithful and she wasn't so—"

Nash stopped talking and went back to rocking on his feet.

He forced a smile. "I loved her, but she didn't love me back. It's okay. We talked this morning, and we're not going to let it ruin our friendship. It would be too hard on the group."

Now guilt hit me. Charlie had avoided our group for the last month almost and then showed up last night with some douchebag-looking guy.

"Yeah, I know what you're saying."

Nash hit me on the shoulder and said, "Dude, please go get something on. You being in a towel is sort of freaking me the fuck out."

I laughed and pointed to the kitchen. "Grab a beer. I'll be out in a second."

"Dude, it's not even nine in the morning and you want to drink?"

"Fine, grab something else to drink. I'll be out in a second."

Hustling back to my bedroom, I pulled on a pair of jeans and a black long-sleeve T-shirt. The temperatures in Austin were on the chilly side but not too bad for this time of year.

When I returned to the living room, I stopped at the sight of my best friend. He looked like he hadn't slept all night.

"You okay?" I asked, sitting down next to him.

"Yeah," he said, making himself sound happier than I knew he really was.

"Looks like we can both be miserable fucks together."

He let out a slight chuckle. "Listen, you might want to at least text Charlie. I don't know what all you said to her last night, but it was enough to scare her. One more thing, Tucker, you've got to stop with the drinking."

I swallowed hard. "I don't feel anything when I drink. No guilt. No pain. No sadness. I'm just numb."

"Yeah well, you're going to lose the bar if you keep getting trashed there like you did last night."

Dropping back, I let my head rest against the sofa while I let out a long groan.

"Fucking hell, why did I let Charleston Monroe back into my life like this?"

Nash chuckled. "Because you never got over her the first damn time she broke your heart."

"Well, this time I broke her heart because I was stupid. Why the fuck was it so important for her to tell me about the stupid marriage bullshit? I should have told her the moment I found out."

I felt his eyes on me. "Not to rub it in or anything, but I told you not to do it."

My eyes closed. "For like the first twenty-four hours, I was seriously out to get her back. Then after we were together and I left her that morning, I felt like shit. I knew I couldn't do it, but I also couldn't tell her. I planned on telling her that weekend, although I was pretty damn sure she was going to tell me first. Then all shit hit the fan with my dad and . . ."

I trailed off; the mention of my father's name made me feel sick. I could still hear those last words I said to him.

"You're a dirty rotten fucking cheater and I hate you."

"I told him I hated him. I called him a cheater and the last words I said were 'I hate you.'"

Nash went rigid next to me.

We sat there for a few minutes, neither of us saying a word.

"He knows you didn't hate him, Tucker."

My eyes burned and I blinked to hold back the tears.

"I don't think so, man. I meant it when I said it, and he heard it in my voice. I was so fucking mad at him though. He cheated on my mom, and he wanted to *explain* it to me. How the hell do you explain that?"

"I don't know. I'm beginning to think that love is just some made-up bullshit."

We looked at each other.

Nash stood. "Fuck this shit. Let's grab some beer and go to the lake."

I lifted a brow. "It's morning still. Don't you have work?"

"Yeah, but I'm the boss. I suddenly feel like drinking and casting some lines."

"Sounds damn good to me. Let me change into something else and grab my poles."

Running down the hall, I heard my phone ping.

Please be Charlie.

I picked it up and saw it was from my sister.

Lily: What's going on? Charlie isn't answering me, you're not answering me and Nash is sending my calls to voicemail.

Me: I'm fine. I'll let Charlie know, as well. Nash is here. We're going fishing.

She didn't reply in a text but instead called me.

"Hey," I said weakly. I still couldn't believe Nash and my sister were hooking up and she was the one to break *his* heart.

"Nash is there? Can you have him call me?"

"I think he'll talk to you when he's ready."

Silence filled the air between us.

"You know?"

Her voice was quiet and a bit shaky.

"Yeah, he told me."

"I'm sorry, Tucker. I knew you wouldn't be happy about it and honestly, it was just . . . two friends having a good time."

There was no fucking way I was talking about this with my sister.

"Whatever, Lily. I need to go. I'll let him know you're wanting to talk to him."

"Thanks. I'm getting ready to head out sailing with . . . um, I just wanted to make sure he was okay."

I let out a sharp laugh. Damn women. Even my own sister.

"He's fine." I said, feeling a bit guilty I was being so short with Lily.

"Don't you dare judge me, Tucker Middleton. I never promised him anything."

"That's between y'all, Lily. I need to go. Be careful today, okay?"

"You too."

"I love you, sis."

"I love you too."

The line went dead, and I opened up a new text message. With shaking hands, I typed out a message for Charlie.

Me: I'm sorry I called you last night. I don't remember any of it. I'm okay. Going fishing with Nash.

Figuring she was pissed and wouldn't reply for hours, I pushed my phone into my back pocket and went about getting my fishing stuff together.

I walked into the living room and set everything down. "You got the cooler?" I asked, reaching for my wallet and making sure I had my fishing license.

"Yep, you ready?"

With a nod, I replied, "Yep. By the way, my sister wanted to talk to you. I told her we were going fishing."

Nash nodded and didn't go for his phone. Instead, he took one of my fishing rods and headed to the front door.

We spent the next six hours floating on Lake Travis—drinking, fishing, and trying to forget our broken hearts. I think the only thing we were successful at in those six hours was the drinking.

Twenty

TUCKER

MY MOTHER STOOD in front of me, attempting to fix the tie on my expensive suit.

"I don't even know why I have to go."

She pursed her lips together. "Because this was important to your father, so it's important to us. Besides, Loyd Adams was a good friend of your father's. You'll be able to meet his son, Darrell. Loyd is grooming him to take over the family business."

I rolled my eyes, thinking of how Charlie's father had done the same with her. Just thinking of Charlie made my insides hurt. She had texted me back the day Nash and I had gone fishing. It had been three hours after I texted her. Her reply was simple and direct.

You scared me. Don't ever do that again.

I wanted desperately to text her back, but I didn't. I couldn't stop analyzing if that had been a mistake.

"Penny for your thoughts," my mother whispered.

Smiling, I let out a breath and then kissed her on the forehead. "I just hate these kinds of things. That's all."

"You won't tonight, trust me. I think you'll be very happy you went."

An hour later when we walked into the ballroom; I groaned at the sight of Noelle.

"Was that your idea of me being happy to go to this?" I asked, jerking my head over to Noelle. It was clear this was one of *those* kinds of events—the one where all the rich families of Austin showed up, donated big money to make themselves look good, and rubbed elbows in the process.

When my mother saw Noelle, she laughed. "Hardly, Tucker. I never did like that girl when you were dating her. She's only after one thing."

Stunned, I stared at my mother and asked, "Do tell, Mother."

She looked at me. "Money. That's all that girl wants. Someone with money to take care of her."

"Well, I own a bar, so I'm not swimming in it."

Lifting her hand and waving to people, my mother walked slowly beside me. "It's the name she likes, son. Your father's business is a good one that makes money, and someday that money falls to you. That's all that woman sees."

I huffed. "And you know this how?" I asked, leaning closer to her.

Pausing, she looked up at me. "Your sister, of course."

I glanced around the room, looking for my sister. Finally, I saw her on the arm of some rich-looking asshole.

"Who is that Lily is with?" I asked my mother when she walked away from the latest person offering her their condolences.

Her eyes searched the room and she smiled. "Mark Peterson. Your father wanted the match."

I frowned. "What do you mean?"

She shrugged. "He pushed your sister toward Mark. Told her it would be a good match and that he liked Mark."

"So, she's only with him because it's what Dad wanted?"

My mother's sad eyes met mine. I wasn't sure if she was missing my father, or if maybe I had hit the nail right on the head.

"I'm not sure, Tucker. You'll have to ask her that."

I sighed loudly. "This is fucking crazy. How is it all these parents are dictating how their kids live their lives? Dad couldn't just let Lily be happy with Nash? Why was that? He doesn't come from a wealthy family? Doesn't work for the business? This is her happiness, Mom."

All she did was nod. "I've already talked to her about it, and she won't listen to me. She said she enjoys being with Mark. That he makes her happy."

"Bullshit," I mumbled under my breath.

An older couple approached us, and my mother brushed her hand at me as if to say the conversation was over. I smiled, answered when spoken to, and sipped water. I'd have given anything for a shot of vodka.

My entire body came to life as I glanced over my shoulder. The moment I saw her, I felt my breath hitch.

Charlie.

She stood in a small group of people. Her smile looked beautiful on her face, but I knew it was fake. She was putting on a show. This was boardroom Charlie, as Lily and Terri called her. The girl who put up a fake persona when she needed to. That wasn't the woman I had fallen in love with. The woman I fell in love with was the fun, carefree Charlie. The one who had a damn shaved cat and liked when I whispered dirty things in her ear. The one who tried to be strong because she was raised to be that way but had moments of weakness that she'd only shown me.

She laughed politely at something someone said, and then it looked like she excused herself. When she turned, our eyes met. She stopped and a small smile moved across her face.

Was she finally done being pissed off at me?

I returned the smile with one of my own. I wanted to go to her. Tell her how fucking sorry I was that I hurt her. Tell her that we were both wrong.

Taking a step toward her, I was hell bent on doing just that. But I stopped the moment I saw him come up behind her. Dipping his mouth to her ear, the guy she was with at the bar said something to her that made her nod her head. She turned to face him as he continued to speak to her.

My heart dropped when I saw his hand land on her lower back and guide her over to another small group of people. Charlie glanced back at me with a look I couldn't read.

"Looks like Charleston Monroe found her a catch."

My head jerked to my right were two women were talking while eyeing Charlie.

"Darrell Adams is indeed a catch. Her company is helping Darrell's with some merger or something. Rumors going around are saying they could be the future power couple."

The weight on my chest grew ten times heavier with each word they spoke.

"Can you imagine if those two got married? She's one of the richest women in Texas, and Darrell's family isn't that far behind."

They moved farther away and tried to keep their voices low, but I followed them, staying behind them so they wouldn't know I was there.

"Plus, I heard he's good in bed, big dick and all, but that his fiancée cheated on him. Rumor has it that daddy is pushing him to get married."

The other girl gasped. "Do you think they're going to get married?"

"Why not? If Darrell has to get married, who better to marry than Charleston Monroe?"

My fists balled up. They had it all wrong. It was Charlie who was the one who needed to get married, and it looked like she found the perfect guy to play the role.

I turned so quickly I ran into someone.

"I'm sorry," I curtly said, making my way over to my mother.

"Mom . . ." I interrupted a conversation she was having with two younger guys, both my age.

"Tucker! I wanted to introduce you to . . ."

"I need to leave. Emergency at work."

Her eyes filled with worry. "Is everything okay?"

Shaking my head, I leaned down to kiss her cheek. "No."

It was the truth. Nothing was okay. Everything was fucking wrong, and I was pretty sure I was the cause of so much of this.

"Will you be okay getting home?" I asked.

She placed her hand on my arm and gave it a slight squeeze. "Of course, thank you for coming sweetheart."

Forcing a smile, I nodded and turned to head to the exit. Before I stepped out of the door, I chanced one more look into the room and found Charlie. She stood next to Darrell, but neither of them had their hands on each other. They simply stood there like the perfect couple that they were.

Twenty-One

CHARLIE

NOTE TO SELF: I don't like this crowd. Avoid all dinners like this in the future.

Two hours of standing on my feet and working a room full of people was not my idea of excitement. Darrell, however, was in his environment. He thrived on the people, the business talk, the promise of future deals and golf games.

I scanned the room for Tucker. I saw Lily on the arm of some good-looking guy, who was clearly not Nash. Continuing my search, I found Patty.

The second I saw Tucker in his tux, I wanted to rush over to him. Beg him to forgive me for being so damn stupid. Tell him I panicked and that I was really in love with him. The look in his eyes, though, when he saw me walk off with Darrell was unmistakable. He was angry. Hurt. I needed to find him and tell him it wasn't what he thought.

"Darrell, I'm getting a headache. I'm going to step outside and get some fresh air."

My "date", and I used the word very loosely, glanced down and gave me a half-a-second look. "Sure. Okay."

Excusing myself, I walked to the outdoor balcony that overlooked the Texas Hill country. I closed my eyes and let myself dream of another life. One where I designed a house on the land I bought just outside of Austin. One where I sat on a horse, enjoying the sun shining on my face.

"So, found another guy already? When's the wedding?"

The sound of my best friend's voice startled me out of my daydream.

Turning, I faced Lily. By the look on her face, I had to question if we'd ever really been friends at all.

"Excuse me?" I asked.

"Couldn't rope my brother into marrying you, so you found someone else?"

I narrowed my eyes and glanced past her. If she wanted to play that game then fine. "I'll gladly answer your twenty questions if you answer mine. Who's the guy? What happened to Nash?"

The way Lily's body went stiff, I had to wonder if I poked a hornet's nest.

"We're no longer together."

Wow. I wasn't expecting that. "Did Tucker find out y'all were sneaking around behind his back for the last year?"

Her arms crossed her chest. "No, I met Mark and something sparked between us."

I lifted one brow. "Is that so? Wasn't he the guy your father kept trying to get you to go out with?"

"Don't you dare judge me, Charlie. You lied to my brother and had every intention of tricking him into marrying you to save your ass."

"Maybe in the beginning, but I wasn't going to go through with it."

"Right," she scoffed.

"What's your problem with me, Lily? I get your father passed away and grief makes you do stupid shit, but what honestly is your beef with me? Funny how I didn't treat my 'friends' the way you are treating me after my parents passed away."

Lily rolled her eyes. "You had everything, Charlie. My brother idolized you from the first moment he saw you. He fell in love with you in college, and you did the same. You were so stupid to walk away from that."

My eyes widened. "Me? What about you on the arm of the guy your father wanted you with? How can you stand there and *judge* me!"

Tears filled her eyes. "It's complicated."

Now it was my turn to fold my arms over my chest. "Really? Because even though you never talked about you and Nash, I know you cared about him."

She wiped a tear away, and as her eyes filled with sadness, I felt the urge to pull her into my arms.

Her steel guard finally broke.

"Oh God, Charlie, I messed up so bad."

Burying her hands into her face, she let out a loud sob. Rushing to her side, I grabbed her and guided her over to a bench where we both sat down. I held her close to my side as she cried.

"Please tell me what's going on, Lily. You haven't been the same since your dad passed away."

When she finally got herself together, she took in a shaky breath.

"A month or so before my father passed away, I had to attend some fundraising event. Mark was there, and I don't know what happened. I mean, Nash and I had a fight a few hours earlier about me not wanting to tell Tucker about us. He had been pushing more and more about it, and I was so worried Tucker would be angry. Plus, if we came out as a couple to Tucker, it would get back to my folks. My father would have been so disappointed in me. Anyway, Mark flirted big time that night, and I had a few drinks. One thing led to another, and Mark and I were in the bathroom of the restaurant having sex. We didn't even use protection, and I have no idea why. Maybe we were both so caught up in it neither of us thought about it."

My hand came up and covered my mouth.

"Oh. No."

She nodded. "I cheated on Nash, and the day my father passed away, I found out I was pregnant. It's Mark's baby."

My heart dropped to my stomach, and I felt sick. "Oh, Lily."

"I was so stupid. I loved Nash."

"Loved?" I asked, wiping a tear from her cheek.

"I still do, but I know if he found out I cheated and got pregnant, he'd never forgive me. For a couple of weeks, I tried to tell him about Mark. Tried to tell him about the baby. Instead, I pushed him away from me. I told him about Mark the other day, and that I had strong feelings for him. I broke up with Nash before he found out what a piece of crap I am. I'm so sorry I lashed out at you at the wake. I was so mad at myself, and you were an easy target. Nothing happened with Noelle and my brother. She was all over him that day, but I swear to you, they are not together. At all."

My head spun. Lily's conversation was all over the place.

"Wait, Lily, slow down. You're jumping from one subject to another."

"I know," she said in a weeping voice. "I need you to know that I never meant those awful things I said. A part of me wanted you to leave because I knew you would think Tucker was hooking up with Noelle. The way she was hanging on him and him not being in his right mind. They didn't sleep together though. She told me earlier that Tucker was a fool who was still stuck on you. And he is. His drinking is out of control and he's miserable. He loves you, Charlie. Please don't marry this guy you're with. Please give Tucker another chance."

My breath caught in my throat.

"I'm not marrying, Darrell. I don't have to get married now."

Her eyes filled with confusion. "What? But you're dating this guy . . . aren't you?"

Shaking my head, I took her hands in mine. "No. He's a family friend, and my company is doing some work for him. He asked me to come tonight because he recently broke up with his fiancée and didn't want to be here alone. The vultures and all. He's young, rich, good looking, and very much single."

Lily wiped her tear-stained cheeks.

"Wait, did you say you didn't have to get married now?"

I nodded and smiled. "It's a crazy long story, but I'm CEO of CMI, and no one can take that away from me unless I want to give it away."

She threw herself into my arms. "Oh, Charlie! This is wonderful news."

I hugged her back. "I know. I've been trying to get some things straight in my head before I talk to your brother. When I saw him here tonight, I was over the moon at the idea of talking to him."

Her smile faded. "He left. Mom said he seemed upset and took off. Said he had an emergency at the bar."

"Shit," I hissed out. "He saw Darrell and probably got the wrong idea about us."

"Probably."

I rubbed my temples and then dropped my hands. I was a shitty friend. Taking Lily's hands in mine, I faced her.

"You're pregnant?"

"Yes. Two months."

"Does Mark know?"

Lily nodded. "He's over the moon. He asked me to marry him last night and I said . . . I said yes."

"Are you happy?" I asked, giving her hands a slight squeeze.

She shrugged. "This would have made my father happy."

"That's not what I asked, Lily. I asked if you were happy about this."

Another tear slipped from her beautiful green eyes.

"I care about Mark a lot, and I'm sure once the baby comes and we're married we'll be fine."

"But you don't love him?" I asked.

"I think I do. He's a great guy and makes me feel good."

"Sexually, or just in general?"

Her cheeks blushed. "Both. He does things to me that Nash didn't. It's completely different with him. He likes . . . doing different stuff to me and I like it too."

I smiled. "He's into kinky shit, huh?"

She chuckled while letting out a quick sob. "Yeah. He likes tying me up and having sex in public places. It's sort of hot. He went down on me in the limo on the way here, and that is something Nash would never have done. I don't think I've ever come so hard in my life knowing the driver could hear us. It was . . . thrilling. I feel guilty saying that I like the way Mark makes me feel and that I'm falling in love with him because I really do love Nash. I'm confused."

My heart broke for her.

"If I've learned anything these last few months, it's that life is short. That we're not granted tomorrow and if we don't stand up for the things we want, they slip away and there isn't a damn thing we can do about it. If I could give you any piece of advice, Lily, it would be to tell Nash the truth. I'm sure he's hurting and confused and even if it ruins your friendship, the truth is out there."

She nodded. "He won't forgive me. Maybe if I wasn't pregnant, but carrying another man's child, he . . . he won't forgive me."

Her head dropped to my shoulder. I knew she was right. Nash didn't come from the same type of families as Lily and I did. His father owned a construction company that he pretty much forced Nash to work for. He didn't drive $100,000 cars around like Lily, Tucker, and me. Hell, even Blake came from a well-to-do family. Nash would never truly fit into the life Lily made for herself. And with her father gone, she would surely step up her role in his communications company. She wouldn't be CEO, but she'd be heavily involved, and that wasn't Nash's scene.

A thought occurred to me though. Lily had never given Nash the chance to try to fit into her world. She'd kept their relationship a secret, and it wasn't until recently that even I found about the two of them. If she had just been honest, where would they both be now?

Pain hit me right in the chest. Who in the hell was I to judge?

"I need to find Tucker," I said. "Will you be okay?"

Lily nodded, pulling out a small compact mirror and groaning when she looked into it.

"Christ, I look like shit."

Standing, I leaned down and kissed her on the forehead. "You look beautiful."

My eyes caught the sight of the guy Lily had been with. "Mark is coming."

Taking in a shaking breath, Lily stood, smoothed out her gown and smiled. "He's a good guy."

I grinned. "I'm sure he is, but please think about what I said. Nash deserves the truth."

Lily nodded and a somber look moved across her face.

"Hey beautiful. Everything okay out here?"

I watched as Mark wrapped Lily up in his arms. He kissed the top of her head and smiled at me. "You must be Charleston Monroe. Lily has talked a lot about you."

My eyes darted back to Lily. "All good, I hope."

I winked and he laughed.

"All good. It's a pleasure meeting you. I knew your father. He was a good man. Did a lot for the community, as well as your mother.

My heart swelled at the mention of my parents. The hurt was still there, but as the days went on, the hurt faded to pride at the mention of their names.

"Thank you for saying that. They were both amazing people."

We stood there in silence for a few moments before I finally said, "Well, if you'll both excuse me, I have somewhere urgent I need to be."

Lily smiled at me and said, "Good luck."

With a smile, I replied, "I don't need luck, I've got love on my side."

Twenty-Two

TUCKER

THE KNOCK HAD me lifting my eyes to the opening door. Nash walked in with a smile on his face. He held a garment bag.

"Where are you going?" I asked, tossing the pen on my desk and arching a brow.

"I'm not going anywhere, but you are."

I laughed. "No can do. I'm behind at work, and all those days you let me get trashed put me even further behind with shit."

It was true. I was behind with everything except payroll, and the only reason that was okay was because I had an accountant who handled that shit.

Hanging up the bag, he turned to me.

"Dude, is that a suit in there?" I asked.

"Yep," he said, sitting in one of the chairs in front of my desk.

"Okay, you want to tell me why you brought me a suit?"

"You're going to a dinner."

"I am?" I asked, my brow arched up in amusement.

"Do you remember what you said to me last weekend? When you came to my house upset and wanting a drink?"

"Yeah, I said I was never letting another woman into my life again."

Nash smiled and nodded his head. After seeing Charlie with that Darrell douchebag at the benefit, I left and started heading to a bar. I was ready to get drunk but turned around and went to Nash's place instead. He gave me a glass of Coke, nothing else, and we talked for a few hours. He talked about Lily. I talked about Charlie. Both of them had broken our hearts and left each of us feeling lost in our way. I still couldn't figure out what in the hell my sister was thinking. Nash confessed last weekend they had been seeing each other for about a year without anyone in the group knowing. All because my sister thought I'd be pissed. Hell, Nash was a great guy. The kind of guy who would work hard to give her the things she wanted. He didn't make the type of money Lily made, and even though he thought that was why she ended things, I knew my sister wasn't that way. It was something else. Something I had hoped to talk to her about tonight when we met Mom for dinner.

"Yes, you said that, but you also said you loved Charlie."

"So?"

"So, I need you to trust me and get your ass in the suit."

My brows pulled in tight. "What's going on, Nash?"

"What if I told you that if you went, your life would change forever?"

With a gruff laugh, I asked, "How?"

Leaning forward, Nash placed his arms on his legs and stared me straight in the eyes.

"In the best way imaginable."

The only way my life could change like that was if Charlie burst through that door and told me she loved me and she wasn't marrying that dick.

"I doubt it."

"Will you just go on faith here, Tucker? Please?"

"Nash, you walk in here with a suit, tell me to put it on, and say I'm going somewhere. Why? Where am I even going?"

The corners of his mouth rose. "I can't tell you."

"Why not?"

"I promised I wouldn't."

"Who did you promise?"

"Charlie."

That made my breath hitch and my heart speed up.

"Charlie?"

The bastard leaned back, shot me a cocky grin, and answered, "Yep. Charlie."

"When did you talk to her?"

He shrugged. "We talked a few times this week. She said she needed me to help her with something, and I'm helping."

Leaning over my desk, I gritted my teeth. "Is this her way of getting me to go to her fucking wedding?"

Surprised by my words, Nash shook his head and laughed.

"Dude, will you please just put the fucking suit on and be out front at three? A limo will be here to pick you up."

He stood and headed toward the door.

"And if I don't go?" I asked, making Nash pause at the door before turning to face me.

"If you don't go, you'll regret it the rest of your life. I can promise you that. I've got to get back to work. I'll talk to you later. Three o'clock, dude. Don't fuck it up."

The door to my office shut, and I spent the next ten minutes staring at it, the suit bag, and my phone.

When I couldn't take it any longer, I picked it up and sent Charlie a text.

Me: What's going on?

She replied almost instantly.

Charlie: Nash drop off the bag?

Me: Yes. What's going on?

Charlie: I know I don't deserve this, but I really need to talk to you.

Sighing, I typed my reply, hitting each key a little too hard.

Me: And you need me in a suit to talk? I don't have time for games, Charlie. I'm tired of playing them because neither of us ever wins.

My phone rang, and it was her name flashing on the screen. I knew the moment I heard her voice, I'd do whatever she wanted.

"I'm busy at work. What's this about, Charlie?"

"The voicemail you left me, where you said you loved me."

My heart jumped to my throat, and I couldn't find the words to speak.

"Do you still feel that way?"

Closing my eyes, I replied in a whisper, "Yes."

"Then please do this for me. I'll explain everything when you get here."

She ended the call without even saying goodbye.

"Fuck!" I cried out, dropping the phone onto my desk. "Goddamnit, why is Charleston Monroe my fucking weakness?"

I had no idea who I was asking since I was alone in my office.

Glancing at my watch, it was two thirty. Nash said a limo would be out front at three. Standing, I headed over to the garment bag and zipped it open. It was one of my suits. Nash must have taken it from my closet.

With a heavy sigh, I took it out, headed to the private bathroom in my office, and changed. Luckily, Nash put shoes in the bottom of the bag. Once I was dressed, I took a look at myself in the mirror. I hadn't shaved in two days and a good amount of scruff was on my face. My hair was in need of a cut and looked like I just rolled out of bed. But doing a once-over of myself in the mirror, I still looked pretty good. Had a bad-boy vibe going on, and I kind of liked that.

Grabbing my phone and wallet, I left my truck keys since I would be heading off in a limo. Where in the hell was I going, and what was going on?

As I made my way through the bar, I got a few whistles.

"Damn, look at you, boss!" one of the bartenders called out.

"Sign me up for a piece of you, honey."

That one I had no idea who had said it, and since the only people in the bar were my employees, I chose not to look around.

Before walking out the front door, I tossed over my shoulder, "I'll be back later."

"Have fun!" a few voices called out as I stepped out of the building and headed toward the black limo that was already parked out front.

The driver stepped out, opened the back door, and motioned for me to get in.

Once I got in, the man was in the driver's seat and talking to me over an intercom.

"Mr. Middleton, there is champagne chilled if you'd like some."

"No, thank you," I replied.

The limo pulled out and started down the road. He made a few turns and went through downtown Austin and down Guadalupe Street. He turned left on Twenty-Fourth and finally pulled into the Neill-Cochran House.

After he parked, he got out and opened my door. "We're here, Mr. Middleton."

I stepped out of the car and smirked. "I see that. What are we doing here?"

He frowned, then simply pointed for me to head up the stairs of the old grand house. It was now a museum of sorts.

Stepping into the house, I stopped in the foyer and looked around. "Hello? Charlie?"

I glanced up to see Charlie standing at the top of the staircase. She was dressed in a beautiful light blue dress that made her eyes pop.

"Did you know they say this house is haunted by a woman named Anna?" she asked as she descended the stairs.

The corner of my mouth rose in a slight smile. "Really? I never pegged you as a believer in the paranormal."

She smiled and my legs felt like jelly.

"I've been known to surprise you a time or two."

I chuckled. "That's true."

The way she gracefully moved down the staircase had me holding my breath. My heart pounded in my chest so hard I heard it in my ears.

Stopping at the last step, she looked me over, her eyes dancing with lust.

Digging her teeth into her bottom lip, she softly said, "You look handsome."

"And you look beautiful, as always."

Her cheeks flushed pink.

Damn, I wanted to tell her how much I missed her. Longed to have her in my arms, be buried inside of her.

"Want to tell me why you had me get dressed up and had me brought here?"

A sexy smirk moved across her face.

"To the point. I like it."

She stepped off the last step and walked past me down the hall. Glancing over her shoulder, she motioned with her index finger for me to follow her.

As I walked behind her, I couldn't help but stare at her perfect ass. My dick jumped in my pants, and I tried to think of something other than squeezing it and hearing her call out my name when she came.

Charlie walked into a room and stopped in front of the white fireplace. Above it hung a picture of an older woman dressed in a beautiful ball gown.

"When I was a little girl, my pappy and grammy brought me to this house. I fell in love with everything about it, especially this room. Something about the pink walls in here and fancy decorations. I remember telling my grammy that something amazing was going to happen to me in this room, but I really never knew what. My mother always told me I'd get married in this house."

I swallowed hard as I kept my eyes on Charlie while she walked around the room.

"I've been to a number of weddings here over the years and every time, I remember that day, but I never thought the idea of a wedding here would come true."

"Charlie . . ." I started to speak, but she faced me and held up her hand.

"Please, let me talk first."

My mouth snapped shut and I nodded.

She took in a deep breath and moved to the window. "I never thought it would come true for two reasons. One was my father pounded it into my head that I needed to focus everything on CMI Consulting, and that meant there was no time for a man in my life. But then I met a man who changed everything."

Her hand lifted and she ran her finger over something on the window.

"When I walked away from him, I knew I would never get married because he was the only man I'd ever loved and would ever want to marry."

My eyes widened and I tried to speak. Tried to move. All I could do was stand there and watch her trace the same pattern as she spoke.

Charlie turned to face me.

"These last couple of weeks I've been going over the time we spent together. Each moment I've replayed a hundred times in my head."

She looked down and took in a deep breath, and then her eyes lifted to meet mine.

"I love you, Tucker. I've always loved you and only you. And I'm sorry I lied to you."

Taking a step forward, she held up her hand.

"That weekend, I was going to tell you the truth. I swear to you, I was."

"It doesn't matter, Charlie. I fucked up too. I hid the truth from you as well because I was so damn afraid you'd leave and find someone else to marry you."

She shook her head. "The only person I want to marry is you. There's no life after you, Tucker. You are my life."

My heart slammed in my chest. "I'll marry you right now, right here, if you want."

Smiling, she finally made her way over to me, stopping just short of me.

It didn't take me long to reach out and pull her to me. Slipping my hand into her pinned-up hair, I pulled her mouth to mine. The kiss was slow at first, until she opened her mouth to me. Then I lost all self-control. My hand dug into her hip, pulling her against me. Charlie groaned in delight when my hard length pressed into her.

After kissing for what felt like forever, we pulled apart.

"Would you really marry me right now?" she whispered, our foreheads pressed together and our breathing labored as though we'd just run a marathon.

"Yes. I love you so much, Charleston. I've been a shell the last few weeks. Losing my father and then you."

She pressed her lips to mine while wrapping her arms around my neck.

"I love you too," she spoke against my lips.

"Is that why you had me get dressed up? Are we getting married?"

What came out of her mouth next nearly knocked me off my feet.

Twenty-Three

CHARLIE

WHEN TUCKER TOLD me he'd marry right here and now, I almost started to cry. I didn't deserve this man, but I was a greedy bitch, and I wanted him.

Forever.

"Is that why you had me get dressed up? Are we getting married?"

I smiled. I wanted Tucker to know I wanted to marry him, but not because it was to save my position at CMI. It was because I loved him and wanted to spend the rest of my life with him.

"No. I have no intentions of marrying you today."

His mouth dropped open, and he took a step back, visibly upset by my words.

"I want to marry you but on our terms. When we're ready."

He looked so confused. It was adorable.

"Wait, I'm confused. Why are we here and dressed up if we're not getting married? I thought you had to—"

I kissed him again, and he moaned into my mouth as he pulled my body closer to his. It didn't take much for either of us to get lost in one another.

"Charlie, you're making me crazy, both physically and mentally," he whispered against my lips.

His hands slid up and down my body, driving me mad with desire. I needed to stay strong or I'd be dragging him off into a closet and having my way with him.

Note to self: Tucker's kisses make it impossible to think straight.

When we finally needed air, I took a step back. My chest rising and falling with each breath.

"I asked you here because I wanted to do something, and I wanted to do it in this room."

His brow raised and his eyes burned with something naughty. "I'm all up for whatever you have planned."

My tongue darted out and ran over my lower lip, pulling a groan from Tucker's mouth.

Taking his hand in mine, I brought him over to the sofa and we sat. I closed my eyes and blew out a deep breath.

"Charlie? You're starting to worry me. What is it?"

I opened my eyes and faced him.

"Tucker, I fell in love with you the first moment I saw you. The first time you took my hand in yours, as innocent as it was, I knew it was more than friendship."

"I feel the same way, baby," Tucker whispered, his hand coming up to the side of my face, causing me to lean into it.

"The marriage clause my grandfather tried to set into action is bogus. My father had it removed, but let's just say I had to fire a few people who deceived not only my father and myself, but the board as well."

"What? You mean, you don't have to marry anyone to stay CEO?"

I shook my head. "No. It would never hold up in court anyway and the piece of shit lawyer tried telling me and the board it would take months, maybe even over a year, to contest it."

Tucker let out a visible breath and shook his head in disbelief.

"So, you don't have to get married?"

With a huge smile on my face, I got ready to jump off the cliff and straight into the future I wanted and deserved. I just wasn't sure that Tucker would join me in the free fall.

"No, I don't have to get married, but I want to get married."

His brows pulled in tight.

"Tucker Middleton, will you do me the honor of marrying me and letting me become your wife? Maybe let me walk around a big country kitchen barefoot and pregnant—once or twice?"

I had to bite back the laugh I wanted to let out. The shocked look on Tucker's face was priceless. He sat there in stunned silence before I lifted my brows and spoke.

"Um, your silence is sort of sending me the wrong answer, so . . ."

Shaking his head to clear his thoughts, Tucker smiled the most beautiful, brilliant smile I'd ever seen.

"God, yes, Charleston. Yes, I'll marry you and knock you up as soon as you're ready."

Laughing, I jumped into his arms, our mouths pressed together. The second I opened my mouth to him, our tongues danced in a sweet rhythm. Tucker pulled me closer to his body, and the feel of his hard length pressed into my stomach made me groan in need.

"Your place or mine?" he asked as he broke the kiss only long enough to speak.

My hand pushed through his hair, giving it a tug back so I could answer him.

"Mine. It's closer."

Fifteen minutes later, we were at my penthouse. The door shut and my hands were all over Tucker, desperately trying to get him out of his clothes.

"Shit! Why did I have you wear this suit? Too many layers."

Tucker's hands were on my back, unzipping my dress. When it fell off my shoulders, his mouth was on my neck, then down my neck to my breasts. My heart raced like never before as he cupped one and then kissed along the cleavage of the other. His finger glided over my sensitive nipple. Even through the thin lace of my bra, I felt the heat from his hands and fingers.

"Tucker!" I gasped, while fumbling with this stupid zipper on his pants. "I need you inside of me. Now."

"I want to kiss your body, baby. Every inch of it."

The dress fell to the floor, leaving me in only my white lace bra, matching panties and white heels.

Tucker's lust-filled eyes moved over my body as though he was seeing it for the first time. "Jesus, you take my breath away every damn time I see you. Sit on the sofa."

I inhaled a sharp breath at his command and quickly followed it. By the time Tucker was next to me, he had stripped out of his clothes and stood before me naked. My insides shook with the anticipation. Him touching me, kissing my body like he promised. Giving me the attention I had missed so desperately this past month.

My body jumped when his fingers ran lightly over the edge of my bra. "You're so beautiful, Charlie."

Opening my mouth, I tried to speak but nothing came out. The only thing I could focus on was Tucker's large hand wrapped around his impressive shaft. My eyes slowly watched him move over it, the small bead of pre-cum beginning to make its way out.

I dropped to my knees from the edge of the sofa, taking him in my mouth. The hissing sound that escaped from his lips made me smile and propelled me to work faster. I took him deeper while he laced his fingers in my hair, guiding me to the perfect rhythm.

"God, Charlie. I need . . . need you . . . to stop."

With one last suck, I let his cock fall out of my mouth and peered up at him. Reaching down, Tucker lifted me and covered my mouth with his. My bra was quickly discarded, and when I felt his hands touch my hips and slowly move to my panties, I broke the kiss and stripped them off.

"Sit."

Tucker's voice was full of desire.

I dropped back onto the sofa and waited for him to bring me to a place only he could.

His hands gently pushed my legs apart, and it didn't take long before I was squirming and pushing my hips into his face.

"Yes. Yes. Tucker, yes!"

Stars exploded behind my eyes as I gripped his hair within my hands. I wasn't even sure what all I said; all I knew was that I had never had such an intense orgasm. When I thought it was over, his mouth was on me again. His fingers worked inside me in the most delicious way.

"I can't. No more, Tucker!"

The pleas coming from my mouth fell on deaf ears because I was soon falling again. This time my body shook, and I nearly screamed for Tucker to stop. My mind and body were all over the place because at the same time, I never wanted it to end.

I was in a state of euphoria. Nothing in the world mattered except for this man and this moment.

"I'm not making love to you on the sofa with that damn cat staring at me again, woman."

Tucker's words brought me back to Earth. I glanced over to see Mr. Pootie sitting on the arm of the sofa. I couldn't help but laugh.

Scooping me up, Tucker nearly ran to the bedroom.

We had so much to talk about still. I needed him to know what my plans were for the future. I needed to know his plans. How soon would he want to get married? When did he want kids? Where were we going to live?

Gently, he laid me on the bed and crawled over me. His mouth kissed me on the lips. "You're thinking too hard, Charlie."

"We have so much to talk about."

His gray eyes seemed to sparkle as he gazed into my blue. "We'll talk . . . after I make love to you. Then fuck you in the shower, then make love to you again before I take you out to get something to eat."

A smile moved over my face. "Let's order in."

Guiding him into me, I arched my back as he slowly pushed in. The feel of our two bodies connecting made my chest flutter.

"I love you," I whispered against his lips.

"I love you too, Charleston."

My mouth turned up as he continued to kiss me. I loved how he called me by my full name when he made love to me. There were so many ways in which I loved this man, and I wanted to show him all the ways starting right now.

"Say it again," I demanded.

He lifted his head so we could look into each other's eyes. Slowly moving out and then ever so slowly pushing back in, he spoke.

"I love you, Charleston. You're mine and you'll always be mine."

"Always," I choked out as a tear trailed down my cheek. Tucker quickly kissed it away as he slowly made love to me.

He did exactly as he promised. He made love to me, fucked me in the shower, then made love to me again on the sofa before calling in an order of Chinese takeout. Mr. Pootie sat in between us on the sofa as I ate my General Tso's chicken and crab rangoon. Tucker ate sesame chicken, and I was pretty sure Mr. Pootie was working hard on getting some of Tucker's food.

"Your cat is giving me a weird look."

"No he's not," I stated, attempting not to laugh because Mr. Pootie was indeed giving Tucker a weird look. If I didn't know any better, I would have sworn he was about to jump onto Tucker and fight him for the container of food.

"Okay, can you make him go away? It's bad enough his weird haircut is creepy, but that look in his eyes is *really* freaking me the fuck out."

This time I did laugh.

"He's sweet. Don't be mean to my baby boy."

"What are we going to do with him when we have kids?"

The question came from him like second nature. He shoved food into his mouth and turned to me, waiting for my answer.

My insides warmed, and my heart raced with happiness.

"We should probably talk," I said, setting my container down and turning on the sofa. I sat with my legs crossed and Tucker did the same thing, except he kept his food clutched in his hands and away from Mr. Pootie's paws.

"Okay, let's talk," Tucker said with a smile.

"Where do you see yourself in five years?" I asked.

He looked up in thought for a moment and then pierced his eyes on mine. "With you, in a house, probably outside of the city because I'm pretty sure we both hate living in the city. Maybe a baby, but for sure a dog."

My brow lifted. "A dog?"

The most brilliant smile lit up his face. "Seriously, Charlie? The dog is all you got out of that?"

Now it was my turn to give him a smile. "Yes, because I see all that too."

Tucker looked surprised. "Really?"

"My dream is to build a house, maybe on the land in Marble Falls, raise a family, and be a wife and a mother."

It took Tucker a good thirty seconds before he moved to put his Chinese takeout on the coffee table and focus back on me.

"Wait. Charlie, you're the CEO of your family's company. I mean, I have no doubt you wouldn't be able to handle that job and be a mother, but living so far from CMI, could you do that?"

I nodded. "Yes, especially when I'm no longer CEO."

His face dropped. "So, wait. I'm confused. I thought you said you were CEO."

"I am," I stated. "But it was never my dream. It was my father's, and I've spent the last ten-plus years doing everything for my father. I could walk away from CMI Consulting as a very rich woman. It's not about the money, and I do care very much about my father's business. That's why I'm giving myself at least a year to be CEO, take the company in the direction I want it to go, get people on my team who see the same future I see, and then step down and let them run it. I'll still retain a majority of the stock, so I very much have a say. It wouldn't be like I'm turning my back on it. I'll still be involved, just not in the day-to-day things."

Pushing his fingers through his hair, Tucker let out a disbelieving chuckle.

"What will you do if you're not working for CMI?"

"Be your wife. Follow my own dreams. I've always wanted to buy old houses and flip them. You bought your house and remodeled it. I was sort of thinking that might be something we could do for fun. You and me."

Tucker's eyes lit up. "I love that idea. What about kids? I know we've brushed over the subject a couple of times the last twelve hours."

I took his hands in mine and kissed the back of each. "I want kids, but I also think it's important to spend time with you. Just us. Maybe travel some and see some places we wouldn't be able to see with a baby . . . or two. I don't want to have a baby when I'm still at CMI because I'd love to be a stay-at-home mom."

Tucker's face lit up like Christmas morning. He reached for me and pulled me so I straddled him. My warmth pressed against his hardness.

"How many kids do you want?" I asked.

"Two? Maybe three. If we're good at it. Well, I know we'd be good at the making babies thing, but you know what I mean."

Laughing, I pressed my mouth to Tucker's, and we were soon lost in one another. It didn't take long before I was stripped bare and the man I loved moved slowly and gently inside me.

Tucker moved behind me, pulling me tight into his arms as we laid on the sofa in the most amazing after-sex glow.

"Son of a bitch!" Tucker cried out, causing me to open my eyes and see Mr. Pootie's head buried inside of Tucker's takeout container.

Smiling, I closed my eyes again and let my happiness settle around me.

Finally, everything was falling into place. Tucker and I were together and nothing would ever tear us apart.

If only I'd known in that moment how naïve my thinking had been.

Twenty-Four

TUCKER

"PULL!"

Nash pulled the trap thrower and two skeet shot up in the air. I aimed, fired, and hit them both.

"Damn, son! Have you missed one yet?" Nash called out with a laugh.

I smiled as I yelled for him to pull again. Another two went sailing, and I shot them both. One right after the other. Two shots.

"This is why I hate going dove hunting with him," Blake said from behind me. Jim let out a laugh and said something to Blake I couldn't hear.

"You know, you can win money with an aim like that. Oh, wait, you used to do that shit in high school," Nash added while slapping me on the back. "Let's get a beer."

Putting the safety on my gun, I followed him to the back of my truck. Jim tossed me a beer, and I sat down in one of the camping chairs we had set up.

"So, the big announcement is tomorrow, huh?" Jim asked before tipping his beer back. Blake made some sort of grunting sound, and

Nash gave me a stupid grin.

"Yes. The announcement is tomorrow. I don't know why it has to be such a big deal," I added with a sigh.

After Charlie had asked me to marry her, I had turned around and proposed a few weeks later when we were back up at the lake house. We'd been officially engaged for two weeks, and the PR people at CMI insisted Charlie make a formal announcement. After all, one of the richest women in the US was now off the market.

"Because you're marrying Charleston Monroe. How much is she worth?" Jim asked.

I rolled my eyes. "I have no clue."

Blake huffed. "Right."

Tossing him a "go to hell" look, I replied, "I'm not with Charlie because of her money. I have my own money, thank you."

Nash laughed. "Don't be jealous, Blake. Charlie was never going to be into you. She has had the hots for Middleton here since college."

Now it was Blake's turn to roll his eyes.

Jim clapped his hands together. "Well, I know how much she's worth, or at least the ballpark figure. Somewhere in the range of $2.4 billion. I believe her father was nine hundred and something on the *Forbes* list of richest Texans last year, so I imagine our sweet little college buddy will be right up there as well."

"Jesus H. Christ. The two of you together will be a powerhouse. Dude, isn't your dad's communications company worth like $1.2 billion?"

I laughed. "Yeah, something like that."

Nash shook his head. "Damn."

"I'm not part of Dad's business though," I stated.

"You get a trust fund from it, dude, so don't be crying poverty," Blake added.

My eyes darted over to him. "I'm not. Never said I was. What's your problem anyway?"

He held up his hands. "No problem. Just stating that the two of you are worth billions, that's all."

"Yeah well, we all know money doesn't buy happiness, and Charlie and Tucker are two of the most modest people I've ever known," Jim said.

I had no clue what in the hell Blake's issue was. His daddy was from the oil and gas business, and we all knew he was worth more than probably both Charlie's company and my father's put together.

"Anyway, have y'all decided on when you're getting married?" Jim asked. "Terri said Charlie hadn't mentioned anything to her or Lily."

Every time Lily's name was mentioned, I couldn't help but notice how Nash frowned. He'd talked to my sister a few weeks back, and I had no clue what went down between them, but every time she was around, Nash took off. Granted, Lily hadn't been spending nearly the same amount of time with our group that she had in the past. Most of her days were filled with work and Mark. I knew my sister wasn't very happy though. Something about her was different, and I couldn't put my finger on it.

"I need to take a drive to check on one of the fences. You want to go with me?" I asked Nash. Jim and Blake were heading over to the skeet thrower, a bet already in place as to who could shoot the most in a row.

"Yeah, I'll take a drive with you."

I jumped into the truck and headed out over the pasture to the west side of the ranch. My family had owned this land for three generations. Five hundred acres just outside of Blanco, Texas. After Charlie took a ride with me out here, she opted for building a house on this land, rather than the land she'd bought in Marble Falls. We'd already met with Nash out here and picked the building site and went over the plans for the house. It meant a lot to both Charlie and me that Nash was the one building our home.

After a few minutes of driving in silence, I spoke.

"So, you ever going to tell me about what happened between you and my sister?"

From the corner of my eye, I saw Nash look at me. "You don't know?"

I faced him, my brows pulled in. "No. Should I?"

He looked surprised but then turned and stared out the front window.

"I figured you would have known before I did."

Now I was confused. "Why would I? Dude, I didn't even know y'all were dating."

"She's pregnant. With Mark's baby."

Slamming on the brakes, I threw my truck into park and faced Nash. "She's what? Are you sure it's Mark's baby? How far along is she? I thought y'all just broke up after Dad died."

I threw him a million questions, but I was stunned. Why in the hell would my sister not tell me she was pregnant?

Nash's forehead creased, and he wore a pained expression. I swore tears shone in his eyes.

Shit. What did you do, Lily?

"Lily cheated on me with Mark. She found out she was pregnant and she didn't know how to tell me, so she broke up with me. Originally she told me she had feelings for Mark and that was why, but the other day she told me the truth. I guess they fucked in the bathroom at some work function and didn't use a condom."

My heart dropped to my stomach. "Was she . . . was she with you after that?"

He nodded. "Yeah. We've always used protection though, but it still hurt like a motherfucker when she told me."

My hand rubbed over my mouth and chin. I had no idea what to say to him. I hated that he was hurting, and I hated it even more that it was my sister who was the one who hurt him.

"Fuck, Nash, man, I don't know what to say."

He shrugged. "I'm sorry it was me who told you. I figured Lily would have told y'all by now."

The mood in the truck was even more somber. "I think my mother knows. When I asked her about Mark, she told me it was Lily's story to tell me. Why wouldn't she tell me?"

"I don't know. Maybe because we're best friends. I know she worries still about hiding our relationship, and again, Tucker, I wanted to tell you. It killed me keeping it from you."

Reaching over, I grabbed his shoulder and gave it a squeeze. "Don't worry about it. We all do stupid shit when it comes to women. I want you to know I would have freaked out at first, but there's no one else I would have wanted my sister with. You're a damn good guy, Nash."

He gave me a lopsided grin. "Thanks, but I'm not a rich guy."

"Lily doesn't care about that."

"Maybe, but I lost her to a guy who is, and that's a hard fucking pill to swallow."

I couldn't argue with him on that one. "I know this isn't what you want to hear, but maybe this is for the best. Maybe Lily wasn't the one."

His entire body sagged and when he spoke, his voice cracked. "I wasn't the one for her, but she was the one for me."

Nash echoed the same words I had said more than seven years ago when Charlie broke my heart. I had a happy ending; I didn't think my best friend was going to have the same. Not if my sister was carrying another guy's child.

"Would you forgive her? For the cheating and all?"

Nash drew in a deep breath and pushed his hand through his dark hair before finally answering. "I could forgive her, but I don't think I would ever trust her. There would always be some sort of doubt in the back of my mind, and I hate I'd feel that way. The only problem is, she didn't ask me to forgive her, or even ask if I would be willing to take her back. A part of me would have, Tucker. I'd take her back, and I'd help her raise the baby because I love her. There's something different about her though. I think she loves this guy, or at least loves being with him. Coming back to me wasn't even an option."

"Well, it might be because she's trying to avoid a scandal in the company. Although, if she's pregnant, I'm surprised they're not engaged."

"They are."

Thud.

I didn't think my heart could drop any harder. "What in the fuck? Since when?"

"I don't know," Nash replied. "She told me they were getting married within the next few weeks. Going off to some fancy island and having a private ceremony or some shit like that."

"Damn, dude. I'm really sorry."

A part of me wanted to drive back to Austin and go straight to my sister. See what in the hell was wrong with her. How could she not tell me any of this? I was livid.

"Do you think Charlie knew?" I asked.

"Not sure. I don't think Terri does. She asked me this morning what was going on with Lily. She has pulled back from hanging out with Terri and Charlie as well."

"Yeah, the only time I've seen her is at my mom's once a week when we meet for dinner. Charlie has been there, but now that I think of it, they didn't really sneak off to talk or anything."

"Whatever. It is what it is, and I have to move on and put her behind me. All I know is, I'm not planning on opening my heart to anyone anytime soon."

I laughed. "You say that now, but someday, dude someday."

He snarled his lip and shook his head, silently telling me to fuck off.

"Come on, let's check that fence and then head back. I have to meet Charlie at her place by six. The *Austin American-Statesman* wants a photo for the story tomorrow."

"Why last minute?" He asked.

"CMI press sent out the announcement just a week ago, and it was the first time our schedules worked out to have it done."

He nodded and we spent the rest of the drive to the fence in silence and most of the drive back to Jim and Blake with nothing but small talk. No mention of Lily came up again. I don't know which of us was happier about that—Nash or me.

"TUCKER! IT'S GOOD to see you!" Marge exclaimed, standing from her chair and moving around her desk. "The photographer from both CMI PR and the *Statesman* are here."

"Oh joy," I mumbled, earning me a quirk of Marge's brow. It was her silent way of telling me to behave. It sort of reminded me of the nanny Lily and I had when we were younger. At dinner parties, she was constantly by our side, making sure we acted appropriately.

Walking through the door, my eyes nearly popped out of my head. Standing in front of me was Charlie. She looked beautiful, as always. She wore a black pencil skirt with a light blue dress shirt that was tucked neatly into the skirt. Her hair was pulled up with just a few strands of hair down framing her stunning eyes. She looked my way and gave me a once-over. The corners of her eyes crinkled with a smile, and she flashed me a come-hither look. Her blue eyes sparkled as I drew closer to her, and I had a hard time catching my breath.

This woman was mine. This amazing, strong, smart, sexy-as-fuck woman was mine.

Leaning down, I kissed her on the lips before moving my mouth to her ear.

"I'm so fucking turned on right now. I want to lift that skirt up and fuck you over your desk."

Her breath hitched, and she grabbed my arms. Slowly pulling back, she stared up into my eyes before lifting up on her toes and whispering against my ear.

"Good thing I'm not wearing panties then, isn't it?"

The room tilted, and I felt like I was about to drop to my knees.

"For the love of God, tell me you're kidding."

With a wink and a step away from me, she replied, "Nope. Serious as all get out."

I closed my eyes and dropped my head back, letting out a groan.

"Oh, it won't be all that bad, Mr. Middleton."

Lifting my head and searching for the voice, I found a tiny woman off to the side. She wore a badge that read *press*.

"I'm Lisa Hart from downstairs in PR."

Shaking her hand, I grinned. "Nice to meet you, Lisa."

"This is Val, she's the photographer with the *Statesman*."

"Pleasure," I said.

Val clapped her hands. "Okay, let's get the show on the road."

We spent the next thirty minutes having at least four cameras on us, all taking pictures.

"Why is everyone so concerned about our engagement?" I asked.

Charlie kept smiling and replied, "Beats the hell out of me."

"Turn this way please," the CMI PR photographer asked.

"Smile big! You're the new power couple!" Lisa called out.

Charlie and I glanced at each other. The look in her eyes said she wasn't the least bit happy about this, and I couldn't help but agree with her.

Another voice chimed in from a lady I hadn't seen before.

"Ms. Monroe, do you think you'll get backlash with Mr. Middleton being the owner of a bar?"

I tensed and Charlie moved her hand over my back.

"And you are?" she asked in a sweet-as-pie voice.

"Nancy Freedom, *Austin American-Statesman.*"

Charlie looked over to Lisa. "Reporters? I thought this was just photos."

Lisa's face went white. Oh hell, I sort of felt sorry for her. This should be interesting. I could hear the bite in my future wife's voice. I found myself wishing I could sit in on a board meeting with her sometime. I'd probably be hard as a rock when it was over.

"Um . . . yes . . . Ms. Freedom, everyone was instructed that this was a photography session only. Not an interview."

The reporter smirked. "Well, I'm here. The question has been asked."

Charlie stepped away from me. "I believe you've gotten enough photos."

"You're not going to answer my question? There have been rumors going around this is an arranged marriage. Is that true, Mr. Middleton? How do you think your late fathers would feel if they knew this bit of information?"

Before I even had a chance to speak, Charlie was all over this woman.

"Ms. Freedom, I'm not sure who your sources are, but I can promise you this is not an arranged marriage. As far as Mr. Middleton owning a very successful and top-rated bar here in Austin, keep your eyes open. We have a lot more things planned for us."

Charlie took a step closer. "You see, I'm not only good in the boardroom, but I'm well versed in other areas as well."

My mouth nearly dropped open. The reporter was taken aback, and Marge looked like she was about to faint.

The reporter forced a smile. "Can I quote you?"

"I'd be very careful what you print about what was said in this room today. I believe my lawyers have been itching for some fun lately."

This time I couldn't hide my smile.

"Right. Well, like Ms. Monroe stated, I believe we have enough photos. Ms. Freedom, you're not given permission to use anything that was said in here today since I was unaware you were a reporter and let into the room."

Marge and Lisa soon had everyone pushed out of Charlie's office. When the door closed, Charlie's body slumped in exhaustion. I made my way over to her and drew her into me.

"That was hot as hell, baby. Seeing you put that reporter in her place."

Charlie's arms wrapped around my neck.

"What did she mean by power couple?"

I shrugged. "Don't know, don't care. As far as I'm concerned, it's just me and you."

"Mr. Pootie too," Charlie said with an evil grin.

"Yeah, that little bastard."

Hitting me on the chest, she walked around to her desk and sat down. "Let me send out two emails and then I'm done for the weekend. How was skeet shooting out at the ranch?"

The memory of Nash telling me about Lily raced back.

"Good and bad."

Her eyes lifted to mine; she was intrigued. "What was bad?"

I moved about in my seat, not sure how to go about this.

"Did you know Lily was pregnant?"

Charlie sat back in her seat. "Yes. She told me the night of the benefit when we saw each other."

My eyes widened in surprise. "You knew and didn't say anything to me?"

"It wasn't my place to say anything. As far as I knew, Lily told you and you hadn't said anything to me."

"She told you that night?"

Nodding, she replied, "Yes. She was pretty upset that she hurt Nash. She told me she still loved him, but that Nash . . ."

Her voice trailed off and she started chewing on her lip.

"But Nash what?"

"Um, I'm not really sure you want to hear this. You being her brother and all."

Leaning forward I gave her a hard look. "Tell me, Charleston."

Moving in her seat like she was uncomfortable, she swallowed hard and answered me.

"She said Mark fulfilled her in ways Nash couldn't."

Anger raced through my body. "So, it is about the money. My own sister is hung up on fucking money?"

"What?" she asked.

I stood and started to pace. "Nash told me today that if Lily had asked him to forgive her, even with the baby, he would have. He said she didn't, and he thought it was because he didn't have the type of money Mark did. I told him he was crazy, that Lily wasn't like that. I can't believe this." Looking at Charlie I asked, "Is that why she never told anyone about them dating? Because she was embarrassed Nash wasn't rich?"

Twenty-Five

CHARLIE

NOTE TO SELF: Make plans to kill Lily for putting me in this spot.

How could she have not told Tucker all of this?

Standing, I held up my hands to get Tucker to calm down.

"Hold on, that's not it. Take a deep breath and sit back down."

"What? My sister is consumed by money!"

I rolled my eyes and walked around the desk, grabbing him by the upper arms. "No, she is not. She's consumed by sex. Mark is into kinky sex and tying women up, and Lily likes that. I guess Nash is more of a vanilla kind of lover."

Tucker's face scrunched up. "Gross. I didn't need that mental image, Charlie."

With a grin, I winked. "Sorry, but you left me with no choice."

He shook his head and asked, "So you're saying my sister is only with Mark because he likes to get his freak on and so does she?"

"No, I'm saying he's different, and I truly think Lily has feelings for him. Do I think she loves him? No. In a way, Lily did this to herself. She never allowed herself and Nash to have a chance. She kept their relationship hidden, and I think that put a strain on her. Sneaking around instead of showing affection. Truly being together and not just sneaking off and being dishonest. She doomed their chances before they even really had one."

"Damn, why in the hell did she hide her relationship with Nash?"

"I can think of two reasons. You being the main one, and probably what happened between us back in college."

He scrubbed his hands over his face. "So you're saying she was afraid if they broke up, it would be weird for the rest of us in the group?"

"Maybe. It's a good possibility. Either way, she's with Mark and they're getting married. I can't believe she didn't tell you any of this. Does your mom know?"

"I have no clue," he replied with an indifferent expression. "I'm sure she does. She said something about Lily needing to tell me why she was with Mark because it was her story."

Wrapping my arms around his neck, I reached up and kissed him lightly on the lips. "I'm sorry I didn't tell you. I honestly thought you knew and just never mentioned it."

Tucker's arms moved around my waist, pulling me flush against his body.

"Well, that's their drama, and I want no part of it. I love you," he whispered, his nose rubbing over mine.

"I love you too."

"Let's get out of here. I need to have your naked body under mine."

Warmth pooled in my belly, instantly causing an ache between my thighs.

"Are you really not wearing any panties, Ms. Monroe?"

My teeth sank into my lip, and I slowly shook my head. "Nope."

A low growl came from the back of Tucker's throat and made the pulsing in my body stronger. I needed him as much as he needed me, but there was no way I was letting him fuck me in my office. Not with cameras rolling. It was bad enough we'd already talked dirty to each other.

"Let me send these two emails and then I'm all yours."

"Always," he replied back in a soft voice.

Reaching up, I ran my fingers through his dark brown hair. Our eyes locked as I replied, "Forever."

~

I COULDN'T WIPE the smile off my face even if I tried. I sat in my office chair, staring out the window feeling happier than ever before. This past weekend had gone by entirely too fast. Tucker and I drove out to the ranch, met with a contractor, and narrowed down where we were going to build a house. Then we headed to Fredericksburg, where we spent Saturday night at a bed and breakfast. It was the perfect place to be since the engagement announcement hit Saturday. We missed all the craziness of the press that waited for us. At least, we missed it all until we got back home late last night. There were so many reporters and photographers camped outside my condo it was unreal. And for what? It wasn't even like we were anybody important.

Sighing, I let my mind go back to the amazing evening and day we spent. We only left twice to get food. The rest of the time we were naked and in bed, making love between some of our own kinky fooling around. I needed to send Lily a thank you card. All her talk of the kinky shit she did with Mark gave me a few ideas of my own this weekend. I was a new fan of being tied up, and Tucker loved the whole ice-and-hot-water bit I did while giving him head. He would have died if he knew the idea came from his baby sister.

My cheeks heated as I thought about Tucker's long, thick cock in my mouth. His tongue pressed against my clit, my hands gripping the sheets as he made me come over and over.

Picking up my phone, I called him.

"Hello, beautiful."

"Hey, handsome."

"How's your day been?"

I sighed. "Long already. I can't get this weekend out of my mind and it's . . . well . . . it's making me needy."

The sounds of a chair moving across a floor came over the phone.

Then a door shutting, then another door.

"Okay, I'm in my office now. Are you calling me for some phone sex?"

Laughing, I twirled a piece of my hair in my finger as I looked out over the city.

"No, remember what I told you, the cameras?"

"Right. The last fucking thing I want is for Blake to find out and watch you make yourself come."

I shuttered at the thought. "I seriously doubt his brother would risk his company, but now that you planted that in my head, maybe it's time to disable this little security system my father put in place."

"Yes. Then I can have sex with you anytime I come visit."

"Consider it done this week."

My office phone buzzed.

"Hold on. Yes, Marge?"

"Ms. Monroe, there is someone here to see you."

Frowning, I looked at my calendar and then at the phone. Why in the world was she calling me Ms. Monroe? Unless the person here to see me was standing in front of her, which wouldn't be the case unless it was an employee.

"Do they have an appointment?" I asked.

"I really want to hear you moan out my name. Go to your bathroom. There's no cameras there, right?"

I giggled and hushed Tucker.

"No, they do not."

"Well, Marge I'm busy right now, have them make an appointment and I'll . . ."

The phone beeped, indicating Marge took it off speaker. Balancing my cell phone in one hand, I picked up the desk phone. Before I could even speak, Marge was talking.

"Charlie," she said in a hushed voice. "I really think you need to see this young woman."

Young woman?

"Why?"

"Why, what?" Tucker asked.

"No, I'm talking to Marge. Hold on, Tucker."

Marge was silent for a moment before she started talking in an even quieter voice.

"Because she introduced herself as the mother of Tucker Middleton's daughter and demanded to see you. Security called me, and I told them to have her come up before she made a scene."

My entire body tensed. Had I just heard her right?

"Did you say—?" I asked, my voice trailing off.

"Yes. She is here with a little girl, and she is saying Tucker is the father."

The entire room felt like the air had been sucked out of it. I fought to breathe. Fought to keep down the bile that was now in the base of my throat.

"Give me . . . give me three minutes before you send her in."

"Just three?" Marge asked.

"Yes. Three."

Hanging up the phone, I pulled my cell phone out and stared at the picture of Tucker that popped up on the screen.

"Charlie? What's wrong, Pumpkin?"

I swallowed hard, glancing at my watch. "There's . . . um . . . there's a woman here claiming to be the mother of your . . . child."

Tucker laughed but soon realized I was serious.

"What in the fuck? I don't have any kids, Charlie, you know that."

A minute was nearly gone. Standing, I made my way into the private bathroom, checked my face, and then told Tucker I needed to go.

"Charlie! Don't you dare fucking hang up!"

Making my way back over to my desk, I pulled in a deep breath. "I'll call you back."

"What? Charlie! Charlie!"

I hit *end* and set my cell phone face down on my desk.

Breathing in through my nose and out through my mouth, I attempted to calm my racing heart.

Oh God. Tucker has a little girl? He has a child? Did he know?

The room felt as if it spun.

No. If he knew he had a child, he would be a part of her life. This is insane.

My phone buzzed on my desk. Flipping it over, I saw Tucker's name.

Another deep breath and I set the phone down and hit Marge's call button. Inside I was freaking the fuck out, but on the outside, I was cool as a cucumber.

"Send them in, Marge."

A few moments later, the door to my office opened and a beautiful dark-haired woman my age walked in. Glancing behind her, I saw a little girl sitting in one of the chairs. Her eyes met mine for a brief moment before she looked back down at her doll.

I swallowed hard. She looked like she was five or six years old.

As I stood up, I forced myself to breathe and lifted my chin, extending my hand to the woman.

With a heavy heart, I plastered on a smile and forced my voice to remain calm and even, which was a monumental feat.

"Charleston Monroe, you are?"

"Lindsey Cooke."

My mind went through all the people we knew in college. Did Tucker meet her in college?

Glancing over to Marge, I smiled bigger. "Thank you, Marge. If I need anything, I'll let you know."

Marge looked at me and then at the woman in front of me.

"Ms. Cooke, is your daughter okay without you?"

The woman glanced over her shoulder and waved to her little girl. It gave me the opportunity to look at her better. She looked nothing like Tucker.

Nothing.

"She's fine. Thank you."

Marge looked at me as if she was waiting for me to agree with the woman. How in the hell was I supposed to know?

With a small shrug, I proceeded to ask Lindsey Cooke to sit down. "Please, have a seat, won't you?"

She took a seat, and Marge reluctantly headed out of my office. Giving one more concerned look, I grinned and nodded for her to close the door.

"So, how can I be of assistance to you, Ms. Cooke?"

The smile on her face was pure contempt, and one I'd seen a million times in a boardroom.

"I want money."

Leaning back in my chair, I grinned.

"Direct and to the point. I like it. Now, tell me why in the hell I would give you money?"

She laughed, and it made my skin crawl.

"Because I've got a little bombshell out there, and I'm pretty sure you don't want it getting out that your fiancé knocked up an old girlfriend and left her to raise their child all alone. Especially when he's worth as much money as he is."

Damn those fucking papers. Why do they have to put what people are worth?

"You do realize that Mr. Middleton is set to inherit that money later on down the road?"

She settled back in her chair, crossing her perfectly fit legs. "He gets a trust fund each month. From what I've been able to figure out, it's a pretty big one. And you, why, you're the richest woman in Texas."

I laughed. Again. "Hardly, but thank you for thinking so highly of me."

"Listen, you have a bunch of zeros and that's all that matters. I want six-hundred-thousand dollars to keep my little secret."

Agitation bubbled up in my chest, and I had to take a deep breath before I lost it on this piece of scum. Leaning forward, I placed my arms on my desk and looked her in the eye.

"You honestly believed you could walk into my office, lay a claim that hasn't even been proven, and demand I give you money?"

She nodded. "If you don't, I'll go to the press and talk."

I held up my finger and said, "Wait just one second. You do realize they will ask you if you have proof. What are you going to show them?"

Her smile faltered for a moment. "Do you really want it to get to that stage, Ms. Monroe?"

"Yes."

My reply caught her off guard. There was something about this woman. Her demeanor said one thing, but her eyes said something different. They were almost desperate.

"Excuse me?"

"Yes, I think the first thing we need to do is a paternity test. If it shows that Tucker is indeed the father, then he'll take responsibility. I mean, isn't that why you're here? For Tucker to take responsibility? Be a father to this young girl?"

"Um, no."

Lifting my brow, I asked, "No?"

"I don't want Tucker involved in her life. I've done fine this long without him."

Leaning back in my chair, I smiled. "So, what you're really after is money, Ms. Cooke? You want me to pay you to make you go away and not cause problems with the press."

She nodded. Her once strong confidence slipped.

"No."

Her eyes widened in shock. "No?"

I shrugged. "No. I'm not going to let you walk into my office with some trumped-up claim that my future husband is the father of your child and pay you to go away. I don't work that way. I'm beginning to wonder if you even know who Tucker is."

When she smiled, it actually made me shiver. I was hoping like hell she didn't notice it. She obviously knew Tucker; I just wasn't sure how well she knew him.

The door to my office flew open, and Tucker came rushing in. Marge was hot on his heels.

"He moves quickly. I couldn't stop him."

"It's okay, Marge." I motioned with my hand that everything was fine. Tucker stormed over to us while Marge shut the door quietly.

"What in the fuck is going on here? Who is—"

When Tucker stopped at the sight of Lindsey Cooke sitting in front of me, he paused. And so did my heart. His mouth opened, then closed.

Then it opened again.

My entire body went stiff, and I had to fight the urge not to get up and run to my bathroom.

He knows her.

For the first time since this woman walked into my office, my confidence slipped.

And my fear that this really could be Tucker's baby skyrocketed.

Twenty-Six

TUCKER

I STOPPED IN my tracks when I saw Lindsey sitting in the leather chairs opposite of Charlie.

Holy fucking shit. Talk about a blast from the past.

"Lindsey?" I asked, startled by her appearance.

"Hello, Tucker. It's been a while. How have you been?"

My head jerked over to see Charlie. She was attempting to remain calm but clearly freaking out inside.

"I'm fine. You want to tell me what in the hell kind of game you're playing?"

"I'm not playing a game. I was just about to agree to do a paternity test since Ms. Monroe seemed to think we didn't know each other."

Charlie cleared her throat.

"Exactly how do you know Ms. Cooke, Tucker?"

I could hear the hurt and anger in her voice, but I knew all Lindsey heard was strength.

"We met about six years ago after we graduated UT."

Glancing back to Charlie, she shot me daggers.

Charlie stood. "Do you have reason to believe that Ms. Cooke's claim that the little girl sitting outside could be your daughter?"

"What? No! I mean, we slept together once, and I wore a condom."

Lindsey grinned. "There's only a ninety-eight percent success rate of preventing pregnancies with a condom."

Anger pulsed through my veins.

"Get real, Lindsey. You and I both know I was so fucking drunk that night I was hardly able to get it up. If my memory is right, I don't think I even finished before I passed out."

Charlie cleared her throat again and folded her arms across her chest.

"I'm not really interested in hearing how the two of you were together, Tucker," Charlie bit out.

"I know I came. At least twice, Tucker."

My eyes landed back on Lindsey. "What do you want?"

"Six hundred thousand and I go away with our little girl and you never hear from me again."

"No," Charlie and I both said at once.

Lindsey sighed.

Picking up her phone, Charlie hit a button. "Marge, I need you to come in here."

Lindsey looked nervous as she glanced between Charlie and me.

The door opened and Marge walked in. It was then I saw the little girl sitting in the chair. She looked nothing like me, but that didn't mean anything. For a brief moment, a sense of dread moved over me, making my chest feel as though someone sat on it.

There was no fucking way that kid was mine. I never even got off that night. I know I didn't.

"Marge, I need you to find a lab that can run a DNA test on Mr. Middleton and the young lady sitting outside. I need to have it done today, and I'll pay whatever it takes to get the results back as soon as possible."

"Yes, Ms. Monroe," Marge said as she wrote a few notes on a pad of paper and headed out the door. Charlie picked up her phone again, dialed a number, and waited.

"Mr. Donovan, I need you in my office ASAP. Drop everything, this is important."

Damn, was it wrong I was so turned on by the authority in my future wife's voice during this shitstorm of a predicament?

I shook my head; now was *not* the time to be thinking about sex.

Lindsey stared at Charlie.

Charlie shot Lindsey a smirk. "Mr. Donovan is my lawyer." Turning away and looking out the large windows, Charlie went on. "Also, be sure to have the recording of today secured and duplicated. Thank you and see you in a few minutes."

Lindsey sat up straighter as Charlie hung up the phone and sat down at her desk. She began looking through something as Lindsey looked from me to Charlie.

"Recordings?"

Charlie barely gave Lindsey a glimpse as she replied, "Yes. I have security cameras in my office that record both video and sound, so your attempts at extorting money from me have all been recorded. Hence the reason for my lawyer to join us."

It was a good two minutes before Lindsey started laughing.

"I see how this is. You're trying to use scare tactics on me. Well, it's not going to work. You want a test done, fine. But until you get the results, I want money to keep my mouth shut."

"No, that's not how this works," Charlie said before I could even answer.

"Ms. Monroe, I don't think you hear what I'm saying. I will walk out of your office toward the first news station I can find, and I will drop a very juicy story in their laps. One that will have your public relations people scrambling to fix. I can't imagine you want that squeaky-clean image of yourself or your company to be ruined."

I took a step back as I watched a look I'd never seen move over Charlie's face. She stood and walked around her desk until she was in front of Lindsey. She leaned against the desk and smiled.

"I don't think you understand what I'm doing, Ms. Cooke, so let me break it down into words you can comprehend. I'm going to sue the living fuck out of you for extortion. I'm going to have that DNA test done so that it proves Tucker Middleton is *not* the father of your little girl and you can never come back and claim it again. I'm going to release the tapes where I have you demanding I give you money to the same media outlets you go to and I will . . . *destroy you.* Your daughter will be taken away from you, your life as you know it now will never be the same, and I have no idea how long your ass will sit in jail. So, now that I spelled it out, do you understand how this thing will work from here on out?"

The door to Charlie's office opened and a man in a suit walked in. He was on the phone with someone as he walked over to Charlie's desk and set down a legal pad.

"Yes, send them over to Ms. Middleton right away." He glanced up and looked at Charlie. "Start an hour ago?"

She nodded.

"Yes, an hour ago up to five minutes ago and that should be sufficient."

Lindsey wrung her hands in her lap.

"Ms. Monroe, I've been brought up to date by Marge. The lab is on their way up right now and will be here in less than five minutes."

"Wait. What?" Lindsey said with panic in her voice.

"A recording of the last hour should be hitting your mailbox . . ."

Charlie's computer pinged with a notification.

"Right about now," Donovan finished with a smile at his efficiency.

When the lawyer had walked into Charlie's office, she made her way back around to her desk and sat down. She typed something in. She hit her mouse and turned her laptop so Lindsey could see it. Her mouth fell open when she saw the video proof of herself walking into Charlie's office. When Charlie turned up the volume, Lindsey stood.

"Fine. You made your point. I'm leaving now."

"Sit. Down. Ms. Cooke," Charlie demanded. "We are getting that DNA test done."

"It's not his kid. I saw the announcement in the paper, and I needed money."

"So you decided to try and get it from me by lying that the kid was mine?" I cried out.

"I was desperate." Lindsey's voice sounded desperate, and the look on her face was too.

"Please don't do this. My daughter is all I have."

"Why did you do it?" Charlie asked. "Why do you need the money?"

Lindsey dropped her head and stared at the floor. "My husband has a gambling problem. We're five-hundred-thousand dollars in debt, at least that's the amount that I know of. I'm about to lose my house, and I don't know what to do. I panicked and thought if I asked you for money, you'd want to keep your image clean."

"Don't you think six hundred thousand is a lot to ask for?" I asked, not feeling the least bit sorry for this piece of shit.

Charlie's phone buzzed.

"Yes?" she asked.

Marge's voice came over the phone. "The lab is here."

"Send them in, along with Ms. Cooke's daughter."

Lindsey looked frantic. "She's not your daughter, Tucker. I'm sorry I lied."

"I never thought she was. I can't believe you did this."

Tears filled her eyes. "Please don't press charges against me. Please."

Three people walked in with Lindsey's little girl in tow. She looked scared to death. Lindsey went over to her and picked her up. Burying her face into the girl's hair, she said, "I'm so sorry I did this, pumpkin. I'm so sorry."

Charlie walked over and looked at two of the people. "Take hair samples and that's it."

Lindsey looked at Charlie. "She's not his!"

With a stone face, Charlie said, "We're going to find out for sure."

"Charlie, why don't we . . ."

Her gaze moved to me, and I stopped talking.

"You weren't the one who had someone come into your office and ask for over a half-a-million dollars. I was. Forgive me for wanting to make sure this isn't your child, and let's hope no other exes walk into our lives and demand money."

And before I knew it, Charlie walked out of her office, Marge trailing behind her. Mr. Donovan stayed in the room and made sure all the proper paperwork was filled out.

"I'm sorry, Tucker," Lindsey whispered to me.

The only thing I could do was shake my head. I had nothing to say to her.

One of the gentlemen walked up to me and said, "We will have the results by tomorrow morning."

Nodding, I replied, "Sounds good."

Charlie walked back into the office and went straight to Donovan. They talked in a hushed voice, and he looked as though he was arguing with her about something. When they finally broke apart, Charlie made her way over to where Lindsey and her daughter still sat.

"Much to my lawyer's disapproval, I'd like to help you out."

Lindsey's eyes lit up and she stood. "What do you mean?"

"I mean, I'm going to have a trust fund set up in your daughter's name."

Standing in front of Charlie, I took her by the arm and moved her back some. "Charlie, that's not my kid."

She gave me a weak smile. "I know, but it doesn't matter. I want to help them."

My brows furrowed, "Why?"

"Because I can. I know what I'm doing. Trust me, Tucker."

My heart warmed, and I wanted nothing more than to pull her into my arms and kiss her. Charlie never talked about all the amazing things she did for people, but I knew. I knew even before we were together. I'd seen her at functions, and I'd seen the generous amounts of money she and her family gave to causes. It wasn't just money she gave either; it was her time as well.

"I love you," I softly said, kissing her on the forehead.

Her hand landed on my chest as she replied, "I love you too." Stepping around me, Charlie walked back over to Lindsey.

"I'm not doing this for you or your husband."

"We're divorcing," Lindsey mumbled. "I don't want him around Laney anymore."

"Good. I think that is a smart thing to do. The trust fund will be put in your daughter's name and will be available to her either when she goes to college or at the age of twenty-five. In the meantime, you'll let Mr. Donovan know how much it is to pay off the mortgage for your home. Is the title in both of your names?"

She shook her head. "No, I purchased it on my own before we were married."

Charlie nodded. "Good. Once your home is paid for, a small amount of money will be able to be withdrawn from an account that will be set up. Once the money is taken out each month, the account will be closed for future transactions until the following month. This is your second chance, Ms. Cooke, don't screw it up."

Lindsey stood, holding her daughter in her arms. "Why are you doing this?" she asked.

"Because I believe in helping people who need help, and although you don't deserve it, your daughter does. Now, if you'll please kindly leave and go with Mr. Donovan, I have work I need to get to."

I watched as Lindsey did what Charlie asked. Once the office door was shut, I watched as Charlie let out a sigh.

"I'm so sorry, Charlie."

Holding up her hand, she looked at me. "Not now, Tucker. I'm emotionally exhausted, and I have a meeting I need to prepare for. Can we talk about this tonight?"

"Of course." Making my way over to her, I pulled her into my arms and pressed my mouth against hers. I hated that this person from my past caused her pain and stress.

Her body melted against mine as she opened her mouth more and we kissed like we hadn't seen each other in days. When my fingers laced through her hair and tugged, she moaned, which went straight to my cock.

Whispering against her lips, I begged her for more. "I want you, Charlie."

"Oh God, Tucker. You're going to make me cancel this meeting." Her voice was deep and full of need and desire.

"Cancel it. Come back home with me."

"The bar?" she questioned in a low voice, both of us very aware of the cameras that we once hated but now sort of loved.

"Fuck the bar."

Charlie pulled back and stared into my eyes. "Let me tell Marge I'm sick and have her reschedule some things. It might take me a few hours to get out of here, but we can spend the afternoon together."

A huge smile broke out over my face. "That's my girl and that works." Kissing her on the lips, I added, I'll meet you at your place."

Rushing out of her office, I pulled out my phone and made one phone call. My girl was clearing her day for me, so I was going to do something for her.

Twenty-Seven

CHARLIE

"ARE YOU OKAY?"

My head turned to see a woman my age dressed in a pantsuit staring at me.

"Excuse me?" I asked.

"You look flushed. Just making sure you're okay. Do you need some water or anything?"

Smiling, I felt my cheeks blush. I couldn't tell her I was daydreaming about Tucker doing naughty things to me.

"I'm fine. Thinking of my fiancé whom I'm about to meet."

Her face morphed into a wide grin. "Playing hooky, huh?"

I laughed. "Yes, something like that."

Her brows lifted. "Better not let the boss find out. I'm sneaking down to Starbucks for an afternoon treat since mine is in a budget meeting."

Tilting my head, I studied her. This girl had no clue who I was. The building CMI occupied ten floors, so she had to know I worked here. She got on the elevator on the seventeenth floor, and I was coming down from the upper floors, which were all CMI.

From the floor she just entered the elevator on, I knew she either worked in accounting or human resources when I asked, "What department do you work in?"

"Accounting. I'm a numbers kind of girl, but I'm only an administrative assistant right now. My boss is a dumbass and thinks that because I'm young, I don't have the know-how to do the job, even though I do most of *his* work. I've been passed over for three promotions."

She frowned and mumbled something under her breath that sounded a hell of a lot like *fucker*.

"Why have you been passed up?"

Looking around the elevator as if anyone else was with us, she replied, "I think it's because he has the hots for me and wants to keep me at his beck and call." She shuddered as if the idea of him made her ill.

"Really?" I asked, my curiosity and anger even more piqued. I needed to find out who in the hell this jerk face was and nip this shit in the bud.

With a small shrug, she said, "Yeah, I've caught him more than once checking out my ass. Jerk. Do you get that problem too? Guys eyeing you up like you're a piece of meat? Last guy who tried to touch me got a knee in the groin."

"Good for you," I said, giving her a high five and chuckling.

"What about you? What area do you work in?" she asked, the sweetest smile on her face. I liked this girl. I liked her a lot.

"I work on the top floor. The name is Charleston Monroe," I stated, extending my hand to the now shocked woman.

She knew who I was by my name.

Reaching for my hand, she mumbled, "Oh. Shit."

Her face turned ten shades of red before she finally spoke. "Lacy Stark. Please, *please* ignore everything I said."

She spun on her heels and faced the elevator doors. Pulling out my phone, I sent Tucker a quick text.

> *Me: Leaving, but need to handle one thing. Won't take more than five minutes.*

Putting my phone in my purse, I faced her.

"Let's grab a coffee and talk a bit more, Lacy."

Her face looked like someone had just told her that her favorite dog was dead. "I'm getting fired, aren't I?"

"No," I said with a short giggle. "You're about to get promoted."

Lacy followed me out of the elevator and into Starbucks. I ordered a tea; she ordered the largest, most potent coffee I thought Starbucks sold.

As we took a seat, she closed her eyes and took in a deep breath before looking at me and speaking.

"I don't ever talk like that, and I'm sure you're going to say, 'Sure you don't,' but I felt like I connected immediately with you, as strange as that sounds. We're both the same age . . . I think . . . and, well, it's not an excuse for bashing my boss and all."

Holding up my hand, I leaned toward her and said, "Breathe, Lacy. It's okay. Most people take one look at me and don't utter a word. I'm glad you spoke up. I want to know if these kinds of things are happing at CMI. First things first though. I want you tomorrow to report directly to my office at eight. I'll let my assistant know to be expecting you."

"O-kay. May I ask why?"

With a smile, I said, "I'm moving you up to be my executive assistant."

Her eyes widened in disbelief. "But . . . but . . . Marge?"

"Is amazing and going nowhere, but she actually needs some additional help. I'm going to be starting a few new projects, and I'm going to need someone who is crazy about numbers to head it up."

"Head it up?"

I took a sip of my tea. "Yes. You stated you're a numbers kind of gal."

Her head nodded frantically.

"Good. When you go back upstairs, I want you to go to Marge's desk. She'll be expecting you. She'll help you with the transfer and alert your previous boss so that it's all taken care of by tomorrow."

Lacy's mouth opened and closed a few times before she finally stood and rushed over to me, hugging me.

"I know this is so inappropriate, but I don't really care! I'm so happy!"

With a few pats on her back, I urged her to sit back down.

"So, I've got to run."

Lacy grinned like a schoolgirl.

"I'll see you in the morning, Lacy."

"Yes ma'am."

Standing, I gave her a soft grin then made my way to the door. My body ached to be in Tucker's arms and with how pissed off I was right now, I really needed a distraction.

When I got outside, I hailed a taxi, pulled up Marge's number, and waited for her to answer.

"I thought you were taking the rest of the day off."

Smirking, I replied, "I am. There's a young woman my age headed up to your office in the next few minutes. Lacy Stark. She's my new executive administrator, and you're going to oversee her work.

"Oh, finally you found someone you liked."

Marge had been asking me for weeks to hire another assistant. The poor woman worked long hours and never complained, and I knew she wanted someone new to help offset the load. I had other plans for Lacy though. I had a feeling this girl wouldn't be my assistant for long.

"Find out who her worthless boss is and have him meet me in my office at seven forty-five tomorrow morning. Sharp."

"Got it. Anything else?"

"Yes, have someone from HR in there as well."

"This just got interesting. Anything else?"

"Make sure Lacy is moved up to the top floor by the end of the day."

"Will do."

"And Marge?"

"Yes, Charlie?"

"Take next week off . . . on me."

"For once, Charleston Monroe, I'm not arguing with you."

"Have a good evening, Marge."

"You too, Charlie."

Hitting *end*, I leaned back and closed my eyes. This had been one hell of a shit-filled day, and I was ready to relax. If any other unplanned things popped up, I was going to lose my shit.

My phone buzzed in my purse, causing me to search for it.

Without looking, I answered. "Hello?"

"Hey, doll. You almost here?"

Sighing, I replied. "Yes. Almost."

"Perfect, see you in a few."

The line went dead. Pulling it from my ear, I stared at it.

"That was weird," I whispered to no one other than myself.

After paying the taxi driver, I climbed out of the taxi and walked through the lobby of my building.

"Good afternoon, Ms. Monroe."

My gaze swung over to the new doorman, Jake. "Hey, Jake."

"Rough morning?"

Scoffing, I replied, "You could say that."

The ride up the elevator to my penthouse apartment seemed to take forever. When the doors opened, a wave of the most heavenly smell hit me. Glancing down to the floor, I smiled when I saw the rose petals.

Walking up to my doors, I unlocked them and gasped at the sight before me.

Tucker stood in front of me, dressed in a tux. My mouth went dry, and my knees almost buckled at the sight of him. He looked so beyond handsome and hot as hell.

"Oh my," I whispered.

He lifted his arms and that was when I saw Mr. Pootie, dressed in a tux as well. I covered my mouth and attempted to hold back my laughter and tears at the same time. Mr. Pootie was not happy about the current events.

"What is going on?" I asked, dropping my hand to my side.

Tucker flashed me a crooked grin that showcased his dimple; my heart melted.

"Do you trust me?"

"Of course I do."

He motioned with his finger to follow him.

"I thought you would have been sprawled out naked and ready for se . . . ahh—"

My words cut off at the sight of our friends standing in the living room.

"I'm pretty sure you were about to say sex," Nash said, his brow lifted. When I caught Lily on the other end of the group, I smiled. I was glad to see her and Nash in the same room, even if they were as far away from one another as possible.

Picking up a pillow from my sofa, I threw it at Nash. I scanned the group of friends standing in front of me. Nash, Blake, Jim, Terri, and Lily were all dressed in suits and dresses. "What are y'all doing here?"

Tucker handed Mr. Pootie to Terri then walked over to me. The way he moved in that tux had my insides quivering, and I was silently wishing we were alone.

"Charleston Ava Monroe. You are the most amazing woman I've ever met, and today was another example of your kind and thoughtful heart. You continue to amaze me day in and day out, and I don't want to wait another minute longer."

Terri walked up to me and handed me a white garment bag.

Joy bubbled up in my heart as I took the bag and looked back at Tucker.

"I don't need a big production, and I know you don't either. All I need is you, our friends, and . . ." Tucker turned to point to Mr. Pootie, who Nash was now holding up and waving a paw at us. "And even Mr. Pootie."

"What . . . what are you saying?" I asked, a sob slipping from my lips. I knew what Tucker was saying, but I needed to hear him say the words that would melt my heart.

"I'm saying let's get married. Right now."

"Here?" I asked, peering around the room.

"Sort of. All I need you to do is get changed, and Terri and Lily will do the rest."

Twenty-Eight

CHARLIE

MY HEART RACED. Excitement like I'd never felt flowed through my veins, and I couldn't control my happiness. I jumped up and down like a little girl and rushed toward a waiting Lily and Terri. They both practically pushed me into my bedroom.

When the door closed, they demanded I get undressed.

"Okay, so hold on. Tucker planned all of this in the three hours since he left my office?"

Terri nodded. "Yep. When that man sets his mind to something, he gets everyone on the same page."

"But weren't you all at work?" I asked as Terri started to pull my shirt out of my skirt.

"Yes, but when your friend calls and says his girl had a bad day and he wants to marry her to make it all better, you drop everything to make it happen."

Laughing, I placed my palm on my forehead. "Oh my gosh, is this really happening? And was Mr. Pootie really wearing a tux? Where does one get a cat tux on short notice?"

Both of my best friends laughed.

"That was all Nash," Terri said. I couldn't help but notice the sadness that appeared on Lily's face. It was gone so quick that if I hadn't been looking at her, I'd have missed it.

"Of course he did," Lily said with a strained chuckle. She was trying; I had to give her that.

I was ushered in the shower after I was stripped of my clothes.

"Put this hairnet on," Lily demanded.

"I just took a shower this morning," I exclaimed as the plastic cap was placed over my head and I was shoved under the water.

"Clean your va-jay-jay. It's going to be your wedding night."

"When was the last time you got waxed?" Terri asked through the bathroom door.

Sighing, I responded. "You know, this is all very weird. Y'all are telling me to clean my lady bits and asking about my grooming habits!"

I heard muffled voices from the other side of the door and decided they had both abandoned me for other things.

It was then everything really hit me.

"I'm getting married. Holy hell. I'm getting married."

Note to self: Get Tucker his wedding gift!

Standing under hot water, careful not to let it touch above my neck, I daydreamed about what Tucker did. How everything would look, where it would be. I was sure I was going to be whisked off in a limo and taken somewhere romantic.

But where? It was a weeknight. How in the world had Tucker arranged this in three hours?

The knock on the bathroom door startled me.

The door opened and Terri called out, "What are you doing? Let's go!"

"I'm coming, hold on."

When I walked out of the bathroom, I nearly dropped to my knees.

"Oh. My. God."

Tears pricked at my eyes, and two tissues appeared in front of my face at the same time.

"It's the dress," I whispered. "How? Where?"

"When we went dress shopping a few weeks back and you tried

this one on, it fit you like a glove. You mentioned if you and Tucker ever ran off and eloped, this was the dress you'd do it in. I told Jim how beautiful you looked in it, he told Tucker the story, and the next day Tucker asked me to go buy it. So I did."

Spinning to face Terri, I gaped at her. "You've had this dress since then?"

She nodded.

My stunned gaze looked between the two of them. "How long has Tucker been planning this?"

"It was something he wanted to do to surprise you. He knew y'alls wedding was going to be more of a show, and he wanted to do something more for the two of you. He had it all planned out in his head, so putting it together wasn't that hard. Plus, he had a tux left over from a charity ball our parents put on last summer."

I grinned. "I remember that ball. I was there and nearly choked on my own spit when your brother walked into the room in that tux."

We all giggled.

Taking my hand, Lily headed to my vanity. "Come on. Let's fix your hair, makeup, get your dress on, and then we need to get to the chapel."

"Chapel?" I asked.

Both of my friends ignored me as they fussed over everything. When Lily got the dress, I couldn't help where my mind took me.

Tucker slipping it off, his hands on my body, touching and kissing me everywhere.

I stood and slipped on the sleeveless lace and tulle gown. The satin on my warm and overly sensitive skin made me flush. Lily winked as if she knew exactly where my thoughts had just been.

"The halter and the sweetheart neckline together is beautiful," Terri said as she started the task of buttoning all the buttons on the back.

"Tucker is going to be pissed when he has to unbutton all of these."

The three of us laughed.

"I forgot it had a train," I said softly, looking at myself in the full-length mirror I had in the corner of my bedroom.

"I can't believe it fits you like a glove. It's like it was meant to be."

"It's a far cry from the dress I'd be wearing for a public wedding."

"Oh, don't worry, I'm sure your PR people will be forcing you to put on some huge fairy-tale display of a wedding."

My eyes pooled with tears. "This is a fairy tale."

They each wrapped an arm around me and hugged me, sandwiching me in between the two of them.

"Shoes? What shoes should I wear?"

Lily rushed to a bag sitting on the bed

"This is your something new." She pulled out a Jimmy Choo shoebox and opened it. Terri and I gasped at the nude high heels covered in crystals.

"Lily! These shoes are like two-thousand dollars!"

Terri smacked Lily on the arm. "Thanks a lot for showing me up. All I got her was sexy blue lingerie for tonight."

With a roll of her eyes, Lily shrugged. "You only have a surprise wedding once. Besides, I bought them for me when I found out I was pregnant! We just happen to be the same shoe size."

Laughing, I pulled her in for a hug.

"Thank you, but these are my something borrowed, not new."

"How about both?" Lily said with a wink.

"Perfect."

Terri handed me a box wrapped in beautiful paper. It was so stunning I didn't even want to unwrap it.

"It's for tonight. Unwrap it then."

I kissed her on the cheek. "Thank you, Terri."

"It's going to be Tucker who thanks me, that's for sure."

"We need to get going. Tucker just texted and said everything is ready."

My hands started to shake.

"Holy shit, I'm getting married."

"You're getting married . . ." Lily and Terri said at once as they gathered up the train and we headed to the front door.

"Wait! Don't I need flowers?"

Terri ushered me through the door. "Taken care of."

"Oh." My hands began to shake more, and I soon found myself being pulled not toward the elevator, but to the door that led up to the private rooftop patio that was mine.

"The roof?" I gasped.

Neither of my friends said a word as they opened the door and Nash and Jim greeted us. Both Lily and Terri took one of Jim's arms and slowly climbed the steps, but not before they each gave Nash instructions on how to carry and drop my train when we reached the roof.

Extending his arm for me, Nash asked, "Are you ready to marry him?"

A bubble of sadness settled in my chest. This was my father's job. To give me away to the man I loved. My mother should have been here, adjusting my hair and telling me how I looked just like her on her wedding day.

Tears filled my eyes, and Nash pulled me to him.

"I miss them, Nash."

He gently gave me a squeeze. "They're here with you, Charlie."

Nash was right. I felt my parents' presence. They were with me. For a brief moment I thought about the letters I still hadn't read. They were tucked safely in my nightstand. I made a mental note to pull them out and read them.

When I pulled back, I took in a deep breath and let it out.

"Is he ready to marry me?" I questioned, my teeth digging into my lip as nerves took center stage.

"He's more than ready to marry you. I've never in all the years I've known him seen him this happy."

My mouth trembled and I fought hard to keep my tears at bay.

"Then take me to him," I managed to get out.

As we climbed the steps, my heart raced faster and faster. Excitement mixed with nerves and made the most amazing feeling that fluttered both in my chest and stomach. When we reached the top, Lily, Terri, and Jim had already stepped outside.

I nearly lost my composure when I saw Patty standing at the top of the stairs. She was the only parent left between Tucker and me, and I was so happy to see she was here.

She handed me the most beautiful bouquet of flowers I'd ever seen.

"These are . . . stunning," I said, pressing them into my face and taking a deep breath.

"Well, they are pretty amazing for a last-ditch effort."

My eyes snapped up to look at her. "You made these?"

Nodding, she gave a small shrug. "In college I worked at a flower shop. I loved working there and was pretty good at it."

"I'll say. They're perfect for Charlie," Nash said.

Patty gave him a sweet smile, but her eyes were filled with sadness. She must have known the truth about Lily and Nash.

"Ready?" she asked when she broke her gaze from Nash.

"So very ready."

Putting my hand through Patty's arm, I was walked outside with Tucker's mother on one side of me and his best friend on the other. This was a clear message to me that Tucker intended on making sure that no matter what, I would be surrounded by people who loved both of us. People who would drop everything and rush around to make a wedding happen in three hours.

When we stepped out and I looked at the rooftop, I lost my fight to keep my tears back. White lights were strung up everywhere and had started to cast light over the rooftop.

There were no chairs, just a beautiful arbor decorated in whites and silver that faced the west where the sun had begun to set. Tucker's family preacher stood under it, with Tucker standing right next to him.

My eyes landed on Tucker. He looked so handsome. When he wiped a tear away, I started crying again. I fought the urge to break free from Nash and Patty and run to Tucker to tell him how much I loved him and how happy he had made me not only tonight, but always.

It seemed like forever before I reached him. It was only then did I see someone standing there with a violin. I'd heard it, but it didn't compute in my brain that they were there on the roof with us.

Patty took my bouquet, and Nash placed my hands in Tucker's.

"I know I'm not your father, Charlie, but I'm more than honored to stand in his place."

My chin trembled as Nash leaned down and kissed my cheek.

He stepped away and I stood in front of the only man I'd ever loved. Tears streaked down his cheeks, and I loved that he was so open with his emotions. Tucker reached up and used his thumbs to wipe my tears away, so I did the same to him.

"I'm sorry Pastor Tim, I know I'm supposed to wait, but I need to do something."

Cupping my face in his hands, Tucker bent over and kissed me. It was soft, slow, and innocent. Brushing his nose over mine, he closed his eyes and said, "You're so beautiful, Charleston. You take my breath away."

My hands clutched onto his arms as I attempted to find my voice. The only thing I managed to get out was something that sounded like "Tucker."

Pastor Tim cleared his throat and Tucker placed a respectable distance between us. I missed the warmth of his lips, the touch of his hands.

When the ceremony started, I didn't even try to pay attention. I stared into Tucker's gray eyes, and he stared back. The only time we broke the connection was when Nash told us it was time for the rings and vows. I laughed when I looked over to see Patty holding Mr. Pootie. He had a black harness on to match his little tux, and knowing Tucker made sure he was a part of today had me getting even more emotional than I already was.

I somehow managed to get through the vows, slip the ring on Tucker's finger, and stay upright when the pastor told Tucker to kiss me. Because kiss me, he did. I don't think I'd ever been kissed like that in such a public display of his affection and when he pulled back, I grabbed his jacket and pulled him back for more.

"Ladies and gentlemen, I give you Mr. and Mrs. Tucker Middleton."

Tucker and I raised up our hands as our friends and family yelled and cheered.

We didn't have a reception afterward; we stood on the rooftop, the pink-and-orange glow of the setting sun fading off to close out the day, with glasses of champagne in our hands. Well, everyone but Lily. She had water.

"To Tucker and Charlie," Nash started, his glass raised. "An example of true love and the testimony that love can overcome anything."

"Here, here!" was called out around us.

"To happily ever after!" Terri added as we all clinked glasses and drank.

Tucker's arm wrapped around my waist, keeping me close to him as everyone chatted about how amazing the ceremony was and they couldn't believe Tucker pulled it all together in one afternoon. It was a reminder of why I left work in the first place. My body was hungry, and it didn't want food. It was hungry for the man standing next to me. The man in the tux who looked hot as hell. The man I needed to have inside of me before I imploded.

Sensing my desire, Tucker leaned down and whispered against my ear, "I promise I'm going to take care of you later."

My knees trembled and my lower stomach pulsed with desire. When Patty informed everyone that she had a catering company setting up food downstairs, I almost wanted to cry. I loved being with my friends and Patty. Loved that I just had the most romantic wedding I could have ever had dreamed up, but I was horny and needed my husband to be all over me.

Everyone started to head toward the steps to head back to my place, but Tucker kept me behind. The glow of the white lights lit up his face, and I was struck again by how incredibly handsome my . . . *husband* . . . really was. He smiled and my stomach flipped. The dimple on the side of his cheek always made my stomach jump, but now that I knew this man was mine, it did something even more.

"I love you so much, Tucker. This day started out to be a pretty messed-up day, and you turned it completely around and gave me the most breathtaking wedding I could have ever asked for or dreamed of. Everything was perfect."

"Not too simple?" he asked with a wink.

Wrapping my arms around his neck, I reached up and brushed my lips across his. "Not at all. It was beyond perfect. Did you time it with the sunset?"

He laughed. "Nope. That was pure fucking luck!"

I joined in on the laughter as he pressed his mouth to mine, kissing me like he had something to prove. He had nothing to prove. He loved me, and that was made so very clear by what he did for me today.

When our kiss broke apart, Tucker placed his head on my forehead. "I forgot some things. Like a photographer. A marriage license. And a wedding band."

Smiling, I let out a contented sigh. "Nash was taking pictures with his camera. We can get the license tomorrow, and I don't need a wedding band to tell me that I'm yours."

"God, do you have any idea how happy you make me? We've come a long way, haven't we?"

"And it's only just the beginning."

With a sexy smile, Tucker took a few steps away, keeping my hands in his.

"I'm going to seduce the fuck out of you tonight."

My breath caught in my throat, and the only thing I could do was let out a moan and count down the minutes.

Twenty-Nine

TUCKER

STANDING IN THE kitchen, I forced a smile as I listened to Blake talk about some caving adventure he was about to go on. Blake had always been interested in caves—both unexplored and explored—and it was usually pretty interesting stuff. Right now though, I just wanted to take my wife into my arms.

My wife.

Holy shit, that sounded crazy. It had me thinking about all the times over the years I had wished Charlie was mine, and now she was.

"Tucker, did you even hear a word a said?"

Drifting my gaze over to Blake, I frowned. "What was that?"

He chuckled and shook his head. "Dude, why don't you just kick everyone out of here and get on with it already. The way you're looking at Charlie is getting sort of creepy."

Nash slapped my back. "He's right. Let me clear everyone out of here and y'all can spend the rest of the night together."

"That sounds great, but can I talk to you for a minute?" I asked Nash.

He pulled his brows in tight but then smiled and looked over at

Blake. "Sure. If that's how you want to spend your honeymoon, but I think Charlie will have something to say about that."

I motioned for him to follow me into the office that was just down the hall from Charlie's bedroom. Even though Charlie rarely worked from home, her office here at the condo was almost as set up as the one at CMI.

Shutting the door, I rubbed the back of my neck and figured out the best way to say this to my best friend.

"What's going on?" he asked. "Is everything okay?"

"Yes. God, yes. I wanted to thank you for everything you did today. I mean, I called you and you dropped everything to help me out and I'll never forget that. I couldn't have done this without you."

Nash smiled. His dark hair looked like he had run his hands through it a million times. The scruff on his face was overgrown, another indication of how busy my best friend's life was. Yet he always made time for me, and that was something I would never forget.

"It's a good thing I'm my own boss. Well, I guess Dad's really the boss."

I gave him a grin.

"You doing okay? What, with Lily here and everything?"

"Yeah."

His voice sounded like he meant it, but his dark brown eyes said something else.

"I know it's hard. I remember those first few times I had to be around Charlie. It felt like my heart was being ripped out."

Nash glanced down at the floor and let out a gruff laugh. "Yeah. It feels something like that. I want her to be happy, Tucker. I really do. She talked to me earlier tonight. You know when I told you I thought I would be able to forgive her?"

"Yeah, I remember."

"She started talking all this nonsense about how she was only with Mark because of the sex and that she still loved me and asked if I thought we had a chance."

My eyes widened in shock. Shit. My sister was messed up more than I thought.

"What did you say?" I asked.

"The truth. That I didn't think I would ever be able to trust her, and that I clearly wasn't giving her the things she wanted or needed. I also reminded her she was carrying another man's baby, and then she started coming on to me."

"Fuck." My hands scrubbed down my face. I didn't really want to hear these kinds of things about my baby sister, but I knew Nash needed someone to talk to. Blake wouldn't give two shits, and Jim was caught up in his own bubble of happiness with Terri.

"Dude, I'm sorry. It's got to be the hormones or something that's making her that way."

Nash let out a fake laugh. "Yeah. Must be. Anyway, I told her no, things would never work out between us now and that we needed to focus on just being friends like we'd agreed to."

Clutching his shoulder, I gave it a squeeze. "I know that was hard, but you're going to be okay."

"Yeah. I know, but it will be a cold day in hell when I let someone else in."

With a sympathetic smile, I added, "Famous last words, dude. Famous last words."

Thirty minutes later and Nash had Charlie's place cleared out of everyone but him and my mother.

"Thank you so much, Patty, for all this food."

Giving Charlie a bear hug and whispering something into her ear, my mother proudly declared it was all her pleasure.

"I love an excuse for any kind of party. I'm glad you were able to pull this together, son. It was simply beautiful!"

With a hug and then a kiss on the cheek, I replied, "Me too, Mom. Me. Too."

"You kids have fun!" Nash called out as he headed out the door and to the elevator, escorting my mother with him.

"Bye! Thank you for everything!" Charlie called out.

"Love you!" I added.

Nash hit the elevator and then turned to me. "Love you too, bro."

My mother chuckled and playfully hit Nash as she said, "I love both of you."

I watched as Charlie's eyes filled with tears. Pulling her back into the room, I shut the door and then pushed her against it. She was still dressed in her wedding gown, and my dick was finally allowed to come out and play.

"Jesus Christ, I've been aching to touch you."

Her teeth sank into her lip as she looked up at me through lust-filled eyes.

"Touch away, Mr. Middleton."

Taking her hands, I pushed them over her head and pressed them against the door while my mouth explored her neck.

"I intend to, Mrs. Middleton."

She groaned.

"Feel good?"

"So good."

Smiling against her skin, I licked up her neck and pressed my lips to hers.

"You taste amazing."

Her body arched to get more contact with mine.

"Tucker! Please. I've been dying since this morning to have you. Don't make me wait another second. I'll have you know that on my last bathroom break I ditched my panties, and I'm pretty sure you haven't removed my garter belt."

It was my turn to groan.

"Fucking hell."

Dropping to my knees, I gathered up the dress and went under it. Lifting her leg, I put it over my shoulder and didn't wait to run my tongue up her folds and to her clit.

"Oh God, yes!"

Charlie came so fast I nearly finished in my own pants like I was a sixteen-year-old teenager getting his rocks off for the first time.

"Tucker. Bedroom!"

Standing, I scooped her up into my arms and carried her though the house. Mr. Pootie, who was stripped out of his tux, took off in front of me.

"No way, cat! Out!" I yelled as he darted into the bedroom.

"He's fine!" Charlie panted as she attempted to get the buttons of my dress shirt undone.

"Charlie, I have performance anxiety when he's in here. You don't understand the struggle."

She stopped and looked at me. Her nose was crinkled up in the most adorable way. It made me fall in love with her even more. Damn it, I couldn't resist her tonight of all nights.

"Fuck the cat. I just want to be inside you."

With a giggle, she went back to work on the buttons. Setting her down, I ripped them off and pulled my shirt off.

"Turn around," I demanded.

When she did and I looked at how many fucking buttons were on her dress, I let out a groan.

"Can I just make love to you with the dress on?"

"No!"

I rolled my eyes and got to work on unbuttoning the beautiful gown.

"Will you wear this at our pretend wedding?" I asked, kissing her skin as it was exposed.

"Our pretend wedding?" she asked while glancing over her shoulder.

"Yeah. Our real wedding was tonight. I mean, we still have to get the marriage license, but in my eyes . . . we're married."

She grinned as she tossed me another look over her shoulder.

"I agree and no. This dress was just for us. I'm not even sure I want to have another wedding."

My fingers stilled on the buttons. "What? Why?"

Turning to face me, Charlie placed her hand on my cheek, her eyes meeting mine. "Because this wedding was everything I ever dreamed of and perfect in every single way. We don't need to put on a for-show wedding."

"But."

Her finger went to my lips. "Finish taking off my dress, Tucker. I want you to make love to me. Plus, I have a gift from Terri I'm supposed to put on."

"No! Not something else I have to take off!"

She slapped me on the chest and shook her head before turning back around. When the last button was undone, Charlie let the dress fall and it pooled around her feet, leaving her standing in nothing. When she stepped out of the dress, I expected her to move toward me. Instead, she picked up the dress, draped it over the chair, and grabbed a large box.

"Be right back!" she called out.

"Ugh! Charleston!"

I did what any other male would do—I got naked and laid on the bed. The events of today came crashing down on me. Everything from Lindsey and her crazy claims that I was the father of her baby to trying to plan a wedding in a few hours. Exhaustion moved over me fast. I closed my eyes and felt my body relaxing.

"Is my husband too tired for sex?"

I grinned and said, "Hell no."

"Then open your eyes and see the present your wife is giving you."

Sitting up, I opened my eyes and my mouth dropped open.

"Jesus," I hissed as I let my gaze roam over Charlie.

She stood at the end of the bed dressed in a light blue lace bra . . . if you could call it that. It was a piece of fabric that went across her tits and barely covered her nipples. In the middle of it was a bow. Moving my eyes down, I saw a thinner piece of satin with another bow, and then a pair of see-through blue lace panties with another bow.

When my eyes finally moved back up her body, our gazes met.

"I'm going to guess you have to unwrap me."

Getting off the bed, I made my way over to her. Her cheeks turned a bright pink, and her chest moved with each breath as she anticipated my touch.

"I should probably tell you, I never was the type of person to carefully open a package. I tend to like to rip the bows off and toss them to the side."

Lifting my hands, I ran my thumbs over her tight nipples, causing us both to let out a strained moan.

"Tucker," Charlie whimpered.

"Oh baby. You are driving me insane."

Her head dropped back, exposing her neck to me.

"Do something about it then."

Her command had me ripping the bows off her body and watching the strings of fabric fall to the floor. When I dropped to my knees, I kissed her stomach while sliding her panties off.

"Get on the bed, Charlie."

Scrambling backward, Charlie scooted up the bed and dropped onto the pillows.

My cock was so hard; I knew the moment I slipped inside her I would be fighting not to come.

Kissing from her toes up her legs, to her stomach, each breast, her neck, and finally to her mouth, Charlie reached between us and guided me right to her warm, wet entrance. Slipping in, I let out a growl from the back of my throat and buried my face into her neck.

Charlie's hands moved over my body lightly, yet they left a burning sensation in their wake. I moved slowly; our mouths pressed together as we kissed and moaned. My heart beat so fast that at times I thought I might pass out.

It felt like this was the first time all over again. I definitely wasn't going to last long.

When I circled my hips, Charlie arched her back and called out my name in pleasure. She gripped my dick like a vise, which sent me tumbling right over the edge with her.

"Oh God!" I grunted as I poured myself into her and she called out my name.

"Best fucking day of my life," I panted as I kissed my beautiful wife.

After a shower and another round of sex, this time pure fucking, Charlie and I collapsed into bed. I wrapped my arms around her body and pulled her flush against me.

"By the way, I'm paying you back for that money you gave Lindsey."

"Okay."

Drawing back to stare at the back of her head, I asked, "Okay? That's it? You're not going to argue with me?"

"Nope," she replied in a sleepy voice.

I kissed the back of her head and said, "Good."

"Are you happy, Charlie?"

Moving in my arms, she rolled on her side and faced me. Her smile was infectious, and I soon wore one of my own.

"Never been so happy."

"It's been a crazy few months. Hard to believe that Christmas is in a few days."

Her fingertip traced my jawline. "I know. What do you want for Christmas?"

"I already got my gift. What do you want?"

With a gleam in her eye, she chewed on her lip before saying, "A puppy."

"A puppy?"

"Yes! We can bring her to work with us, I mean, switch days, and you'd probably have to have her more especially when she got bigger."

"A puppy?"

Nodding like a little girl, she jutted out her lip and said, "Pwease."

Laughing, I grabbed her and rolled her on top of me. She squirmed and lifted her brows.

"So is it me or the puppy who has you excited?"

"It's all you, baby. All you."

"So . . . is that a yes?"

I reached up and cupped her face in my hands. "If you want it to be a yes, then it's a yes. Mr. Pootie is going to have a brother or sister."

Charlie let out a girly scream and then lifted her body off me before sliding over my cock.

"If this is your way of saying thank you, we can get as many animals as you want."

"Good, I was thinking a few goats." She lifted up and dropped back down, causing us both to gasp.

"A horse." She did it again, and this time I moaned with the feel of her on me.

"Or two."

Grabbing her hips, I stilled her.

"Just keep fucking me and I'll agree to whatever you want, baby. We can become like Noah and get two of everything for all I care. Just keep doing what you are doing. Just. Like. That."

Charlie winked and did exactly that.

Thirty

CHARLIE

WALKING INTO THE office, I couldn't wipe the smile from my face if I wanted to. Marge sat at her desk, and on the other side of the room was Lacy Stark.

"Good morning, ladies."

Marge lifted her gaze and eyed me with caution.

"Good morning, Ms. Monroe."

"When we are up here, Lacy, it's Charlie. Everywhere outside of here or in front of other employees, it's Ms. Monroe."

I stopped at my door and let out a chuckle before turning and saying. "Actually, it's now Mrs. Middleton."

Marge nodded, not really paying attention to what I said.

"Robert Hapner and Lynn from HR are in your office like you asked, and wait a minute, what did you say?"

Lacy jumped up. "What did you do on your half-day of hooky?"

Marge looked at her surprised, and then she swung her gaze back to me.

"I got married, but I'll tell you both about it when I take you to lunch later. For now, I have someone's ass to chew out."

"There's the Charlie I know and love," Marge stated. "Also, those tests results came back early. I'm not sure how much you paid them, but they put a rush on the rush."

Winking, I took in a deep breath and let it out. I wasn't the least bit worried. "Thanks, Marge. Come into my office in exactly three minutes."

"Only three, huh? Took your father six."

"This won't take long, trust me."

Opening the door to my office, a gentleman a few years older than me jumped up.

"Ms. Monroe, what do I owe this pleasure of meeting with you about?"

He went to sit as I rounded my desk.

"Don't bother sitting down, Hapner. This is going to be quick. I'm sure you heard by now that Ms. Stark is now one of my executive assistants."

He adjusted his tie. "Yes, I'm not going to lie; I wasn't aware she was looking to move within the company."

Lacy's employee file sat on my desk. I glanced over to Lynn, who was sitting at the conference table. Focusing back on the file, I flipped it open and went through the papers quickly.

"How is that possible when she has put in for four promotions in the last . . . let's see, two years?"

Hapner's face went white.

"Ms. Stark wasn't ready for those types of assignments."

"Really?"

"I disagree with you. I think the reason she didn't get the promotions was because you liked looking at her ass too much."

"Excuse me?"

Standing, I placed my hands on my desk and leaned forward.

"I will not stand for this type of behavior in my company. If I so much as hear someone whisper that you're looking at them the wrong way, I'll have you out on your ass so fast you won't know what hit you."

"Ms. Monroe, there must be some sort of misunderstanding. I respect Ms. Stark very much and would never treat her that way."

"Good. Then you'll feel the same way about your new administrative assistant."

Turning back to Lynn, I raised a brow and she nodded.

"Right. Looks like he will be starting this afternoon."

Hapner cleared his throat. "He?"

Lifting my eyes to meet his, I asked, "Is there a problem with that?"

After clearing his throat more times than needed, he shook his head. "No. No, of course not. It's just I figured I'd be picking my own secretary . . . I mean . . . administrative assistant."

Leaning back in my chair, I smiled. "I'm sure you will be very happy with who HR hired to fill Ms. Stark's position."

The door to my office opened, and instead of Marge standing there, it was Lacy.

Well played, Marge. Well played.

"Mrs. Middleton, your meeting is in ten minutes."

With a smile plastered on my face, I reached my hand across my desk. "Was great meeting you, Mr. Hapner. We'll be talking soon, I'm sure."

The poor bastard. It was sort of painful watching him look between Lacy and me. He finally snapped out of it and shook my hand before turning on the heels of his dress shoes and walking out of my door. Lynn stood, gave me a knowing smile, and followed Hapner out the door.

"Thank you, Lacy," I said as I sat down. When she closed the door, I grinned like the Cheshire cat.

"I think I may actually miss this job."

Six months later

"OPEN YOUR EYES."

The sound of Tucker's voice against my ear made my body shiver.

"I'm nervous!" I squealed as he chuckled.

"Just open them."

A rush of air left my lungs as I stood and looked at our finished house.

"Oh my. Oh wow. Holy crap."

Turning, I jumped into Tucker's arms as Nash let out a relieved-sounding laugh.

"You like it?" he asked as Tucker spun me around and then put me on the ground.

"Like it? Nash, it's beautiful. I can't believe y'all got it built in four months."

Tucker wrapped his arm around my waist. "Perks of having him for a best friend."

I stood and stared at the two-story house in front of me. It was perfect. It was simple yet filled with all the fun things I wanted. Some I didn't need but still wanted.

"It's fucking huge!" Tucker croaked out.

My face heated. It was a big house. Nine-thousand-square-feet huge.

"I needed an office," I stated.

"Okay, what about the other five bedrooms?" Tucker asked as we walked toward the house. We hadn't been out in a month and totally left the finishing touches to Nash. He didn't disappoint.

"One is ours, one is a guest room, and the other three are for little Tuckers."

My husband's eyes lit up.

I ran my fingers over the wood pillars on the front porch. "I love that you used the same wood and finish that's in Sedotto."

"Yeah, I do too," Nash said.

We walked into the house and did a quick tour of it before the three of us ended up on the giant covered patio outside. A bottle of champagne sat in ice, and I turned to Nash.

"You do this?"

He nodded. "We do with all our finished homes."

After popping open the bottle, Nash poured us each a glass.

"To new beginnings," Nash said with a grin.

"New beginnings," Tucker and I echoed.

Lifting the glass to my lips, I paused and focused my eyes on the sign hanging up over the outside bar.

The rules of seduction.

Under the title was a list of rules on how to seduce the one you wanted.

My hands went to my hips, and I turned to face both men.

"Who put up that sign?"

Tucker and Nash exchanged looks and then started laughing.

"What better of a housewarming gift than a sign that reminds y'all of how you finally came together."

Hitting Nash on the arm, I faced Tucker.

"We all know who the master of seduction is. I don't need any rules."

With a quirk of his brow, Tucker replied, "Really? If I'm not mistaken, I'm pretty sure I turned the tables around on you in that department."

"Maybe you should actually go and read the sign, sweetheart. You might learn a thing or two."

Nash couldn't contain his smile as Tucker let out a gruff laugh.

"Please. There is nothing on this sign that I don't already know."

I watched as Tucker got closer to the sign. Nash moved to my side and bumped my shoulder.

"Congratulations, Charlie."

My stomach fluttered and I replied, "Thank you, Nash."

Feeling a warmth rush through my body, I closed my eyes and thought back to the day I opened the letters from my parents, not long after Tucker and I got married.

To my dearest Charleston,

If you're reading this, something has happened to me. My sweet girl, my dream for you is to find happiness. True happiness. Follow your heart, Charleston, even if it leads you down an unmarked road.

Love you sweetheart!

Love, Mom

Dear Pumpkin,

As I sit here, I'm watching you play on the living room floor. My sweet little ten-year-old mini me. It was your mother's idea to write you these letters, and I admit I've been staring at my page for an hour now. I want you to know how much I love you. I know you will grow up to be an amazing woman, and I know I'll most likely be hard on you. Please know one thing, I only want you to be happy. I want you to follow your heart, even if at times it doesn't seem like that's what I want.

I know you'll make both your mother and me proud, and if you're reading this, that means we won't be there for you when you need us, not physically at least. We will, however, always be with your Charlie. Always. Never forget that.

I love you with all my heart.

Daddy

OPENING MY EYES, I looked up at the sky and smiled before focusing back on my husband.

Tucker started to read the sign.

"Seduce my mind and you can have my body. Find my soul and I'm yours forever."—Anonymous

"What's this envelope taped on here?" Tucker asked, taking it off and opening it. He stood frozen for the longest time before turning and meeting my gaze.

The picture of the sonogram was in his hand as he read the letter I had written him.

Tucker,

The last time I wrote you a note, I didn't mean a single thing I wrote down. This time, I have no regrets about anything in my life. In fact, you've made me the happiest woman on Earth. Thank you for loving me and being the amazing husband you are. I hope you're ready for the next phase.

Parenthood. This is going to be fun! Mr. Pootie is going to flip out when he finds out he's going to be a big brother!

I love you,
Charleston

"Are you serious?"

I nodded with tears in my eyes knowing Tucker would be just as happy as I was.

"No fucking way!" he exclaimed. "We just started!"

"Looks like you've got some powerful swimmers there, buddy," Nash called out as I hit him in the stomach.

The moment Tucker started my way, I started his. We met in the middle, and I threw myself at him.

"Charlie, we're having a baby?" he asked, his voice cracking from emotion.

"Yes. We're having a baby."

He spun me around and cried out, "Best fucking day of my life!"

When he finally put me down, I took his hand and placed it on my stomach.

Our eyes met, and I was taken aback once again by how much I loved this man.

"You and me forever."

Leaning down, he softly kissed me and whispered, "Forever."

The End.

Entice Me

LOOK FOR *ENTICE Me,* Nash and Kaelynn's story, coming spring 2019!

Since the moment Kaelynn Dotson walked into my world, I haven't been able to think, eat, or sleep. After having my heart broken by the only woman I've ever loved, Kaelynn has ignited something deep down inside me—a flame so hot that I cannot ignore, no matter how hard I try.

I vowed to never open myself up to a woman again, but there's something about Kaelynn that is drawing me to her.

There's just one problem.

She's hiding something from me. Trust is something I need, but when it comes to Kaelynn, all the lines seem to be blurred. I know I should take this as a warning and walk away, but for some reason, it's only enticing me more.

I moved to Austin, Texas, with only one thing on my mind—to help my friend Morgan start a new business. What I wasn't expecting was her brother. Nash Barrett isn't like any other man I've ever met. He's confident, sexy, and not afraid to be himself. It's a refreshing change compared to the men I grew up with back in Utah.

Trying to fight my attraction to him is becoming harder by the day. We come from two different worlds, and even though I'm trying to live in his world, I'm scared the truth will come out.

I'm living a lie.

I'm not the girl from a middle-class family in Utah like Nash thinks. I'm the heiress to a billion-dollar fortune, and that's not what he's looking for. He's had that before, and it left him scarred.

If the truth comes out, I'll lose the only man I've ever fallen in love with . . . I'm not sure I'm willing to give him up.

Thank you

A HUGE THANKS to everyone who made this book possible. Elaine, Hollie, Callie, and Christine! I couldn't do this without y'all, so thank you!

Laura and Tanya, thank you for being the first eyes on the book and giving me your feedback.

To my readers, I hope you enjoy this new series. I love y'all to the moon and back!